A NOVEL

BRICK

NOV 2013

Dear Reader:

Oh, how I love Allison! This book had me completely captivated to the point where I could not even work on my own for a few days. *Brick: Double Dippin' 4* is the way to keep the ball rolling with exciting characters and storylines that can only come from the mind of a brilliantly imaginative person such as Ms. Hobbs.

Brick in on the warpath, searching for the person who beat Misty beyond recognition and he is not taking any prisoners. His anger having lain dormant for years as he tried to make a marriage work with Misty's own mother, it has now been unleashed and anyone with any common sense needs to stay the hell out of his way. But there is still a tender side of Brick, and a complete stranger, with as many issues as himself, brings out his tenderness. Anya has come to Philadelphia seeking revenge against the men who kidnapped, raped, and then stoned her mother to death. She will not rest until justice has been served in the form of vengeance. What happens when two people hell-bent on ridding the world of violent offenders become violent themselves? Read this book and find out. It is a shocker.

The prior books in this series are: *Double Dippin'*, *Big Juicy Lips: Double Dippin' 2*, and *Lipstick Hustla*. Also make sure that you join Allison on Wednesday nights as she conducts her weekly chat at 10 PM EST. The topics are always sensual and on point.

As always, thanks for supporting me and the Strebor Books family. We strive to bring you cutting-edge literature that cannot be found anyplace else. For more information on our titles, please vi t us at Zanestore.com. My personal web site is Eroticanoir.com and my online social network is PlanetZane.org.

Blessings,

Zane

Zane
Publisher
Strebor Books
www.simonandschuster.com/streborbooks

"Baby, she's dead. We can't help her."

"Misty is not dead! Move out the way, Baron. I have to try to do some CPR on my baby."

"She slipped away peacefully."

"Nooo! This can't be. She was fine when I checked her last. And she…" Thomasina froze mid-sentence. Suddenly the meaning of Brick's words washed over her like an icy tsunami. "My God, Baron! What have you done?" Thomasina covered her mouth, her eyes huge with fear and disbelief.

"Her life was pure hell, Thomasina," Brick said. He stood up and reached for his wife, offering her comfort.

She shoved Brick away, and fell on the bed, trying desperately to shake Misty into awareness. "Misty, wake up. Wake up for Mommy!"

Brick tugged his wife's arm. "She's at peace."

Frantically, Thomasina placed two fingers against the side of Misty's neck. "She's not dead!" she exclaimed. "She still has a pulse!" Brick dodged from Thomasina's path as she raced from the bedroom to call 9-1-1.

Brick understood that it was a mother's nature to go to extraordinary lengths to save her child, but he knew without a doubt that Misty was dead. And he was responsible for taking her life. Brushing a shaky hand over his first love's face, Brick closed Misty's unseeing eyes.

Breathlessly, Thomasina returned to Misty's bedroom with the phone pressed against her ear. "Ma'am, I don't know what happened. I came in my daughter's bedroom and found my husband holding her, telling me she's dead. But he ain't a doctor and my daughter still has a pulse, goddamnit. Now tell me exactly what I need to do until the ambulance gets here."

Thomasina listened to the voice on the other end of the phone, and then spoke in a trembling voice, "I know a little CPR, but I'll

CHAPTER 1

From an unfathomable distance, he could hear his wife calling him. Too choked up to speak, Brick lay in silent agony with his arms wrapped around Misty's still warm body. For most of his life, Brick and Misty had been friends. And lovers. Despite all the dirt she'd done…despite his determination to keep Misty out of his life, their bond had not been severed… not even when he married her mother.

Thomasina entered her daughter's bedroom and gasped. She blindly grasped the doorjamb to maintain her balance. "Baron! Why are you lying in bed with Misty?" Though she spoke in a hushed tone, there was unmistakable panic in her voice.

With his back to his wife, Brick could only respond with an anguished groan.

Thomasina stumbled across the small bedroom. She shook Brick's massive shoulder roughly. "Misty's too weak and frail for you to be all over her like that. Let go of my child before you squeeze the life out of her."

"She's gone, Thomasina. Misty's gone!" He croaked out the words. He reluctantly released Misty, gently resting her head upon the pillow.

One look at Misty's vacant gaze and Thomasina shrieked. "Oh, Lord Jesus no! Call 9-1-1, Brick! Why the hell are you just laying there? Hurry! Do something!"

need you to walk me through it." Her panicked eyes darted from Misty's unmoving body to Brick's tear-stained face.

Trying to calm down, Thomasina inhaled deeply. "The paramedics are on their way, but right now it's up to me and you to try to get Misty breathing again."

Brick had felt the life leave Misty's body; there was no hope in reviving her. Still, he had to appease his distraught wife. With the back of his hand, Brick wiped tears away. "Whatchu need me to do?"

"The woman on the phone said we have to get Misty off the bed. Lay her on the floor."

Brick lifted Misty's frail body and tenderly lowered her onto the floor.

"Here, talk to the 9-1-1 lady. She's gonna guide me through it." Thomasina handed Brick the phone, and knelt beside her lifeless daughter.

Brick took the phone but didn't say anything to the emergency medical dispatcher. Thomasina seemed to know what she was doing. He watched as Thomasina pushed down on Misty's tiny chest with both hands, counting loud and desperately with each compression. When she reached number fifteen, she began breathing into Misty's mouth.

A sudden and urgent pounding on the front door brought a frightened yell from Little Baron's bedroom.

"Let the paramedics in!" Thomasina shouted. She urgently began the compressions again, paying no attention to her toddler son's cries.

Having no more use for the EMD, Brick ended the call and rushed out of the room. Out in the hallway, he hesitated briefly when his son let out another distressful wail. Little Baron began throwing a fit when he caught sight of his father. He screamed at the top of his lungs and shook the railing of his crib. But Brick kept moving. There was no time to pick up and console his frantic child.

"It's all right, lil man! Daddy's gon' be right back to get you!" Brick yelled as he bounded down the stairs.

෧෨

Thomasina rode in the ambulance with Misty. Brick stayed behind, getting himself and Little Baron dressed. The ride to the hospital was solemn. His young son seemed to sense that this was a somber occasion, and accepted being strapped in his child seat without squirming or uttering a word of complaint.

Brick shook his head, imagining Thomasina getting hysterical and becoming inconsolable when the doctor pronounced Misty dead on arrival.

But once she regained her composure, Thomasina was going to demand some answers. From Brick. He was the last person to see Misty alive, and he imagined that the cops would probably want to have a word with him, too.

He swiped his hand across his sweaty forehead. The deafening sound of his rapidly beating heart filled the car.

It had been a mercy killing. Wait…no…he didn't actually kill Misty. He'd only assisted. Misty begged for that lethal cocktail. She was of a sound mind when she'd swallowed each and every one of those pills. It was straight-up suicide. Misty wanted out of that useless body. She wanted to be with Shane.

But Thomasina wouldn't understand. Shit, at this point, Brick didn't understand. Like old times, he'd allowed Misty to have her way.

Damn, Misty. Fuck was I thinking? It wasn't your time yet. I can't believe I let you talk me into that crazy shit!

Grim-faced, Brick drove slowly, taking the long route to the hospital.

ACKNOWLEDGMENTS

To my publisher, Zane, a chance meeting with you changed my life, taking me from self-published writer to bestselling author. You've always been supportive of my work, giving my career the boost that put my books into the hands of thousands of readers. I'm honored to be your friend and part of the Strebor family.

Charmaine Parker, I'm so proud of you. I thoroughly enjoyed your first novel, and now I'm waiting for book number two!

Cairo, we bonded during that train ride from Baltimore to Philly. I treasure our friendship.

Daaimah S. Poole, fellow author and good friend. Thanks for helping me out. You always come through and I'm so grateful.

Yona Deshommes, thank you for always looking out, and helping me take it to the next level.

Karen Dempsey Hammond, it would take at least one more lifetime for me to repay the many kindnesses that you have extended over the course of our friendship. Thank you, my friend.

To all my readers and the fans of the *Double Dippin'* series… this one is for you!

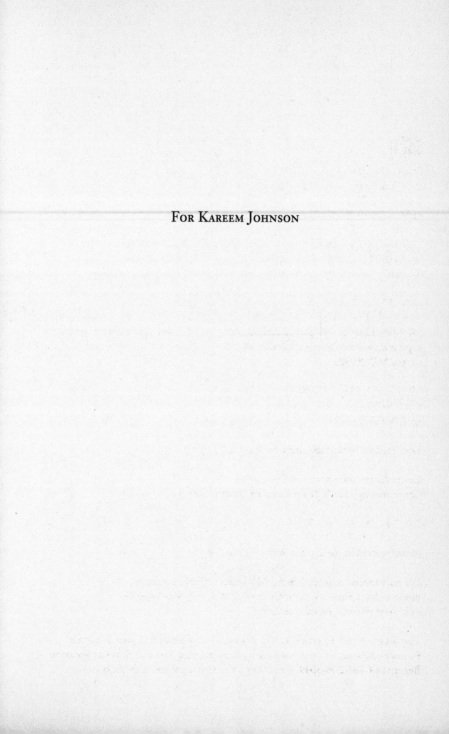

FOR KAREEM JOHNSON

Strebor Books
P.O. Box 6505
Largo, MD 20792
http://www.streborbooks.com

ISBN 978-1-59309-417-1
ISBN 978-1-4516-5687-9 (ebook)
LCCN 2011938444

First Strebor Books trade paperback edition July 2012

Cover design: www.mariondesigns.com
Cover photograph: © Keith Saunders/Marion Designs

10 9 8 7 6 5 4 3 2 1

Manufactured in the United States of America

For information regarding special discounts for bulk purchases, please contact Simon & Schuster Special Sales at 1-866-506-1949 or business@simonandschuster.com

The Simon & Schuster Speakers Bureau can bring authors to your live event. For more information or to book an event, contact the Simon & Schuster Speakers Bureau at 1-866-248-3049 or visit our website at www.simonspeakers.com.

ZANE PRESENTS

ALLISON HOBBS

A NOVEL

BRICK

SBI
STREBOR BOOKS
NEW YORK LONDON TORONTO SYDNEY

CHAPTER 2

Brick parked in the visitor's garage at the hospital. Carrying his sleeping son in his arms, he made slow strides toward the elevator.

Inside the visitor's lounge, he found Thomasina wringing her hands and pacing. Her face was a mask of grief and anxiety; her eyes red and puffy from crying. Having dressed hurriedly, she was wearing pajama bottoms, a T-shirt, and flip-flops.

Guilt-ridden, Brick used his free arm to hug his wife.

"They had to pump Misty's stomach. The doctor said she overdosed on pills. She's barely clinging to life, but they're not giving up." Thomasina eased out of Brick's embrace and glanced toward a set of double doors that were marked: No Admittance. "There's a whole team of doctors working on her back there. Oh, God, please let my baby pull through."

Brick frowned in confusion. *Misty's still alive? How can that be possible?*

"The doctors can only do but so much. We need the Lord's help." Thomasina had a desperate look in her eyes—like she'd wished she could trade places with Misty.

Brick felt torn between the two women he loved. Thomasina wanted her daughter back, but from Misty's perspective, life wasn't worth living. Misty would be devastated if she woke up and found herself, once again, trapped inside that broken body and confined to a bed.

Thomasina gazed at Brick with an eyebrow arched. "I can't figure out how Misty could have overdosed. I'm the one who administered her medication, and I followed the doctor's orders to a tee."

"You didn't do anything wrong, baby," Brick mumbled guiltily.

"But no one else had access to her meds, Baron. Only her nurse and me. The nurse had the past few days off, so that leaves me. And there's no way I would have overdosed my own child!"

"I know," Brick muttered.

"It's going to take a few weeks for the toxicology report to reveal exactly what drugs were in her system."

"We'll get through this." Hoping his words were true, he gave Thomasina's shoulder a quick squeeze.

"I'll never forgive myself if I was so absent-minded that I overdosed my poor, sickly daughter." Thomasina had a tortured look in her eyes and Brick couldn't allow his wife to blame herself for another moment.

"I gave Misty the pills," he confessed softly. Unable to look Thomasina in the eye, he kept his gaze downcast. Needing to do something with his nervous hands, he readjusted his son's body weight, shifting the toddler's sleeping body from his right side to his left.

After resting Little Baron's head upon his left shoulder, Brick stole a glance at Thomasina. Thomasina's eyes had turned to slits. Her lips were tight. "You did what?" she asked incredulously.

"I can explain."

She uttered a sound of shock. "I can't believe what I'm hearing. You're responsible for this?" She bent at the waist and moaned. "You were supposed to be helping Misty. How could you do something so cruel?"

Brick hung his head. After a long uncomfortable silence, he

looked up. "Thomasina, please listen to me. You know Misty was suffering. She was in so much misery…she didn't want to be here any longer."

Too shocked to speak, Thomasina stared at him with horror all over her face.

"It was what she wanted," Brick explained. "Misty had been planning her suicide for a long time."

"Misty was paralyzed. She was completely helpless, so how the hell could she get a hold of enough pills to almost kill herself?"

"Hear me out, baby," Brick pleaded. "She wasn't swallowing the pills that you gave her. She was spitting them out, using her good hand to toss her meds under the bed."

Thomasina glared at Brick; her lips were bunched together in fury.

"Baby, I know you're mad at me, but it wasn't my idea. After Misty had stashed what she thought was a lethal dosage, she begged me to gather 'em up from under the bed and put 'em in her mouth."

"What you did was attempted murder," Thomasina hissed.

"You gotta look at it from Misty's perspective. She was in a lot of pain. Mentally and physically. For her, every day was torture… a slow death. She cried like a baby, telling me how miserable her life was. When she begged me to help her, it was a hard decision, but I love Misty…like a sister," he added. "It seemed like the right thing to do."

"You had no right to go behind my back and try to execute my daughter."

"Execute!" Brick reared back in indignation. "That's kind of harsh. You weren't there, Thomasina. You didn't hear Misty begging and crying. You have no idea—"

"I'm the one giving her those stretching exercises that cause her to cry out in agony, so don't tell me that I don't know. I can't count how many times she's told me she wanted to end her life, but I wasn't foolish enough to listen to her."

His wife's words hit him in the gut. "I'm sorry. I realize that I should've talked to you about it. But Misty begged me not to."

"She played you, Baron. Can't you see that after all this time, Misty still has you wrapped around her finger?"

"Nah, it's not like that," Brick objected.

"I sent you into my baby's room to cheer her up; not to kill her." She looked him up and down sneeringly.

The look of disgust on his wife's face filled Brick with shame and remorse. He hadn't seen her wearing that repugnant expression since the days when she had disapproved of his relationship with her daughter.

"Hand me my son," Thomasina demanded, as if their young child was no longer safe in his father's arms.

"I got him," Brick protested, holding Little Baron tightly.

"Hand me my child, you monster!"

She hates me! The room began to spin. Feeling lightheaded and defeated, Brick relinquished their child. "I'm not a monster," he protested.

"It's over, Brick."

"Baby, please. Don't talk like that." He reached for her.

Repulsed, Thomasina recoiled from Brick. "Misty has never been an angel, but she's my daughter and I'll always love her, whether she's right or wrong. But you…" Thomasina twisted her lips in disdain. "I can't bear the sight of you."

"I wasn't thinking straight, baby," Brick said desperately. "We've built a strong relationship. Don't throw it all away."

Thomasina made a chortling sound. "You threw it away. A strong relationship is built on trust and I can't trust you, nor can

I forgive you. Not after this." She shook her head emphatically.

"It's asking a lot, but you have to let me prove myself. Misty caught me in a weak moment."

"I know what you're capable of, Baron. I watched you maim and kill a man right in our kitchen."

"I was defending my family."

"You didn't have to take that man's life. I begged you to let the police handle it."

"He was reaching for his knife. It was self-defense," Brick said without a trace of remorse.

"You kicked the knife away, so why'd you have to strangle him to death?"

"The nigga deserved something way worse than death," Brick responded. "Suppose that junkie had made it upstairs and had a knife up against Little Baron's throat?"

Thomasina gasped at the thought. She kissed her son on the cheek and gently patted his back. "Well, thank God, that didn't happen. Look, I've tried to put that night out of my mind. I've made a lot of excuses for your cold-blooded tendencies…"

Brick couldn't hold back a wounded, guttural sound. He couldn't help it; his wife was throwing all kinds of hurtful slurs at him.

"I've also tried to convince myself that you're a normal human being," Thomasina continued.

Deep frown lines creased Brick's forehead. "Whatchu saying? You think I'm an animal or something?"

"I'm calling it like I see it," Thomasina said coldly. "I had hoped that you would cheer Misty up, but I made a big mistake; sending a heartless killer into my precious daughter's bedroom."

"You got it twisted, but that's cool. I'm through begging. Whatchu gon' do, Thomasina—have me arrested? I hate seeing you suffer, but I'm not going to keep apologizing for trying to help Misty get out of her miserable life."

"I don't need to call the cops on you; the Lord deals out the best justice. In the meantime, make sure when I get home, you're not there. Pack your shit and find a new home. I don't want you anywhere near me or my son!"

His worst nightmare had come true. He was being cast out into the cruel, cold world. Alone again. No family. No home to call his own. Terrifying childhood memories flashed across his mind. Then Brick pulled himself together, reminding himself that he was no longer a child. He was a big, grown-ass man, and he had no choice but to make it on his own.

"I'll move out today," Brick conceded. "I'm sorry we had to end up like this, but seriously, Thomasina, you can't stop me from seeing my son."

"The hell if I can't, you ruthless murderer," she spat.

Brick flinched, but he didn't contradict her.

At that moment a female doctor emerged from behind the set of double doors. She approached Thomasina, acknowledging Brick with only a brisk head nod. "Mrs. Kennedy, your daughter made it, but I'm afraid she's comatose."

Thomasina squeezed her eyes shut briefly as she absorbed the information. "How long will she be in a coma?"

The doctor shook her head. "There's no way to know for certain. It could be days. Weeks. And unfortunately, she may never come out of it. The good news is that she survived. At least she has a chance."

"Oh, my God. Can I see her?"

"Yes, but only for a few minutes." The doctor turned around. Walking briskly, she pushed through the doors designated for hospital staff.

Without giving Brick as much as a glance, Thomasina rushed behind the doctor, carrying Little Baron in her arms.

Brick's eyes followed his family until they disappeared behind the restricted set of double doors. He stood motionless for a few moments. Reluctant to leave, he wondered if he should stick around and give Thomasina a ride home. *Nah, she'd rather take a cab than look at my face.*

Resigned to the idea of a future without his wife and son, Brick dragged his feet toward the exit sign.

CHAPTER 3

I'm finally outside the prison gate. I look around, but I already know what it is. It's not like I had my hopes up for anything. I wasn't expecting to see a big welcoming committee, but I did expect to see *somebody!*

After ten years behind prison bars, seems like at least one person would be out here to meet me. But nobody showed up. Nobody! Not even my own mother. My mom only visited me three times in ten years. Always complaining that the trip takes too long, and her health isn't up to par.

Everybody can kiss my ass. My family and so-called friends let me sit and rot in prison. Once I get shit poppin' in Philly, I ain't tryna hear nothing from nobody. If they ain't talkin' money, then I can't hear 'em.

After I get my cake up, the first thing I'ma do is throw myself a welcome home party. Yeah! With strippers! Only pretty bitches that got their head game tight can get in. I'ma see if I can get a liquor company to sponsor my big bash.

I plan to go holler at Evette as soon as I hit Philly. The last two years of my bid, she was the only person that consistently wrote me. Sent me cards and letters. Kept a little something on my books, and accepted my phone calls, while all these other mufuckers counted me out.

At first, Evette was only a prison pen pal. Then we got closer.

Started talking about having a future together. She's thirty-six years old; she got ten years on me. The weird thing is, Evette and I have talked on the phone and communicated through the mail, but we ain't never met in person.

I asked her… Nah, lemme keep it real, I pleaded with her to send me some naked flicks. She refused. In fact, she refused to send me any pictures at all. I asked her if she was tryna hide the fact that she's a big girl. I really wouldn't give a fuck how much she weighs. Pussy is pussy—as long as it's wet and juicy. That's my philosophy.

She claims that she's a normal weight. I asked her to describe herself. According to Evette, she's average-looking, and slightly visually impaired.

Slightly visually impaired! What the hell does that mean? Is the bitch half-blind or all the way, ugly?

One day we were on the phone, and she asked me how I felt about marriage. Wanted to know if marriage was in our future.

She had a nigga on the spot. All I could say was, "Uh…yeah, sure, we can do that."

But now that I'm out, I hope we can kick it together without her bringing up the topic of marriage. I'm not tryna marry anyone right now. Matter fact, I don't wanna be with one chick. I got to make up for lost time and spread this dick around. Ain't no one keeping this dick on lock; especially not a handicapped broad.

Evette used to end every letter by saying she was holding me in prayer.

Well, being that I'm not incarcerated anymore, and I don't need her to hold me in prayer, I hope she realizes that the only thing she needs to hold now is my dick. In her mouth. 'Suck it, bitch,' I'ma be saying. Then I'ma slide it deep inside her coochie.

I hope I don't have to knock no cobwebs outta no dried-up pussy. I want that pussy to be so hot, that it's sloshing and dripping. Saturating her panties.

Squish, squish. That's all I wanna hear while I'm deep-stroking.

My mind drifts back to the last time I had sex with a female, and I can't help from twisting my lips in disgust. The last piece of pussy I had was as dry as the Sahara Desert. Even that bitch's mouth had a drought going on. Her tongue felt like sandpaper. Scratched up my dick. *Fuckin' bitch!*

Merely thinking about the night of the crime is extremely disturbing. I can feel my chest beginning to tighten in outrage. They shouldn't have sent me up over no pussy and a little bit of horseplay. Shit! We were only fucking around. It wasn't about nothing. That ho's dehydrated pussy wasn't even worth ten years of my young life.

The therapist I was seeing in the joint told me I should distract myself from negative recollections by thinking about my most pleasant memory.

But I don't have any pleasant memories. I bullshitted that therapist, made up a bunch of happy shit so he'd recommend me for parole.

Nope, I'm tryna do the exercise, but I can't think of no good memories. The only thing on my mind is bodying any bitch that looks at me the wrong way.

I lost a whole decade over a ho, and I'm mad as shit about it. That bitch had it coming; the real crime is I spent ten years in a cage over some bullshit.

That ho's dehydrated pussy wasn't even worth the kind of time they gave me.

CHAPTER 4

At home, Brick peered inside Misty's bedroom. Heartsick, he stared at her empty bed.

I tried to help you, Misty. I fucked up. I never meant for you to end up in a coma. Now I have to live with that guilt.

Your mom's through with me. She called me a monster, but only God can judge me. The only thing that's gon' keep me from going crazy is finding the muthafucka that ran you over. You said it was a female, right? But I don't care...man or woman, I'm serving up some stiff justice. I'm not giving out any express tickets to hell. Whoever tried to kill you is gonna suffer a long, horrible death.

Inside his and Thomasina's bedroom, Brick began packing, pushing as many items as he could fit into an oversized duffle bag. From the top of the dresser, he grabbed a family portrait. He stared briefly at himself, Thomasina and their adorable son. Taken before Misty got hurt, it was a photo of happier times. Swallowing back sorrow, he pressed the picture frame to his heart and then quickly stuffed it deep inside his bag.

He'd have to rent a room somewhere. A cheap hotel or a boarding house. Brick shoved a hand in his pocket, pulled out a wad of bills and counted them. He had a little over seven hundred dollars. That would get him through until his next payday.

There was a nice chunk of money in his savings account, but Brick refused to touch it. He was proud of the nest egg that he'd manage to put away for his son's education. He told himself that no matter how hard it got out there, Little Baron's college fund was off limits.

Using his cell phone, Brick looked for affordable accommodations. He tapped on an icon and accessed a list of hotels. Moving his finger swiftly, he sped past the high-end hotels, and perused the bottom of the list. He nodded when he spotted a place where he could rest his head without breaking the bank.

Brick left the bedroom and went downstairs. As he passed through the family room, his eyes slowly panned the area, giving his cozy home a solemn, lingering look. His jaw muscles twitched as he detached his house keys from his keychain. With deep regret, he set three silver keys on the coffee table.

Deep in his heart, Brick had always felt the immense joy he'd shared with Thomasina was something he didn't deserve. He'd always feared that his happiness was only temporary. Now that his worst fear had come to pass, he was surprisingly calm. Though his heart was breaking, the rage he felt toward Misty's unknown assailant kept him strong—kept his emotions intact.

When Brick threw the duffle bag in the back seat of his car, he noticed his son's car seat. Missing his little guy already, he sighed bitterly and reached for the seat. He groaned when he remembered that his keys were inside. He placed the child seat on the front porch and raced back to his car, as if running away from the painful reminder...his son wouldn't be riding around with his daddy for a long time.

ഇൻ

Lured by the unbeatable cheap price, Brick approached a smudged glass door that led into the entry of a seedy hotel. The place had been recommended online as an economical lodging for tourists.

One glance at the misfits that were loitering in the lobby told Brick that these guests were not out-of-town travelers. Brick perused the hotel guests and quickly sized them up. Some were so animated, they were practically boisterous, while others mumbled to themselves, shuffling around like zombies, obviously high out of their minds. *Addicts, a couple of pimps, and a bunch of hoes.*

He hadn't been expecting the Four Seasons, but he certainly didn't expect a gutter hole like this. Spending the night in his car would be better than staying in this rattrap.

Prepared to recline in the front seat of his car, Brick turned to leave. From the corner of his eye he spotted someone stepping off the elevator—someone that looked vaguely familiar.

Judging by the way the dude was dressed with half his ass out, his jeans hanging well below his waistline, Brick decided that the young punk had to be right out of his teens…no more than twenty or twenty-one.

Brick felt much older than his actual years. Being married to an older woman had matured him. He'd evolved from being a directionless, weed-smoking thug to becoming a responsible family man. He heaved a sigh, realizing that he could no longer consider himself as being responsible. After what he'd done, most people would consider him completely reckless.

From the time he'd put that first pill onto Misty's tongue, he'd knowingly begun the process of unraveling everything he'd worked so hard to build.

But… What was done was done.

If he were lying up in bed paralyzed, he'd want someone to put him out of his misery. Trouble was, he'd failed Misty. She was possibly worse off than before. And that was a damn shame.

He watched the slim-sized dude as he sauntered over to the front desk and exchanged words with the clerk.

I've seen that skinny-ass, young bull before. Curious, Brick crept over to the counter to eavesdrop and to get a better look.

"Yo, I can't sleep in that room if the air ain't working," the dude said.

"It'll be twenty dollars more if you want to upgrade," said the disinterested clerk. A fitting representative of the sordid hotel, the clerk had bad teeth, a terrible case of acne, and greasy dark hair that hung in his face.

"I ain't paying for no upgrade. It ain't my fault that y'all shit be breaking down every other day." The skinny bull jerked his body in aggravation.

"Take it up with management," the clerk dryly responded.

"I'm taking it up with you, mufucka!" The dude leaned across the desk, threateningly. "I'ma boss; I call the shots!" he growled at the clerk. "I'm 'bout to black out, man. I'm two seconds from snapping, yo. Man, you don't want it. I'm tryna tell you, if I make a call, me and my peoples will take over this bitch!"

The young chump was talking real reckless, Brick noticed. He doubted if a dude his size could survive a strong wind, let alone handle a hostile takeover. Brick chuckled to himself.

Squinting as if to sharpen his vision, Brick edged closer. He studied the angles of the young bull's dusty, brown-skin face. He couldn't place him, but his gut feeling told him that this loud-mouth sucka had something to do with Misty.

"They be trippin' up in this piece, man. Always tryna beat a muthafucka." The slim dude directed his words to Brick. Brother to brother…thug to thug.

Grimacing, Brick nodded, denoting his shared disgust of the business practices of the shabby hotel.

Sensing that Brick might have second thoughts about checking into the seedy dive, the clerk dismissed the scrawny dude and offered Brick a forced smile. "Can I help you?"

"I came to inquire about weekly rates," Brick stated gruffly.

"We only rent rooms on a daily basis."

"What's the daily rate?"

"Fifty-six dollars. Check-out time is noon."

"That'll work," Brick replied. One night in this dump was more than enough time to figure out the connection between this loudmouth sucka and Misty.

"Did you forget about me?" the dude with the sagging jeans interrupted. "How you gon' just ignore what I was saying? I need some muthafuckin' air in my room, and I ain't paying extra! My shawty is pregnant, yo. If she loses my seed, I swear to God, I'ma sue everybody. I'ma own the place!"

Unfazed by the angry rant, the clerk pointed to a box on the desk that was labeled, 'complaint' in hand-scrawled, black letters. "Put your grievance in writing."

"This is bullshit. Don't y'all got any fans or something that I can take up to my room?"

"You can try the hardware store down the street," the clerk offered disinterestedly.

"Now I gotta text my shawty and tell her to bring some money down here. Man, y'all gon' have to come off some serious paper if she gets sick from having to drag her pregnant ass down to this lobby." He glared at the clerk and then pulled out a cell phone. Frowning at the screen, he began rapidly working his fingers and thumbs as he texted.

Suddenly, the hairs stood up on the back of Brick's neck. Watching this nut bull fucking with his cell phone brought back memories. Now he knew exactly where he'd seen this dusty-looking knucklehead. He'd been playing with a cell phone when Brick had first set eyes on him. *That's the clown that was with Misty when she came to visit Thomasina after she gave birth to Little Baron. He was Misty's only worker. He was whining about going to Red Lobster while Misty was working on me...determined to lure me back into the game. If memory serves, Misty called him Troy. Yeah, this nigga's name is Troy.*

Staying in a flophouse like this, Brick concluded the male prostitute was obviously going through hard times without the guidance of Misty. Brick doubted if the kid was involved in what happened to Misty. He didn't appear to have the heart, or the paper, to put a hit out on his former pimptress. But you never know. Anyone that had been close to Misty was suspect; even this lanky fool. If nothing else, he'd be able to give Brick the names of people that had beef with Misty.

Resisting the urge to collar and bitch-slap some information out of the chump, Brick softened his expression. "Yo, cuz, I can switch rooms with you after I check in. I wouldn't want a pregnant woman to have to suffer in this heat."

The dude named Troy stopped texting and looked at Brick. "Good looking, man," he said, breaking into a relieved grin.

Having difficulty holding his affable smile in place, Brick turned his back and filled out the forms that the clerk had given him. He wrote down a fictitious name and address and then slapped some cash on the counter. Without question or even asking for ID, the clerk gave Brick the key to his room.

CHAPTER 5

It took forever, but I'm finally in Philly.

Evette said she was gon' skip work and spend some time with me. I hope she realizes that I want some welcome home nookie the moment she opens the door. No polite chit-chat. She don't need to say shit. I want her to immediately start coming out of her drawers.

I get off the El on Forty-sixth Street. I'm walking and scanning all the little side streets, looking for Ludlow, the street Evette lives on. It dawns on me that I'm not locked up anymore. I'm breathing in fresh air and feeling sunshine on my face, and there aren't any guards around, telling me yard time is over, and to get back inside.

Pent-up rage begins to leave my body. I feel good. Excited about the future.

"Whassup. How's it going?" I say to passersby, giving them a friendly smile. But they all give me wary looks, gazing at me all crazy because I extended a greeting.

Philadelphians are the most evil-ass, unfriendly people in the world. Fuck 'em; I'm a free man.

Evette told me that her house was left to her by her grandfather. It's paid in full. All Evette has to worry about is keeping up with the taxes. I told her I would help with that…but we'll see. I ain't spending no dough until I see how things are gonna turn out between us.

I'm on her street now, and I'm getting nervous. Anxiety is making my heart beat fast. Am I actually about to get my dick wet?

Evette better not be wasting my time talking about getting me reintroduced to society. She claims that she can help me become a productive citizen. Mold me into the perfect husband. Whatever! I'm only interested in having a spot to call home, some cooked meals, and wet pussy whenever I want it.

I'm about to press down on this babe's doorbell, but I'm feeling kind of skeptical...like I might be on camera, getting punked. I haven't been inside a home in such a long time, all kinds of mixed emotions are jumbled up inside me.

True to her word, Evette is home. She opens the door, and smiles at me. "Look at you! Oh, my goodness, look at you, Kaymar! You're so handsome." She squeezes my right bicep, and then gives me a hug.

Stiffly, I tolerate her embrace. "Hey, Evette. You looking good," I tell her, but I'm lying. I'm horrified to see that one side of her face is hanging. Her eyelid is droopy, and one side of her mouth is kind of zigzag.

I thought "visually impaired" meant that she couldn't read small print without rocking some extra thick eye glasses, but the entire right side of her mug is impaired and sagging all crazy.

Evette's dead wrong. Instead of taking me off-guard and springing her deformity on me, she should've been honest about her condition.

Now I understand why she wouldn't send me any pictures. She figured that one look at her mug and I'd cut off the relationship.

"So, what happened to your eye...and your mouth and shit?" I ask, trying to keep the frown off my face. "What is that? A birth defect?"

Evette looks crestfallen, like she'd hoped that I wouldn't mention her ugly face. Sheee-it! One thing about me, I always speak my mind.

"It's Bell's Palsy. My doctor said it's not a permanent condition. That's why I didn't tell you. I was hoping my face would be back to normal when you got out," she says, trying to sound pitiful.

"Goddamn!" I look away in disgust. "So, lemme get something straight," I say, standing with my arms folded across my chest. "You really can't pick your lip up at all?"

Her good eye blinks rapidly. "No, I can't control my facial muscles on the impaired side," she says, shaking her head.

There's a long awkward moment as I marinate on her words. I decide that I'm furious, and that Evette needs her ass whooped for misleading me into thinking she only had a minor problem with her vision.

But I can't kick her ass. Not right away. I don't want to jeopardize my parole, so I'm gon' have to ease into backhanding this lying bitch.

Digging deep, I gather up some self-control. I force myself to look past her flaws. I focus on her good points. Like her fat ass! Umph! My dick is starting to swell. I'm ready to grab those juicy buns.

Instead of standing around feeling awkward, Evette and I should be getting better acquainted upstairs in the bedroom.

My dick is bricked up and ready for stroking. I'm feeling conflicted emotions, though. It's crazy, but I'm feeling both disgusted and turned on by this scuggly ho. Something about her hideous disability is bringing out the freak in me—giving me real raunchy thoughts.

Before I fuck her, I should put a paper bag over her head…you know, to spare myself from having to look at her. But I can't risk pissing her off. At least not before my parole officer makes a home visit. After I establish this is my address, Evette can crawl up in a hole somewhere. She can die for all I care.

Shit, I might murk this bitch before the home visit if she don't get over here and jump on this dick.

໔ઝ

Instead of taking care of my needs, Evette's still staring at me, flashing a zigzag grin and looking real stupid.

All of a sudden, the smile vanishes from her face. "Have a seat, Kaymar. We need to get a few things straight." Her voice is no longer cheerful. With a serious expression, Evette points to the couch. The couch is old-fashioned and the color is faded; like something her old relative must've left behind. In fact, everything in the crib looks ancient and gloomy.

I sit with my back straight. My hands are folded in my lap, like I'm on a job interview…or in front of the parole board.

"A lot of women don't mind sleeping around, but I've been saving myself for the right man."

"You're a virgin?" I ask with a frown. I'm pissed because I didn't expect to have to be struggling and tryna jimmy my dick inside a tight opening.

"No, I'm not a virgin. But I've been celibate for the past six years. Saving myself for a man who's going to treat me with respect. Are you that man, Kaymar?"

This is some bullshit. Why does this one-eyed hooker feel the need to interrogate me at a time like this? She deserves to be smacked for luring me to the crib to rehash the same ol' conversation we've been having for the past two years.

"I told you a million times, I'ma changed man," I say with irritation in my voice.

"Are you sure?"

My hand is itching to slap her, but if she calls the cops, I'll be in a world of trouble. And I'll be jammed up if she throws me out her ol' raggedy crib. Being that my mother and everybody else in my family has made it clear I'm not welcome, I guess I'm stuck here in this moldy house until I can do better.

I get control of my temper and say, "Yeah, baby. I'm rehabilitated. I got my GED and everything." I put my game face on and add, "I'm a lucky man to have a sexy woman like you." My eyes begin to roam. Her titties are kind of small, but the rest of her body is tight.

"You said you're rehabilitated, but how do I know that's true? Do you have a plan...any job prospects?"

Even though I'd rather be upstairs in the bedroom tearing up some pussy, I put a pleasant expression on my face, like I'm cool with sitting here and listening to her run her crooked mouth.

"After I see my parole officer and talk to a couple of counselors, I can start looking for a job. It won't be long before I have a steady income."

She sighs. "I was hoping we could start looking at engagement rings by next week. I told you I don't believe in shacking up. I've waited two years for you to get out. We need to start planning a wedding as soon as possible."

She's making me frustrated. Got me literally twiddling my thumbs. If I don't do something with my hands, I'm liable to use them to punch her lights out. Pop her in that good eye. How she gon' pressure me to marry her as soon as I step foot through the front door?

Bitch must be as crazy as she looks!

CHAPTER 6

"Do we see eye to eye, Kaymar?" Evette asks.

She has me squirming, talking that eye-to-eye shit. That's not the kind of expression that a droopy-eyed ho should be using.

I play it off. "We can get married. I'm ready whenever you are. But first I gotta find out what I'm getting into."

"What do you mean?"

I shrug. "I'm just saying… I don't wanna get into something as serious as marriage if we're not compatible in bed."

"But we both agreed to wait…" Evette opens the left side of her mouth, and then closes it as she struggles to find the right words. "You told me you'd already waited ten years for sex and that a few more months wouldn't make any difference."

"That was before I saw you and your sexy self." My throbbing dick has me lying and talking all kinds of shit.

Evette gets fidgety. She begins fooling with the silver chain around her neck. I got this bitch cornered! She's invested a lot of money in me over the past two years. Her heart is on the line, too. She put all her romantic hopes and dreams on me, and she wants to make a profit from her investment.

I decide to call her bluff.

"My cousin just got married," I suddenly say. "He's married to a religious girl. Being a good Christian, my cousin's wife wants to help me out. She invited me to stay with them. She says there are sisters in the church lined up, waiting to cook dinner for a good-looking man like me."

I couldn't resist talking about my physical appearance, reminding her I'm a good catch. I'm no slouch in the looks department, while Evette is the type of broad that probably scares children when she goes out in public.

I can see Evette's mind at work. She's having second thoughts about giving up some poontang. I can tell by the way that she's biting on her fingernail. Yeah, I turned the tables on this nutty broad, real quick. Fuck outta here, tryna force me into marriage. She's lucky I'm freaky enough to wanna stick my dick up in a bitch that facially-challenged.

No more Mr. Nice Guy! I stand up and fold my arms. "Show me whatchu working with, baby. Cut out all the dialogue and pull them jeans down."

"Huh? Right here in the living room?"

I nod.

"Don't you want to go upstairs to the bedroom?"

"I don't have time. My cousin and his wife are expecting me to come through. His wife has a big welcome home dinner waiting for me," I say and then begin unzipping my pants.

My pants are halfway down when Evette blurts out, "Maybe you need to go visit your family first, and then come back home." She sounds offended.

I yank my pants up. "Solid," I agree. "That sounds like a plan."

The zigzag side of her lips starts to tremble. She seems close to tears. "I was going to surprise you by taking you out to dinner tonight."

"I'd rather have a home-cooked meal." I turn up my nose at her offer as I button the top of my pants.

"Okay. I don't mind staying home and cooking for you."

I want to laugh in her face. It's obvious I have her in the palm of my hand. "I already made arrangements with my family. Family comes first; you need to respect that."

"I thought you said your family had all turned their backs on you."

"Everybody except my cousin," I lie. I've always been an excellent liar. "Look, you gotta understand some things. Once we're married, I'll put you on top, but until then, you gotta earn that spot."

She nods uncertainly. "What do I have to do to earn the spot?"

"You gotta keep me satisfied." Ready to get my knob polished, I take off my shirt and step out of my pants. Her left eye is gawking at my well-developed physique. I don't know what the droopy right eye is doing; I've quickly taught myself how to block the bad side of her face away from my line of vision.

Standing butt naked in the living room, I begin stroking my shit. I could've popped off right there, but I wanted to squirt inside a warm hole. I slow my hand stroke, back up and sit on the couch.

"Come over here, girl," I say, steadily beating my meat. "Come handle this."

Evette has a trapped look on her face as she slowly tugs off her jeans. She's close to taking off her top, but I stop her, and yank her toward me.

My eyes are closed when she straddles me. Her thighs feel good pressed against mine; I get the shivers. I'm all keyed up since I'm finally about to get me some hot pussy.

Excited, I fit the head of my dick inside her slit. "You're tight," I murmur as I push in a few inches. "I can tell you been saving it all for me...your future husband," I say in a husky voice.

Future husband must be the magic words. Evette goes wild, moaning and groaning, placing sloppy kisses all over my face.

Turning the heat up a few notches, I whisper in her ear, "I've been waiting a long time for this day, Mrs. Crawford."

She's acting like a bitch in heat, bouncing up and down on my pole. She's biting and sucking on my neck. I don't like the way her mouth feels on my neck, but that pussy is super juicy. It's so mushy with her juices, I can't hold back; I skeet. My dick's only been in that pussy for a little under a minute, but she's lucky I ain't bust on impact.

Evette murmurs softly and caresses my face; she's trying to work her lips around to mine.

I grimace. I'm not tryna kiss that droopy mouth, hooker. I'm saving kissing, candy, and flowers for the right girl...someone who deserves to be treated special; not some fuggly ho.

"Yo," I say, leaning away from her. "It's gon' take a minute before I can get relaxed enough to get involved in kissing and all the lovey-dovey bullshit you tryna get into."

She murmurs some kind of an apology and then looks down in embarrassment.

"Don't try to force me into something that I ain't ready for," I grumble. "That shit you doing is a turn-off."

She flinches like I slapped her. Slapping her is a good idea. It takes a lot of inner strength to keep my hands to myself.

I shake my legs impatiently, letting her know it's time to get off me. Evette has the nerve to wrap her arms around my neck, and then lays her pea head on my shoulder, tryna sneak in some cuddle time. "Raise up!" I say gruffly. "You can get some more later on tonight."

The nerve of this ho. At first she didn't wanna give up any pussy, and now she can't get enough of this dick.

Evette slides off my lap, real slow and reluctantly. I smirk with satisfaction at the sight of my jism oozing out of her pussy.

"I have to go upstairs and clean up. Do you wanna take a shower with me? You can lie down and rest while I fix your dinner."

"I ain't got time for a shower. I told you, I gotta go see my cousin," I say as I pull my pants up. Evette is being sneaky, tryna lure me into a sexathon, but I'm not going for it.

And I'm not washing my Johnson off either. I haven't smelled pussy in a long time, and I dig the idea that my groin area has the ripe smell of vagina.

"What time are you coming home?" Evette timidly questions me.

I shoot her a dirty look. "I'm not on your time clock."

"You don't have to be so rude, Kaymar. I only asked you a simple question."

A simple question! I'm furious at the nerve of this bitch. I squint at her, making my eyes narrow and real evil-like. Evette can tell I'm two seconds from knocking her on her simple ass. But I restrain myself. I don't have this bitch figured all the way out. She might be the type to pick up the phone and try to get a nigga locked up. So, until I find out how she ticks, I'ma try to keep from punching her.

"I'll be back around eleven. Is that all right with you?" I say through clenched teeth.

"Eleven o'clock is fine," she answers quickly.

I saunter toward the door, and then I stop, suddenly remembering I spent all my money on bus fare. "I need some money," I state challengingly.

Evette immediately scampers to the dining room to get her purse. She's so afraid of making me angry, she doesn't even take the time to cover her naked ass. When she returns to the living room, I noticed that a big ol' glob of my jism is clinging to her pubic hairs. *Nasty ho!* I say to myself, but my dick is excited by the disgusting visual. My Johnson is stiffening up, acting like it's ready to smash again.

But I don't have time to bang this bitch again. Got people to see and places to go.

Evette pulls three twenty-dollar bills from her wallet.

I take the money and scowl at it like it's covered in shit. "Sixty dollars! Is that all you think I'm worth?"

She tenses visibly...even shudders a little. "That's all the cash I have right now. I'll get more tomorrow."

Sighing, shaking my head, and rolling my eyes, I reach for the doorknob, letting her know how disgusted I am about the measly amount of money she gave me.

"Can I get a little kiss before you leave?" Evette asks, her lips puckered.

I groan real loud. Ignoring her lips, I kiss her on the cheek and bounce.

CHAPTER 7

The elevator reeked of urine and mothballs.

Unfazed by the stench, the scrawny bull looked delighted by the prospect of switching rooms with Brick. "My name's Cash Money, man; you can call me C."

This broke-ass nigga got jokes. Living in a flophouse like this, he got a lot nerve calling hisself Cash Money!

"Marvin," Brick muttered, using the alias that he'd written on the form when he'd checked in.

"What floor we going to? I wanna check out the room; make sure the AC is working," Cash Money said, his finger poised over the buttons.

"It's on the Ninth," Brick said through clenched teeth. It was taking all of his willpower not to beat the shit out of the dude right there in the elevator. Until he learned otherwise, Troy AKA Cash Money was the number one suspect in Misty's near fatal accident.

During the ride to the ninth floor, Cash Money chattered on and on. He complained about the heat and rambled on and on about suing the hotel. But Brick wasn't listening. In his mind, he envisioned getting Cash Money behind closed doors and choking the truth out him.

The elevator came to a bumpy stop on the ninth floor, and Brick silently exited. Bouncing with joy, Cash Money followed closely behind Brick.

Though it was the middle of the day, the hallway of the hotel was shadowy and gloomy. Brick squinted as he made his way to room 914.

Brick opened the door. "Damn," he uttered. With his lip turned up, he surveyed the stained bedspread, dusty furniture, and the filthy, worn carpets.

"I told you, man! Ain't these people got a lot of nerve, charging niggas up for this dump?" Cash Money said and then went over near the air conditioner. Clicking a button, he released a blast of cold air.

"Ah, now that's what I'm talkin' about," Cash Money said, enjoying the breeze. "Me and my shawty gon' be laid up on chill mode for the rest of the day. She gon' be salty when it's time for her to go get that paper later on tonight," he commented with a giggle.

Brick arched an eyebrow. "I thought you said your girl was pregnant. You got her tricking while she's carrying your seed?" Scowling, Brick was two seconds from bashing dude's head into the air conditioner.

All traces of joy left Cash Money's face. "Uh, she *might* be pregnant. We don't know for sure," Cash Money said, back-peddling. "She missed her period, but she ain't seen a doctor yet."

"You tryna scam me out my air-conditioned room?" Brick's face was twisted in a menacing sneer. He didn't give a shit about the room. The mere suspicion that the scum bucket nigga standing before him could've had something to do with Misty's condition had Brick snarling.

"Nah, nah. It ain't even like that," Cash Money said, uneasily. "I don't wanna take any chances—just in case—see what I'm saying? She's liable to get heatstroke cooped up in our room."

Brick inched closer, intimidating Cash Money with a penetrating stare. "Haven't I met you somewhere, cuz?"

Cash Money backed up cautiously. "Nah, man, we ain't never met."

"Yes, we have," Brick said with assurance, nodding his head. *This nigga ain't got no heart—backing up and flinching like a lil' bitch.*

Sensing trouble, Cash Money tried to ease toward the door. Brick blocked his path. His large muscular body became an impenetrable blockade.

"Your first name is Troy, right? You used to work for Misty."

Cash Money gasped audibly.

"Seen Misty lately?" Brick asked with a sneer.

Cash Money's eyes were fixed longingly on the closed door. "I ain't seen Misty since that night…" Realizing that he'd said too much, he stopped talking. His eyes widened with panic.

"Is that right? So you saw Misty the night somebody tried to take her life? Was it you?"

"No!"

Brick stepped closer. "Were you the coward who ran her down and left her for dead?"

Scared speechless, Cash Money claimed innocence by adamantly shaking his head.

"You better start talking, man," Brick advised.

"I don't know what happened to Misty!"

Without warning, Brick lurched forward, delivering a series of vicious body shots that sent Cash Money sprawling.

Collapsed in a stunned heap, Cash Money grunted as he used a forearm to try and sit upright. Frowning and blinking rapidly, he tried to get his bearings. He squinted at Brick. "I remember you now. At the hospital. You're married to Misty's mom."

"That's right. And Misty's my family," Brick said, allowing the man on the floor to grasp the close bond between him and Misty. "Whoever brought harm to her is not gon' be breathing air much longer."

Cash Money swallowed. "I'm not the one you should be coming

for. I was back at the crib; I ain't have nothing to do with what happened to Misty that night."

Clutching the rounded collar of his tee shirt, Brick yanked Cash Money to his feet. "If you don't start talking, mufucka, your pimpin' days are about to be over," Brick hissed.

"I ain't no pimp!" Cash Money sounded insulted. "My girl was tricking before I met her."

"Whatever, man. Tell me about the last time you saw Misty."

"She was on her way to go handle some business."

"With who?"

Cash Money's eyes slid down to his sneaker. "Um…I think she was on her way to see Smash Hitz."

"You lying, nigga. Ain't no flights to Miami that time of the night."

"He was here in town. He was renting out a crib on the Main Line."

"How do you know that Misty was on her way to see him?"

"She woke me up and told me. Then she got dressed. She took the Lambo and rolled out."

"Were you fucking Misty?"

"No! It was strictly business between us."

Brick's eyebrows knitted together in anger. He grabbed the sleeve of Cash Money's shirt, yanking him forward until they were face-to-face. "Nigga, who do you think you talking to? I know Misty like the back of my hand and it's never strictly business with her. You just said she got dressed…so I'm assuming she was naked. Whatchu tryna hide, mufucka?" Brick raised his fist.

Cash Money flinched. He wriggled out of Brick's grip and held his arm up defensively. "I'm not hiding anything. I'm being straight up."

Brick snorted as he slowly walked over to the door and put the security chain in place. Then he began unbuckling his belt.

Cash Money gawked in puzzlement. "Whatchu trying to get into, man?"

"I can't get the truth out of you, so I might as well hang your slimy lil' ass and be done with you." Brick advanced toward him with the belt doubled in half.

Cash Money held up both hands pleadingly. "Yo, I ain't do nothing to Misty. The last time I seen her, she was on her way to see Smash Hitz…to give him back his chain. She took it with her…had it inside the whip."

"Misty never made it to where she was going." Brick looked up in thought. "Smash Hitz repossessed that Lamborghini she was driving, so I guess he got his chain back," he mused aloud.

"No, he didn't get the chain back. His peoples searched the car after the accident, but the chain was gone," Cash Money eagerly added.

Brick gave him a sidelong glance. "For somebody who claims he don't know nothing, you sure have a lot of inside information." Quick as a flash, Brick lashed Cash Money across the neck with the belt. An angry welt instantly appeared.

"Ow…man, I'm tryna be helpful. What's up with you?" Cash Money rubbed his neck gingerly and retreated in the direction of the locked door.

Brick stalked toward him. "Where you think you going? Ain't no way out of here, except through the window. Can you fly, mufucka?" Brick asked in a low, deadly tone.

"What else you want from me? I told you everything I know." Cash Money gave the window a desperate look, as if considering it as an escape option.

Brick thrashed him across the other side of his neck with the belt. Cash Money yelped. Now there were two thick welts on his neck. He gently touched the marks on his neck and grimaced in pain.

"Sounds like you set Misty up." Brick glowered at Cash Money.
"I told you, I ain't have nothing to do with that."

"You think your neck hurts now? Hmph. You gon' feel some real pain after I start tightening this shit around it." Brick shook the belt threateningly.

Terrified, Cash Money let out a strident yell. His cry for help should have alerted someone. But in that hotel, hollering, cursing, and screaming were a part of the everyday soundtrack.

After making a mad dash to the door, Cash Money frantically tried to undo the chain.

Twirling the belt like a lasso, Brick whipped it through the air, cracking Cash Money in the back of the head with the metal end. Dazed from the thump on the head, Cash Money's loud pleas fizzled down to mumbled whispers. In a struggle to keep himself upright, his fingers grasped at the doorframe, but he couldn't hold on. His slight body slid downward.

Cash Money lay crumpled on the floor, facedown. Brick investigated Cash Money's condition by sticking the toes of his boot into his ribs. The frail young man didn't budge. *Punk ass!*

Brick patted the metal belt buckle in gratitude as he observed the golf ball-sized knot that protruded from the back of his victim's head.

Arranging Cash Money in a seated position, Brick propped him in a corner. After securing the belt around Cash Money's neck, Brick smacked both sides of the listless man's face, bringing him back to consciousness.

"Start talking or I'ma choke you 'til your eyes pop outta your head," Brick threatened, giving the belt a hard tug. Cash Money coughed and made gurgling sounds as Brick tightened the leather noose around his neck.

Cash Money groped at the belt. "Take it off," he gasped. "I'll tell you everything I know."

Brick thought about all the misery Misty had gone through and was still enduring. A heartless mufucka had not only broken her spine, but had also used a tire iron to crush her beautiful face.

If this sucker who called himself Cash Money was responsible… if he was the one who had set Misty up, then he didn't deserve an ounce of mercy.

"Take it off, man. Please."

"Fuck you, nigga." Brick pulled the loop tighter.

Cash Money gagged and gurgled. His arms flailed and his legs kicked out spastically in front of him as he was being choked. "Aye, man. Aye. I'ma tell you everything I know."

Brick loosened the noose. "What's your room number, nigga?"

"Twelve-fifteen," he blurted. "What you want my room number for?"

"Misty told me a bitch fucked her up that night. I'ma skin your girl alive if it turns out she's the bitch I'm looking for."

Brick vibrated with rage. He hadn't believed himself capable of harming a woman, but he felt different now. If the bitch in room 1215 was responsible, she was going to suffer a slow and agonizing death.

Noticing the murderous gaze in Brick's eyes, Cash Money started talking fast. "My shawty don't know nothing about Misty. She and I met about a month ago. We're both innocent."

"Why should I believe you?"

"Because I'm telling the truth. Shit, I barely escaped with my own life that night."

"Oh, so there's more to the story. You been holding back on me, man," Brick said accusingly.

"Smash Hitz is looking for me."

Brick frowned. "Say what?"

Cash Money raised a pleading hand. "Give me a chance to explain before you start choking me again."

"Talk, nigga."

"I borrowed the chain Misty was returning to him. When she never made it, he thought I still had his shit, but I didn't. That chain is supposed to be worth a couple million dollars and that nigga wants me delivered to him, dead or alive. Why you think I'm staying in this flophouse? This is my hide-out spot."

CHAPTER 8

Getting close to my old neighborhood, I can feel butterflies in my stomach as I ride the C bus. Not wanting to risk bumping into any of Theodore Belgrade's people, I hop off the bus a couple blocks sooner than I have to.

The Belgrade family is large and crazy. Theodore has six brothers, about five rowdy uncles, and several young and dumb, trigger-happy, nut-ass lil' cousins. Everybody in the Belgrade crew stays strapped, and since I ain't carrying any protection, the last thing I need is to get into a tussle with any of them wild niggas.

Before I go visit my mother, I need to get me something for my head. I see a small crowd of young bulls hanging outside the Chinese store. I know what it is, but I ward them off, shaking my head as they rush me, each one using his own personalized sales pitch.

"You need something?" asks a tall bull wearing tight clothes. These young niggas today are trippin' with their skin-tight, punk-ass shirts and pants.

"You need something? I gotchu, man," a heavyset bull says, and then I realize it's not a bull. It's a female. A butch. Times are truly changing. These lesbian homos are outta pocket...taking their dyke shit way too far.

"I got that green," says a dude with a little bit of slouch in his jeans.

"Give me a minute," I say to the bull that looks more normal compared to the other two nut-ass niggas. I can work with a nigga that dresses like he got some sense.

I dip into the Chinese store to get me a pack of rolling paper. Most niggas my age smoke blunts, but you don't get the luxury of smoking blunts when you in the state pen, and so I lost my taste for cigar leaves. A nigga that's behind bars has to get real creative if he wants to smoke a bag of weed.

Mufuckas that's locked up gotta use the outer wrapping of toilet paper to roll up. Every now and then, I could get my hands on some fool's monthly court subpoena. Subpoena paper is a hot commodity in the joint. Them shits have a texture that's better than Top rolling paper.

"Lemme get a pack of Zig-Zag. And a lighter!" I yell through the bulletproof partition.

"Top paper only," the ol' Chinese broad behind the counter says.

I frown and then nod my head. Hell if I'm gon' be roaming all over the 'hood looking for a certain kind of paper.

The bitch behind the counter is taking a long time to get my shit. She's getting on my nerves, the way she's inching along lifting up this and that. She's making me wanna hurt her.

Keeping my eyes on the front door, I keep twisting around and looking over my shoulder, making sure ain't nobody creeping up on me. "What's taking so long, Miss Kim?" I ask in an irritated voice. *They need to put Grandma out to pasture*, I think to myself.

"Not Miss Kim. Name Miss Chong," the Chinese woman barks.

"Whatever, bitch," I mutter.

While Miss Ching-Chang is meandering behind the counter, I notice this honey-brown skin chick come through the door. Shawty is rocking a tight pair of black shorts and a clingy top with the word "pink" inside a black heart. I give her a long, appreciative look, but she deliberately ignores me and stares up at the sign that lists the food prices.

I scope out shawty's ass, and I can't help from smiling. The words, "Love Pink" are emblazoned across the back of her shorts. There's something real sexy about those pink letters sitting on her ass. I recognize that slogan from a Victoria's Secret catalog that was floating around the joint.

When a female comes outside half-naked, she must be looking for something. I run my hand across the lump inside my pants. Shawty got me bricked-up.

I can tell we're vibing together. I want to brush up against her cute lil' booty...let her feel the effect she's having on me. But I don't want to risk losing my cool and start grinding on that ass, so I get a grip on myself.

I can wait. I'ma give her every inch of this dark meat as soon as I can get her somewhere nice and secluded. I ain't got any money for a hotel room or nothing, so I hope she has a spot where we can chill. If not, I'll figure out something.

I need to let her know that whatever her hot ass wants to do, I'm with it. I don't have any inhibitions. Shawty lucked up. She done bumped into the freakiest cat she'll ever meet.

After leering at her for a few moments, I sidle up to her, and in a low, suggestive voice, I say, "I like that plump ass."

She recoils like she's looking in the face of Freddy Krueger or somebody. "Ew! Get outta my face, pervert!"

At first I'm confused, and I look around, flabbergasted. She couldn't be talking to me; I just gave her a compliment. But she's sneering, so I get insulted. A few moments ago, this bitch was throwing her pussy all up in my face, and now she tryna play me. *Who does this lil' dick teasing, cum slut think she is?* I'm so mad, I'm about to go ham on this ho.

"Two dolla; two dolla!" the Chinese bitch starts shouting. Her mug is twisted up in irritation. It takes me a few seconds to realize she's yelling at me.

"Hold up, Miss Chin Chang...Yin Yang or whatever your name is." I reach inside my pocket and get the money. As I slide the money through the slot, I use my peripheral vision to keep an eye on that smart-mouth dick tease.

Shawty got her lips bunched up. She's looking furious, with her arms crossed against her chest. She's glaring at the food selections.

I stick my purchases inside my pocket, and wonder how long this bitch is gon' take to order her food. She needs to hurry up; I got something for her. I'ma show her who's in charge. I grab my dick and give it a quick squeeze before I step outside and pay dude for a bag of weed.

The sun is setting; it'll be dark pretty soon. Instead of going to my mother's house, I mosey on over to the next corner and watch a group of young bulls shooting craps. I'm not really paying these dice-slinging mofos any attention. I'm camouflaged right now...looking like any other nigga, blending into the backdrop of everyday urban life.

When shawty comes out with her bag of food, I'm gon' peep which way she goes. With my dark skin and dark clothes, I'll merge into the shadows as I stalk my prey. I'ma yank that ass into a nearby alley. Or behind a truck...whatever's convenient.

Some slick-looking young bull walks up and acts like he's watching the crap game. He has a sly grin and a gleam in his eyes. His hand is suspiciously in his pocket, making me think he's a stick-up bull. I recognize a thieving nigga when I see one, and so I take a few steps backward, deciding it's time to bounce. I can wait for shawty on a different corner.

But the grinning nigga's eyes dance in my direction and then grow wide. "Yo, is your name Kaymar?"

Damn, I'm busted. The last thing I need is to be recognized around here. I briefly consider denying being Kaymar; my name is mud in this neighborhood. I want to run but, for some reason, I'm stuck. Frozen with fear. I should've never allowed that lil' ho in the Chinese store to delay me. I shoulda went straight to my mother's house like I planned.

"I don't know you, man," I state. My feet thaw out and I start easing in the opposite direction.

"You're the dude that got sent upstate with Theodore. Your name's Kaymar, right?" the young bull asks again.

Now everybody's gawking at me. Their expressions start to harden at the mere mention of my name. Even the nigga that's holding the dice stops playing and decides to gaze at me with the corner of his lip turned up in disdain.

"That's the snitch—the bull that turned state evidence on Theodore?" a short, stocky dude inquires, and then steps toward me threateningly.

Keeping him away from me, I stretch out both arms and hold my palms out in front of my chest. "Yo, I'm not looking for any trouble, young buck." It was hopeless to try to reason with a pack of blood-thirsty fools, but it was a worth a try.

"Looks like trouble found you," the stocky bull said.

Their voices take on the sound of an angry mob as they advance and then surround me.

I don't stand a chance against this hoard of wild young bucks. All I can do is drop to the ground and curl into a ball.

These fools are acting like my head is a soccer ball. Kicking and stomping my dome like they tryna make a score.

I have to protect my dome, so I manage to pull my arms up and shield my head. Every other part of my body is fair game. After a while, it seems like my body simply goes numb.

The distant sound of a siren saves my ass. *The cops! Yes!* Unwilling to interact with the law, the hooligans quickly disperse.

Taking ragged breaths, I drag myself to my feet, and pat myself down, checking for broken bones. None of my bones are jutting out, so I figure I'm straight. I dust my pants off, but there's not much I can do for my shirt. It's ripped and filthy.

As I limp down the street, making my way to the bus stop, I catch a glimpse of shawty coming out of the Chinese store. She takes one look at me and bursts out laughing.

I want to punch that ho in the face. But I can't...not in my current condition. Angry and humiliated, I hobble away. The sound of her laughter echoes in my ears.

After the ass-whooping I took, I have to exact some type of revenge on somebody.

Ain't nobody to take my anger out on except that bitch at home. I shake my head. Evette has no clue that she's gon' have to pay for this. She's gon' feel my wrath tonight.

CHAPTER 9

After continually choking, kicking, punching and knocking Cash Money around, Brick figured he'd gotten all the information he was going to get for the moment. But Brick had no intention of letting his victim go free.

"Give me your cell phone."

"What for? Yo, I need my phone, man." Cash Money's voice cracked pleadingly.

Brick gripped him by the collar. "Gimme that fucking phone."

"Aye, aye." He grudgingly relinquished his phone. Frowning, Brick scanned the contact list, but saw no familiar names. Searching for a link to Smash Hitz or any of his people, he was particularly interested in out-of-town area codes, but found only local numbers. Figuring that it might come in handy later, he tucked the phone inside his pocket.

Brick took a moment to compose himself. He looped his belt around his waist, and smoothed out his shirt. "Let's roll. It's time to pay your chick a visit."

"She don't know nothing," Cash Money insisted.

"Let me be the judge of that. Let's go!" Brick didn't possess any weapon other than the belt he wore, and yet all he needed to persuade Cash Money to trudge to room 1215 was a harsh tone and a deadly look on his face.

Cash Money's expression was grave; he walked stiffly, as if being forced at gunpoint.

Cash Money rapped softly on the door. "It's me, Anya. Open up." He looked at Brick sheepishly. "I don't have my key on me. I left it in the room."

Brick could hear the TV. The volume was turned up high. Shawty couldn't hear Cash Money's light tapping with the TV blasting. He cut an evil eye at Cash Money, who was being entirely too patient as he waited for the girl to open the door. "Whatchu waiting for? Knock again!"

Cash Money knocked again—softly, listlessly, like he really didn't want his knocks to be heard.

Brick was ninety percent sure the cagey little con man hadn't personally harmed Misty, but he was convinced that Cash Money had had a hand in setting her up for disaster. And he was going to pay with his life—after Brick beat some more information out of him.

He could see himself snapping Cash Money's boney fingers, one by one. After that, he'd stomp on the man's ankles. Brick could break those bones easily with the heavy work boots he was wearing.

He'd crack dude's kneecaps next. He could do some real damage if he whacked those knobby knees with a metal pipe—a piece of steel. He looked around the empty hallway, hoping to set his eyes on something he could use as a weapon. Nothing!

Brick frowned as he envisioned the tool kit in the trunk of his car. *If I had my tool kit on me, I'd nail his palms to each side of the doorframe with my nail gun. Then I'd use my hammer on those knee-caps. Plunge a screwdriver into his eyeballs. Crack a coupla ribs with a wrench. Pull out all dude's teeth, using a pair of pliers. I'd torture the shit out of this lil' grimy-ass Negro!*

"Don't be playing games; this better be the right room," Brick groused.

"It is. Shawty's probably in the bathroom or something."

"You're fuckin' around, man." Aggravated, Brick jabbed him in the ribcage with his elbow. Cash Money folded, letting out a groan.

"Tell your girl to open this door up before she finds you bodied right out here in the hallway," Brick snarled.

Motivated by the threat of death, Cash Money banged on the door. "Anya!" He pounded again. "Open the door, Anya!"

Brick was fuming at the mere suspicion that the female on the other side of the door was involved in hurting Misty. He rubbed his hands together, gearing up for mayhem and murder.

Finally, the door cracked open. The security chain was in place. Through the small opening, a pair of large, curious eyes scrutinized Brick. "Who's that?" a female voice inquired.

"Oh, this is my man, Marvin." Cash Money attempted to sound cheerful.

Brick shifted restlessly. *Unlock the door. Don't make me have to splinter this mufucka with one of these steel toe boots.*

The moment the chain was slid off, Brick stepped forward and shoved the door open, eager to begin his interrogation session.

Anya's physical appearance took Brick off-guard. He'd expected Cash Money's girl to have the rough look of a hardened prostitute. At the least, he assumed she'd be a twitching and fidgety, bone-thin crack whore. But Anya didn't look anything like the stereotypes. Though she had a wrinkled bandana tied around her head, she was clearly a beauty. Her glistening brown skin was scrubbed clean—free of makeup. It was hard to ignore her beautiful dark brown eyes accentuated with natural, thick eyelashes curled at the ends. Cut-off jeans revealed shapely legs and a cheap pair of rubber flip-flops exposed pretty feet and toes that glimmered with green nail polish.

Anya was a dime, Brick observed. But her good looks didn't

distract him. He knew from years of dealing with Misty, larcenous females that were beautifully packaged were often more dangerous than the unattractive ones.

Anya flinched when she noticed the thick welts on Cash Money's neck. "What happened to your neck, C?"

"Keep your mouth shut, ho. I'm asking the questions," Brick said gruffly. The room was miserably hot and stuffy, intensifying Brick's fury.

"Wh-what's going on, C?" There was raw fear in Anya's dark eyes.

"It's all good, baby. He just wanna ask you—"

Brick slammed the door and locked it, cutting off Cash Money's weak explanation.

"It's hot in here," Cash Money balked as he fanned himself with his hand.

Brick snorted. "It's 'bout to get hotter in this bitch if I don't get some answers."

"Why you gotta hold us hostage in a room that ain't got no AC?"

"We're hostages?" Anya's voice came out in a panicked whisper. Realizing the gravity of the situation, she covered her mouth with her palm. Her fear-filled eyes latched onto Cash Money's face.

"Whatchu staring at him for—he can't help you," Brick snapped. Proving his point, Brick smacked Cash Money upside the head.

"Damn! Whatchu hit me for? I ain't even do nothing," Cash Money complained.

"Go sit yourself down over there." Brick pointed to the bed.

Cash Money lumbered over to the bed and dropped down with a heavy sigh. "All this physical violence ain't even necessary, man."

"Turn that loud fucking TV down so I can hear myself think,"

Brick told Anya. "Then take a seat next to your partner in crime."

She raised her brows in confusion.

Focused on getting the truth, Brick didn't buy into her act of innocence. "You got wax in your ears or something? Do what I said and then sit yo' ass down next to your man."

Anya pointed the remote and turned down the volume, but she remained standing, her arms folded stubbornly. "He's not my man; we're friends. And I'm not sitting anywhere until you tell me what this is about."

Brick laughed; the sound held a malicious ring. "If you know what's good for you, you'll sit your lil' ass down right now." He raised a fist. "One blow to your dome, and you'll be in a coma, like Misty."

Anya scurried over to the bed and sat down. She scooted close to Cash Money. "Who's Misty? And what does she have to do with me?" she asked, holding up her hands in confusion.

The girl was playing dumb. Brick squinted menacingly at Anya. "Stop bullshitting. When was the last time you saw Misty?" Brick looked down at Anya's feet.

Perplexed, Anya's eyes followed Brick's gaze.

With his eyes on her feet, Brick mumbled, "You better start talking, ho. It'll be a shame if I have to scatter those pretty lil' toes of yours all over this room."

Anya gasped and reflexively yanked her feet backward. She shot a horrified look at Cash Money. "What the hell is going on?" she whispered.

CHAPTER 10

In the sweltering hotel room, there was the smell of fear and sweat.

"I don't know anyone named Misty," Anya said.

"I already told you Anya don't know nothing," Cash Money chimed in.

Brick lunged toward Cash Money. "Was I talking to you?"

"Nah, but—"

"Why you run your mouth so much?" Brick slapped both sides of Cash Money's face.

"Ow! Damn! I ain't saying nothing else."

After witnessing Cash Money getting bitch-slapped, Anya no longer considered him a protector. She edged away from the skinny dude and turned pleading eyes in Brick's direction. "Listen, I'm telling the truth. I really don't know anyone named Misty. I swear. I've only known C for a few weeks."

Brick snorted. "All it took was a few weeks for to start selling ass for this punk?"

"Whaaat?"

"Your man, *Cash Money*, told me that you're out there hustling your body while he lies back in the hotel, blazing up. That's pimpin', isn't it?"

She shot a hard look at Cash Money. "Why would you lie on me like that? You know damn well I'm not a prostitute."

Cash Money shook his head, remaining mute. With his thumb and index finger, he motioned that his lips were zipped, conveniently following Brick's instructions to keep his mouth shut.

Disgusted, Anya returned her attention to Brick. "Look, I'm going through something. A financial setback. And um...when my money got low, I moved here. I met C here at the hotel. I *thought* he had my back!" She rolled her eyes at Cash Money.

Brick looked at Cash Money. "Why'd you tell me that your girl was tricking?"

Cash Money shrugged.

"Just lying for the sake of lying, huh?" Brick shook his head.

"I'm not his girl, either," Anya said.

Brick lifted a brow.

"Since we were both going through hard times, we decided to share a room...to cut back on the expenses. We're roommates; that's it."

Brick chuckled. "How do you feel about this nut telling me he's your pimp?"

Anger flared in her eyes. "I'm furious."

Brick cast a disdainful look at Cash Money. "If you lied about being a pimp, you probably lied about Misty. I bet you're the person who left her for dead."

Lips sealed together, Cash Money shook his head vehemently.

"Talk, mufucka!" Brick yanked Cash Money's lightweight body off the bed and slammed him to the floor. The unexpected violence caused Anya to let out a little yelp of fear.

Next, Brick placed a boot on Cash Money's scrawny chest, securing him to the floor.

"You crossed the line with me when you brought your skinny ass to my wife's hospital room. Sitting up in there like you were part of the family."

"Misty invited me," Cash Money said in a raspy voice.

"Whatever. I didn't like you back then, and I don't like you now. So just imagine how much pleasure I'ma have when I start pulling out your toenails with pliers. I'll use some chicken wire to snap off your fingers." Brick grinned at Cash Money.

Anya grimaced.

Cash Money began to whine. "I don't know nothing, man. For real, dog."

"You know *something*; you're just not telling me. It's cool, though. One way or another, I'ma get the truth out of you."

"Okay, I'm trying to think." Cash Money tapped his forehead as if to speed up his thought processes.

"I want the names of Misty's clients, her female associates, male hoes, and her dicks on the side. I want the names of anybody she was dealing with—especially women."

"Misty didn't have any female friends," Cash Money said.

"What about enemies?"

"She had too many enemies to count."

"Name names, mufucka," Brick bellowed.

"Uh, she had beef with Baad B...you know, over Spydah."

Anya peered at Brick and Cash Money with great interest when she recognized the names of two famous rappers.

"I know about Baad B. What other females was Misty beefing with?"

Cash Money shrugged. "I can't remember."

Brick kicked Cash Money in the kidney. "Any thoughts?"

"Ugh!" Cash Money grabbed his side and rocked for a few moments. "Misty ain't really deal with females. I don't have any reason to lie about that."

Dude was telling the truth. Misty didn't like kicking it with females. She'd always preferred the company of dudes. Misty rarely let any woman get close. Brick took his boot off Cash Money's chest.

Using another tactic, he turned into the good cop and extended his hand, helping Cash Money to his feet. Maybe a little human kindness would put the little featherweight at-ease.

"You're right, man," Brick said in a friendly tone. "Misty didn't deal with females on a personal level. Do you think one of her workers, or maybe one of her clients, sent a broad to do his dirty work?"

"It's possible," Cash Money agreed as he dusted Brick's boot prints off his shirt. "Misty had some problems with this tranny dude she met when she was in Miami. The tranny was involved with Smash Hitz."

"Smash Hitz!" Anya whispered the megastar's name with awe. Learning the famous rapper was possibly entangled in an affair with a transvestite caused Anya's eyes to widen.

Brick wasn't surprised to learn Smash Hitz dug trannies. Misty only dealt with mufuckas that were into freak shit. Deep in thought, he folded his arms, and allowed his thoughts to roam. *A transvestite!* It all made sense now. Even though Misty had insisted a woman had hurt her, Brick had found it hard to believe a female had the heart, or the strength, for the kind of brute force that had paralyzed her and crushed her face.

Smash Hitz' name kept popping up. Being that Misty knew the man's dirty little secret, the rapper was suspect. Brick needed some contact information on Smash Hitz. A phone number would be good for starters. Things were starting to make sense. Misty was on her way to see Smash Hitz and, out of the blue, a female tried to kill her.

Now Brick realized the perpetrator wasn't an ordinary female; it was a female impersonator. Whoever that transvestite mufucka was, he and Smash Hitz were both as good as dead!

"What happened to Misty's client list?" Brick asked Cash Money in a tone much calmer than he felt.

"She kept her records on her laptop."

Misty's crib and all the contents had been immediately confiscated by the company that owned the property. That company was based in Miami. Brick figured that Smash Hitz probably owned Misty's crib, too. The realtor claimed that Misty had been negligent in the monthly payments on the mini-mansion she'd been leasing. At the time, Brick and Thomasina were so concerned about Misty's health, salvaging her personal belongings had been the furthest thing from their minds.

"Do you know the tranny's name?" Brick asked.

"Nah. All Misty told me was the tranny was pissed off when Smash refused to take her…him…or whatever, out in public. Misty said the tranny threw a fit and wanted to fight when she found out that Smash was taking Misty to the Grammys."

Brick nodded solemnly and stroked his chin as he mentally planned a trip to Miami.

Smash had a security team surrounding him at all times. Still, the man was only human—capable of human error. And the moment he slipped up, Brick planned to be there, spazzin' on his ass. The beat down he planned for Smash Hitz would persuade the man to eagerly give up the name and location of his transvestite bitch.

Brick shook his head, imagining all the bodies he'd have to drop and the long trail of bloodshed that would ultimately lead him to the jealous transvestite that had fucked up Misty's life.

CHAPTER 11

Licking my wounds, I drag myself to Evette's front door, planning to smoke my reefer once I get behind closed doors. I check my pockets, and quickly realize my ten-dollar bag of weed is gone.

They got me for my weed, my Top paper, my lighter—everything. Those niggas was off they rockers, but I'm somewhat comforted by the fact they didn't get the money tucked inside the bottom of my sock.

But I'm still feeling irate over getting my ass whooped, and getting clipped for my reefer. Young bucks nowadays take shit to the extreme. They real extra with their shenanigans.

I could press the doorbell like a civilized person, but after the brutal attack I endured, acting civilized is out of the question.

I pound irritably on the door. "Evette!" I yell in fury. I count to ten, trying to calm myself down, but it doesn't work. It occurs to me to look for a rock and bash out one of the glass panes at the top of the door. Before I get an opportunity to deface her property, Evette finally opens up.

Looking a hot mess, she's wearing a grandma nightgown and has a silk cap on her head.

"What happened to you, Kaymar?" she blurts out as she takes in my bruised face and ripped-up shirt.

Cussing, I shove her out of my way, and take the stairs two at a time. I look in the bathroom mirror to inspect my face. There are knots on each side of my head. It looks like I've sprouted a set of horns. My face is cut, scraped, and swollen.

I'm reluctant to check out the damage to my ribs. Worried they might be fractured or broken. Both sides of my ribcage hurt so badly, mere breathing is painful.

Evette comes in the bathroom. She's standing behind me, looking concerned. She keeps asking me what happened. I ignore her and continue examining my injuries.

Wincing in pain, I take off my shirt. Evette gasps in shock. My whole torso is fucked up. Those lil' niggas had a field day on my black ass. As dark as I am, there are visible bruises all over my stomach and ribcage.

"Some young bulls rolled on me," I finally mutter.

"Why?"

I glare at her nutty ass. "Ain't no reason why niggas roll on somebody. They robbed me and ran off with my bag of weed!" I shake my head. I can't believe that out of all the pen pal bitches in the world, I ended up with fuggly, dumb-ass Evette.

"You gon' just stand there, or are you gon' take care of your man?" I say in a surly tone.

She opens up the medicine cabinet and begins to gather up a bunch of bullshit.

I stand there flinching and cussing as she dabs my facial wounds with a cotton ball saturated with peroxide. I ain't gon' lie...after a few moments pass, I kind of like the tender way she's administering to me. Her gentle touch reminds me of the upstate nurse. *Mmm!* Thinking about the jailhouse nurse is getting my dick hard.

"You got some Vaseline?" I ask.

"Yeah, but I was going to put that on the cuts after I make sure your wounds are clean."

"Hell with them wounds. Put some Vaseline on my dick." I reach down to undo my pants, but a sharp pain shoots through my ribcage. "Ahhh! Shit!" I cry out in agony.

"Make yourself useful, Evette. Help me pull down my pants." It's obvious I can talk to Evette in any ol' grimy way I choose. Clearly, she's allowing me to treat her like she's a piece of shit because I'm her last hope for marriage.

I don't feel sorry for Evette. She should've known better than to get involved with a convict. Besides, she knew when she refused to send me her pictures she was hiding the fact that she's a hideously deformed bitch.

She offered to let me stay here just to keep me close. To trap me. But it's not gon' work. There's not a snowball's chance in hell that I'm ever gon' take a walk down the aisle with Evette.

Meanwhile, as long as I'm living here, I'm gon' make her suffer for trying to dupe me into matrimony.

Evette has a confused look on her face as she carefully pulls down my pants. "It looks like those monsters were trying to kill you," she comments when she discovers more scrapes and scars on my hip and thigh areas.

"Yo, enough with all the comments. Be quiet," I holler. "Grab some Vaseline and jerk me off."

"Huh?"

"Can't you see I'm in pain? I need some quick comfort."

"Why do—"

"Zip it!"

She instantly closes her mouth.

"Now get the Vaseline, so you can take care of your future husband."

She goes and retrieves a container of petroleum jelly from a shelf in the bathroom closet.

Using four fingers, she scoops out a glob of Vaseline. I watch intently as she coats my monster-sized erection with the greasy substance.

Feeling lightheaded from the good feeling, I lean against the sink. "Put some on my nuts, too," I direct.

Following my instructions, Evette lubes up my dick and my nuts. The girl is not easy on the eyes, but I have to give her credit for being a quick study. With one hand, she strokes my shaft, and she uses her other hand to expertly rub my nut sac in a circular motion.

As Evette administers to my manly desires, my thoughts turn to that lil' dick tease from the Chinese store. I want to fuck, but I also want to hit a bitch. That peculiar combination of impulses has me shooting off my wad quickly.

I like seeing dick juice splattered all over the front of Evette's nightgown. That's sexy.

I can feel my Johnson twitching as it begins to recharge. I have a couple more loads up in me. "Take that grandma nightgown off," I hiss. "Why didn't you put on something pretty for your future husband?"

A smile creeps across Evette's lips. She loves it when I refer to myself as her future husband. I'd be willing to bet money this bitch's cum hole is gushing with pleasure. But I'm too injured to give a fuck about the status of her pussy.

At the moment, my head is filled with a lot of freaky thoughts.

Evette takes off the drab nightgown. I don't look at her face. As long as I keep my eyes focused on her naked body, my dick will stay hard.

My dick is still nice and greasy, but I need some additional lubrication for the idea I have in mind. Thoughts of that lil' dick teaser is messing with my head, making me both horny and mad.

"Hand me the Vaseline," I tell Evette. She has to do all the legwork. I'm in too much pain to be moving around.

She gets it for me and holds the container while I dig out a scoop. I rub it into my right palm. "Turn around," I utter. My voice is husky with lust.

"Why do you want me to turn around?"

"Don't ask questions!"

"But I'm not into anal sex. That's nasty," she says pitifully.

"You think I'm a fag or something?"

"No."

"You think I'm a pervert?"

"No, but listen, Kaymar. I...I have boundaries, you know."

"I got boundaries, too. I don't stick my dick in assholes, stupid ho."

"I didn't mean nothing...I only wanted you to know—"

"Zip it! Turn around!"

Too afraid to be disobedient, Evette reluctantly turns her naked ass around. I imagined those pink letters that shawty was rocking on her ass, and I give my dick a couple of strokes. Before I get too caught up, I stop myself and give Evette some attention. I smack the hell out of her ass with my lubed-up palm.

"Oh, God!" she shrieks as I light her ass on fire.

"You love pink, huh?" I say, ignoring the pain in my ribs as I brace to strike her ass cheeks again.

She looks at me over her shoulder. "Pink? What are you talking about, Kaymar?" Evette asks in a frightened and desperate voice.

I don't wanna look at her right now, so I yell, "Why is your nosey ass looking at me?"

Evette yanks her head back around. She's crying and hollering as I sprinkle her ass with a series of slaps and a couple of punches. Her ass changes colors, going from soft brown to bright pink.

Completely aroused, I press my lubed-up groin against her sticky buttocks. Jolts of pain shoot up my sides as I grind hard against Evette's bruised flesh. With a grimace, I endure the extreme discomfort.

"I love pink," I whisper in her ear.

She doesn't have a clue what I'm talking about. But it doesn't matter. Evette can feel the passion behind my words. She wiggles and thrusts and before I know it, she's backing that ass up, pressing against my dick.

"I love you, Kaymar. I'll do anything you want me to do," she tells me as she reaches behind her back and separates her butt cheeks.

"You want me to fuck you in your ass?" I ask, making sure that I'm reading the signs right.

She nods. "If you want to."

"That's not what I want."

"What do you want?" she whispers, trying to twist around and look me in the eye. Even though it hurts to use any of my muscles, I grip her arm to keep her in place.

"Bend over so I can see those pink marks on your ass," I say in a soft voice.

She bends at the waist. Her ass is in the air, at groin level.

I grip my dick and aim upward. With a loud groan, I squirt on Evette's back. With pride, I watch my nutt as it trickles down to the welts on her ass. Those welts remind me of pink letters.

CHAPTER 12

"I need your government name and I want your mama's address," Brick said dryly.

"What do you want that information for?" Cash Money looked appalled.

"Insurance. I can't stay here and baby-sit your ass. But if you decide to disappear, I'll be able to reach out and touch your mother." Brick smirked. "I'm curious to find out if a mother's love is strong enough to withstand torture."

Horrified, Cash Money inhaled sharply. "My mom never met Misty. And she don't know nobody Misty was associated with."

"Doesn't matter. Your mom is going to know where you're hiding. Once I start using sharp tools on her fingertips and shit, I'm pretty sure she'll give up all the tapes, including your date of birth and your social security number."

Cash Money swallowed. "My real name is Steve, man. Steve uh…Harris."

"You're lying already, Troy."

"Oh, yeah. It's Troy Harris. Steve is my middle name." Cash Money looked sheepish.

Brick shook his head. "What's your mom's address?"

"She stays with my aunt right now, uh, in North Philly. Nineteenth and Berks."

"He's lying," Anya said, glaring at Cash Money. "His real name is Troy Morris. His mother lives—"

"Why you putting my business out there?" Cash Money griped.

"You lied on me—told this man I was tricking. And then you brought him to our room, involving me in some drama I don't know anything about."

"I was only kidding when I told dude you was a ho." Cash Money shook his head, as if Anya was being overly sensitive.

"Well, I'm not laughing." Anya looked at Brick. "I'm innocent. I don't know his mother's exact address but I do know she lives near Fifty-Sixth and Media."

"Come on, Anya. Are you serious? You just gon' lead this killer straight to my mom's front door?"

"You should've thought about that before you brought him to our hotel room." She looked in Brick's direction. "If I show you where C's mom lives, will you please let me go?" Anya bit nervously on her bottom lip.

Cash Money let out a groan of displeasure.

She held up her right hand. "Honestly, I don't know anyone named Misty."

Brick could tell the girl was telling the truth. It was obvious she didn't know Misty or any of the people involved. Brick wondered what curveball life had thrown at Anya that had landed her in this dump and with a sleazy character like Cash Money.

"This room is hot like a sauna. I'm ready to get up outta this piece. You ready to roll out?" Brick asked Anya, wiping sweat from his face.

"Can you give me a few minutes to pack? I don't want to be anywhere near this slime ball." She glowered at Cash Money.

"Who you calling a slime ball? Go ahead...leave! Go with dude. Fuck if I care."

"No, fuck you! I thought we were friends. But your grimy ass—"

"You gon' show me where his mom lives or not?" Brick interjected.

Anya nodded.

"Get your shit together, and let's go!"

Hastily, Anya threw clothes and toiletries into a quilted, red overnight bag.

"After all the meals my moms cooked for you, you just gon' throw her under the bus?" Cash Money grumbled.

As she stuffed her bag, Anya looked over her shoulder. "You didn't hesitate to throw me under the bus!"

"I told him you don't know anything about Misty! He wouldn't listen!"

"You ain't living right, C. I didn't come to Philly to get caught up in your drama."

"Whatever, bitch," Cash Money spat.

Cash Money was getting way out of line. Brick was tempted to fold him up with some gut punches, but he was bored with beating on the skinny dude, so he barked at him instead. "Yo, watch your mouth, Troy Morris," Brick said snidely, using Cash Money's government name. "I can touch you and everybody in your family. Remember that!"

Brick strode to the door. Anya fell into step beside him.

"Before you roll out, can I get my cell phone back?"

Brick gave him a dirty look.

"Aye, aye. Keep it. But um…if you not gon' use the room with the AC, can I move my things in there?"

Brick sneered at Cash Money. "You expect me to help you get comfortable? Man, you lucky to be breathing. Fuck outta here!" Brick held the door open for Anya. They exited the hot, stuffy hotel room.

CHAPTER 13

Sitting in the passenger seat of Brick's car, Anya pointed to a row house with neatly trimmed hedges. "That's where his mom lives. The house with the white security door."

"Why should I believe you?"

"I don't have any reason to lie. Come with me; I can prove it." She opened the car door.

"Nah, I'm good. You go. I'll be watching from the car."

"Okay." Anya shrugged and stepped out of the car. Brick half-expected her to make a run for it. He watched her warily as she sauntered down the walkway. Remembering that her overnight bag with all of her worldly possessions was stored in the trunk of his car, Brick relaxed.

Turning his attention away from Anya, he examined Cash Money's contact list and tapped on, "Mom." Brick held the phone to his ear, and listened to the ringing phone on the other end. On the third ring, someone picked up and began shouting in his ear.

"You gotta lot of fucking nerve, calling me from my son's cell phone. Listen, you barbarian, you better stop harassing my son. Troy told me you threatened to come to my house and hurt me. Well, it's gon' take a lot more than some threats to scare me. I'm sick of you thugs bullying my child. Troy's a good boy; he shouldn't have to live in fear, looking over his shoulder all because you think he stole something from you. Troy was raised in the church, and he doesn't steal."

Brick took a breath and attempted to get a word in edgewise, but the woman kept up the tirade. "And another thing, you can tell that little bitch, Anya, that I have a pot filled with bleach and boiling water for her. After I welcomed her into my home—fed her hungry ass—she's got the audacity to bring trouble to my front door. Yeah, I got something for her when I see her. I'ma burn the skin right off her body. Think I won't? Make sure you tell her what I said!" With those hostile words, Cash Money's mother hung up on Brick.

Anya was at the front door, prepared to rap on the front door. Brick honked the horn, and then jumped out of the car. He yelled Anya's name. Rushing toward her, waving his hand, he beckoned her to get back in the car.

Anya turned around; she looked at Brick and shrugged. He gestured for her to move away from the door. She trotted toward him in the knick of time. The door burst open and a tall, thick woman stood in the doorway. Smoke and steam wafted from the pot that she held in her hand. "Lowlife bitch!" the woman yelled.

"Run! Get in the car!" Brick yelled in desperation.

Anya looked over her shoulder. When she saw the smoking pot, she began sprinting toward Brick—racing like Marion Jones trying to cross the finish line.

Anya was half in and half out of the car as Brick peeled away.

After she caught her breath, Anya closed the door and put her seat belt on. She looked at Brick. "Now, you know where C's mother lives. Do you believe me now?" Anya asked, and then burst out laughing.

"Dude might be cowardly, but his mom's got heart. She ain't scared of nothing." Brick chuckled and then his expression turned serious. "I'm sorry for putting you in that situation. I wasn't expecting her to be waiting with a pot of bleach and boiling water. Who does shit like that?"

"That's what was in the pot—bleach *and* boiling water? Goddamn!"

Brick nodded. "That's what she said when I called her." He held up Cash Money's phone.

"Oh, my God." Anya shuddered. "Wow! That's ghetto warfare."

Brick grew quiet. It was hard enough dealing with the fact that he'd failed Misty; he didn't want to be responsible for bringing harm to this innocent young woman.

"Can't blame a mother for trying to protect her son, but I'm curious, can you please tell me what's going on? Who is this Misty chick and what happened to her?"

"I can't get into that with you."

Now Anya fell silent.

"What's your story?" Brick asked merely to make conversation.

"It's long and crazy. My father is out there living on the streets and nobody cares except me. I'd been searching for him for about a month when I...uh...fell on hard times. I feel like giving up, but can't. I won't be down much longer. Once I'm on my feet, I want to help him. Make sure he has decent food; put a roof over his head."

Being homeless had always been one of Brick's biggest fears. He was homeless right now, but he was surprisingly unworried, viewing his situation as more of an inconvenience than a hopeless state of being. His mind was too focused on revenge to worry about a comfortable bed.

"How long has your pop been living on the streets?" Brick asked.

"About seven or eight years. I don't know if he's dead or alive, but I have to try to find him."

"I got a room with AC back at the hotel. I'm not gonna use it. It's yours for the night, if you want it. But I really don't think it's safe for you to stay there, now that you got beef with Cash Money—and Mom Dukes." Brick chuckled uneasily, trying to make light of the dangerous encounter he'd led Anya into.

"Can you give me a ride to the women's shelter in Germantown? I've stayed there from time to time. They may have an available bed."

"No problem." Brick wished that he could be more of a help to Anya, but he had troubles of his own. He didn't need any extra baggage.

Driving along Stenton Avenue in Germantown, Brick noticed one fast food place after another. "You hungry?" he asked Anya. The least he could do was offer the poor thing a meal before he dropped her off at the shelter.

"Kind of."

"Is KFC all right with you?"

"Anything's all right with me. Beggars can't be choosers," she said with a pained smile.

CHAPTER 14

I nside KFC, Brick and Anya ate in silence. Anya tore into a drumstick and then a chicken wing while Brick was still working on the same chicken breast. Big and muscular as he was, Anya was eating him under the table. The girl was hungry.

Noticing there were no napkins on their tray, he got up and grabbed some napkins from a dispenser. "Here you go." He set the napkins down in front of Anya.

"Thanks," she muttered, steadily chewing.

"How old are you?" he inquired.

"I'll be twenty-one soon."

"You don't look any more than seventeen or eighteen."

"Well, I feel like I'm eighty." She gave a weary sigh.

"Where you from, if you don't mind me asking?"

"I was born here in Philly; moved to Indiana when I was a little girl."

"Did your pop stay here in Philly, after you and your mom left town?"

"My mother didn't exactly leave town. She's deceased."

"Sorry to hear that."

"I was eleven years old." She shrugged. "It's been so long, I barely remember her. Anyway, I stayed with my father and grand-mom for a while. After my grandmom passed, my dad wasn't able to take care of me. He sent me to Indiana to stay with my aunt.

Aunt Minerva isn't a blood relative. She's more like a friend of the family. I didn't have an easy life, but I try not to dwell on the past," Anya kept her eyes down as she wiped her hands with a napkin. She was acting as if she hadn't been affected by losing her parents, but Brick could sense the subject made her tense and upset. He was sorry he'd persuaded her to divulge her personal history.

"I'm broke right now, but not for long," she continued in a much stronger voice. "When I get on my feet, I'm going to hire a detective...do whatever it takes to find my father. I'll get him his own crib or he can come back to Indiana with me. It's his choice—whatever makes him happy."

Brick had also lost his mother when he was young, and he felt a connection to Anya. She was lucky to have a support system back in Indiana. Part of what made Brick tick—the dark, treacherous part of his soul—had developed during childhood, when he was whipped and abused, threatened and taunted by the adults that were supposed to be taking care of him.

He wondered if Anya's aunt had treated her right. But since he wasn't willing to share his personal story, it wasn't fair to ask her for details about her life.

Besides, Brick and Anya were only two passing ships. He was on a mission that would end in murder. While Anya, on the other hand, was desperate to save a life.

They were on two separate journeys.

Back in the car, Anya gave Brick directions to the shelter. The women's shelter was on a nice street in a residential neighborhood. Brick popped open the trunk so that Anya could get her bag.

She grabbed her red bag and hurried to the front door. She gave Brick a quick wave when someone opened the door. Brick let out a breath of relief once Anya was inside. Instead of pulling off, he sat in front of the shelter with his motor running, wondering what his next move should be.

He needed money. Couldn't accomplish much without it. He could get a loan from the credit union at work. After he got his hands on some paper, he'd put in for a two-week vacation—or better yet, he'd ask for a leave of absence.

Infiltrating Smash Hitz' camp would probably take longer than two weeks. Finding a way to abduct both Smash Hitz and the tranny broad was going to take patience and cunning.

Now that he'd figured out a way to finance a trip to Miami, he decided to splurge on a clean room in a decent hotel. Still sitting in his car with the motor running, Brick searched the Internet on his cell, and located a hotel near the airport that offered a full kitchen, a living room, and a bedroom. The price wasn't bad, either.

Satisfied with his plan, he pulled out of the parking space and drove a few feet, tapping on the brakes when he reached a stop sign at the corner.

Glancing in his rearview mirror, he spotted Anya. She was leaving the shelter, head hung low. Red bag tossed over her shoulder.

Brick immediately put the car in reverse and cruised backwards until he reached Anya. "What happened?"

"No room. They're only taking women with children. The administrator called a shelter on Thirteenth and Arch. They have two beds open. But it's first come, first serve," Anya said, sounding dejected. "I hate to ask you, but can you give me a ride downtown?"

"Yeah, I can do that." Brick unlocked the passenger door. He felt somewhat responsible for her predicament. If he hadn't shown up at the flophouse, Anya would have continued her daily routine with Cash Money. As pitiful as her life with Cash Money must've been, at least she'd had a place to stay. Now she was out on the streets. Brick noticed the sky was darkening. It looked like it was going to rain.

Suddenly affected by the gloomy sky, Brick thought about his family. Thomasina had always shown him nothing but love; she'd given him the utmost respect throughout their short marriage, and now she hated him. His son was going to be distraught when he woke up in the morning and couldn't find his daddy.

And Misty… *Oh, God. Misty!* His anguish over Misty was all consuming. *I fuck up everything I touch.*

"Is something wrong?" Anya asked, picking up on Brick's sudden mood swing. "I can take a bus and the subway if you don't feel like—"

"You don't have to go to a shelter; you can stay with me," Brick announced, making a sudden decision to take care of Anya for a few days. He'd have a guilty conscience if he left her stranded with nowhere to rest her head.

"You know the deal," he told her. "I got shit to take care of. I'm only getting this room for a few days…a week at the most. After that, you're on your own."

Anya nodded.

೮೧೦೪

Brick swiped the key card. He and Anya entered the cool and nicely decorated hotel room. Carrying a shopping bag filled with milk, cereal, and munchies, he strode to the small kitchen and set the bag on the counter.

Anya lingered in the living room area for a moment, checking out the widescreen TV and the modern furnishings. "Wow. This is nice," she said as she joined him in the kitchen. "Thanks for looking out for me."

"It's not a big deal."

"It's a big deal to me. It's been a minute since I've been in clean place with all the comforts of home." She ran her hands along the surface of the countertops, and then swung open the door to the fridge. "Ooo, they gave us complimentary bottles of water."

Brick chuckled as he began taking items out of the shopping bag.

"You're laughing, but I'm serious, Marvin. People take shit for granted, but I know what it feels like to go without the basic necessities in life."

"My name isn't Marvin," Brick corrected. "I made that up. Call me Brick," Brick said, refusing to divulge his government name.

"Brick? Is that short for brick house?" she asked, laughing as she surveyed his muscular body.

"Nah, another long story. I picked up the name when I was a kid." *A kid transporting bricks of marijuana in my backpack.*

His mind wandered to his horrible childhood. Abandoned by his mother. Abused by his stepparents. Molested and mutilated by the neighborhood drug dealer—the man who'd trained him to sell drugs and who'd dubbed him Brick. Reflexively, Brick's hand went to his cheek, expecting to feel the cruel, jagged scar his molester had left on his face.

Thanks to Thomasina, the scar had been surgically removed. Yet it always came as a surprise and a great relief when his fingers slid easily over smooth, textured skin.

And then there was his past with Misty. Recalling the perverted path they'd taken together filled Brick with shame and regret.

"Hey, Brick, there's another TV in here," Anya called from the bedroom.

Lost in thought, Brick hadn't realized Anya had left the kitchen.

He shook away the painful memories and strolled into the bedroom.

Anya turned down the covers of the king-size bed. "Look at this! Crisp, clean sheets. This is heaven! I'm gonna sleep so good tonight!"

"They only gave us one bed? I asked for a room with two queens," he stated, frowning. "Oh, well. Fuck it. I have to be on the job at seven-fifteen in the morning. I gotta get some rest. I'll deal with the room change after I get off work tomorrow."

"The sofa has a pull-out bed; I can sleep in the living room," Anya suggested.

"Nah, you're all excited over this big bed. I can nod off in the living room."

"Are you sure?"

"I'm positive. Can you excuse me while I take a quick shower?"

"Sure." Anya left the bedroom, giving Brick privacy.

CHAPTER 15

Compared to the grungy, hot room Anya had been sharing with C, this suite was a palace. While Brick showered, she pulled out the sofa bed and made it comfortable with the extra set of sheets and blanket she found in the hall closet.

She was surprised at how compassionate Brick could be. Attitude-wise, he'd done a complete one-eighty. She'd been petrified when he'd come barreling into her and C's room, making unspeakable threats and holding them hostage. Her dislike of him had been immediate and profound. His good looks were hard to recognize while he was terrorizing her. Now that he'd changed his disposition, kindly giving her food and shelter—even offering her the big comfy bedroom, she could appreciate the strong, masculine features that shaped his handsome face.

Anya had no intention of taking advantage of Brick's kindness. The pull-out sofa bed was too small for a big hunk of a man like Brick; she'd sleep here in the living room.

Anya could hear the sound of the water running in the shower; it had a soothing effect. She hadn't felt this safe and protected in a long time. That wedding band on Brick's finger had her curious. Was he married to Misty, the comatose woman?

She had been stunned when Brick and C started talking about the rappers, Smash Hitz and D.B. Spydah. Anya knew someone was after C. She'd assumed he had beef with a local thug. Never in a million years would she have imagined that C was hiding out from a big-time celebrity. And the news that Smash Hitz was into transvestites... Wow! That was some juicy information. Scandalous!

She wanted to be nosey and ask Brick to fill in the blanks about C's involvement with this Misty chick and Smash Hitz, but Anya knew better than to pry. At the moment, Brick seemed to be in a fairly decent mood. The mere mention of Smash Hitz' name might set him off—might prompt him to begin another round of intense questioning. And Anya didn't have any answers for Brick. It was best to let sleeping dogs lie.

She clicked on the TV and gazed happily at the vivid, high-definition images on the screen. A feeling of contentment washed over her. Hopefully, she could stay here with Brick until her money came through.

In a few weeks, she'd be visiting the lawyer. After that, she'd be Miss Independent. With a few million in her bank account, she'd never have to depend on anyone again.

But she wouldn't be able to enjoy the money until she found her father. She had to help him; had to let him know she understood everything now. It was so important for him to know she loved him. That she forgave him.

She'd shower him with material things. First thing on the list would be a home of his own. A decent wardrobe. And a car. Whatever it took to make him feel like a contributing member of society.

And she also had to deal out some personal justice.

Pondering the options money could buy, Anya suddenly decided that Brick might be the perfect man to get the job done. But she needed to act fast...approach him with an offer before he cut ties with her and took off for Miami. *I need someone killed. I can pay.*

Are you interested? She shook her head. Seriously, how could she ask him a question like that? Brick acted like a killer, but he had a personal vendetta against Smash Hitz and the unnamed transvestite. Killing for money was a different story.

She'd wait a couple of days. Get to know him better. Determine if she should try to negotiate a deal. Having Brick take care of the job was more appealing than contacting an anonymous assassin online. Crazy as it sounded, a person could find damn near anything on the Internet. Including a hit man.

Anya reached inside her bag and retrieved a plastic case filled with toiletries. She tugged off her shorts, planning to jump right in the shower after Brick finished.

Brick! That nigga was shot out...crazy as hell when he was angry. But damn, he was hot! Assuming his wife was the chick in a coma, the poor man could probably use some loving. Anya sure could. She was long overdue for some skin-on-skin action.

While staying with C, it was easy to ignore his sexual advances; she wasn't feeling him like that. But Brick. Whew! His name should be Mr. Muscles. His arms were cut and looked as hard as steel. She could only imagine what his bare chest and all the rest of him looked like. Yeah, Brick could get it. Trouble was, he didn't seem to want it.

Anya sighed. She was too intimidated by Brick to flirt with him. Maybe he didn't think she was attractive enough. She stood in front of the wall mirror. Frowning, she scrutinized her face. Her eyebrows needed to be waxed. She unloosened the knot in the back of her scarf. Her hair was a wreck. Dry and in desperate need of a perm. But there was nothing she could do until she could afford to go to the hair salon.

Her wardrobe sucked, too. It was hard to make a fashion statement with only a few tops, a couple pairs of jeans, and some shorts. Nothing glamorous. Nothing that was feminine or sultry enough to entice Brick.

She turned away from the mirror and slumped down on the sofa bed. Sulking, she tied the bandana around her head. She didn't even feel sexy enough to try to be seductive. Brick might feel disrespected if she came at him all half-ass and dead wrong. Having already experienced his lunatic tendencies, Anya decided to leave Brick alone. He was a loose cannon, capable of whipping her ass and possibly breaking a few bones during the process.

Curled up on the pull-out bed, Anya closed her eyes and fantasized that Brick was tossing her around, smacking her ass and fucking her like he was a wild-ass stallion. Ramming her, taking out all his frustrations on her pussy. *Ooo, damn.*

Substituting dick with a finger, she pulled her panties to the side; her middle finger traveled to her hot spot.

ဆာ

By the time that Brick finished showering, he found Anya softly snoring. He was ready to switch rooms with her, but shawty was knocked out. She was lying on top of the covers and wearing only a bra and panties. Brick respectfully covered her with the blanket. He turned off the TV and switched off the lamp.

Back in the bedroom, he noticed a missed call on his cell. *Thomasina!* Had she called to tell him that Misty had passed? In a sudden panic, Brick set the phone down. His heart was thumping and he needed a moment before he talked to his wife. If Misty was gone, he'd need all the emotional strength he could gather to try and console her mother. Then again, maybe Misty had made a miraculous recovery. Maybe Thomasina was willing to forgive him.

He called Thomasina. "Hey, babe."

There was no response on the other end. Only sobbing. Choking, mournful sobbing. Brick's heart sank. "What's wrong—Misty didn't make it?" he questioned.

"She's still alive. But she's slipping away fast. The doctor doesn't expect her to make it through the night."

"Do you want me to come over?"

"No! I hate you, Baron. I never want to see you again. Misty didn't stand chance. I'm her mother; I was supposed to protect her, and I left my helpless child alone in the room with you, a ruthless murderer!" Thomasina wept bitterly. After she regained her composure, she stated coldly, "I'm going to see a lawyer; I'm getting out of this marriage."

"Thomasina," he said in a strangled voice. "No matter how guilty you think I am, I swear, baby. My hand to God…what I did, I did for Misty. Why can't I make you understand? Baby, she was sick of living. She wanted to find peace."

"I'm sick of you telling me that you did what was best for my daughter. She was paralyzed and she was unhappy, but my child was alive! Before you took it upon yourself to overdose her, she could talk—communicate. On good days, my daughter could laugh and smile. Misty could talk to me. Now she's on the brink of death. You had no right to take matters into your hands. Oh, God! I shouldn't have allowed you to be anywhere near her."

"I respect everything you're saying. Do what you gotta do. Look, I don't have a permanent address yet, so send the papers to my job. I'll sign them, Thomasina. I'm tired. I won't fight you on this."

"You're tired? Oh, poor Baron. What about Misty? Do you think after you sign the divorce papers, everything will be all right? You should be behind bars for what you did to Misty. Do you hear me, Baron?"

"Yeah, I hear you," Brick mumbled.

"Don't worry about your next permanent address; I have one for you. The state penitentiary, you murderer! My lawyer will be sending the divorce papers to the pen." Thomasina took a deep breath. "I'll never forgive myself for letting you into my daughter's room. But you're not getting away with it. You're sick in the head, Baron. Nothing but an animal!" Out of breath and running out of insults, Thomasina disconnected the call.

There was no getting through to her. She was out for blood. Not only was their marriage over, she wanted him to be behind prison walls for the rest of his life.

೮೦೦೩

Brick slept fitfully. Two restless hours passed, but sleep refused to claim him.

It seemed he'd just drifted off when the alarm sounded. The sun shone through the window. Time to get up and go to work.

With the morning light came a brand new perspective. Brick felt a renewed sense of righteous anger. He wasn't giving up until Misty's assailants had experienced his special brand of retaliation. After he caught up with Smash and his tranny—after he'd relieved both of them of some of their body parts, he'd be willing to turn himself in—if that's what Thomasina wanted. He couldn't undo what he'd done, but if his incarceration gave Thomasina any measure of peace, then so be it.

CHAPTER 16

Last night, Evette and I shared a few tender moments. I ain't gon' front; sleeping in the bed with Evette is nice.

She disrupted my sleep twice last night. The first time, she woke up whimpering and talking about she needed some Tylenol because her ass was tingling.

"Whatchu mean?" I asked, rubbing my eyes.

"I can't sleep. My butt hurts, real bad. Maybe some Tylenol will stop the stinging."

There were only about four Tylenol pills left in the bottle and I needed those for my sore ribs and whatnot. I could have let her lie there and suffer, but I can be a nice guy every once in a while. So I decided to take care of her welts and bruises. But not with Tylenol. I run shit in this house, so the remedy has to be my way.

I told Evette to scooch down and suck me off.

"Don't swallow," I instructed after I shot a load in her mouth.

"Spit it out." I cupped my hands in front of her mouth and captured the nutt that I'd busted.

In my mind, I was pretending to be a doctor treating a patient. I smeared my nutt all over her wounded ass. Acting as a medicinal balm, my semen was put to good use.

A few hours later, Evette was at it again, whining and complaining about her sore ass. Before I could even wake all the way up, she had wiggled downward and was slurping on my Johnson.

Her head was bobbing up and down furiously as she worked hard to pull another nutt out of me.

The average nigga would feel perturbed if he had to keep waking up out of a good sleep to administer first aid. But I didn't mind at all. In fact, I enjoyed it. Truth! There's something real satisfying about tending to a sick patient in the wee hours of the morning.

With the moonlight shining through the window, the atmosphere was warm and peaceful. I gently slathered my dick juice over her butt cheeks while she lay on her stomach. She had her face pressed into the pillow, so her words were muffled, but she lifted up her head and clearly said, "I love the way you treat me, Kaymar. You're so kind."

Those words of appreciation made a nigga feel real good. Got me feeling like healing bitches might actually be my true.calling.

Then a few moments later, she said something else…some mumbled shit that I couldn't make out. Her words were garbled, but it sounded like she said, "After we get married, I want you to spread your cum all over me, every night."

Now correct me if I'm wrong, but seems to me Evette was hinting that she wants me to take it up a couple notches. Start whooping her all over: Ass, arms, legs, thighs, back… I wonder if she wants me to spank them lil' titties, too?

I'm confused right now. I don't know what love is supposed to feel like…but I'm feeling so good right now, this feeling has to be damn close to love.

I look at the clock and it's six in the morning. Evette is still sleeping, but she has to get up in a minute and get ready for work. Her job requires sitting, and I'm not sure if she'll be able to apply any pressure on her sore butt.

I lift the covers up to check and see how her ass wounds are doing. She wakes up a little. She murmurs a sound when the cool air breezes on her body.

I frown at the sight of her naked booty. Hard cum is caked on her ass. I don't like the way it looks. I go in the bathroom and bring back a warm washcloth.

"Evette!"

"Hmm?"

"Wake up."

She shifts slightly and then gets real still when I apply the warm cloth to her butt cheeks, soaking off the dried-up cum.

"Listen, you gotta be a little late for work today. I gotta doctor you up before you leave the house. Okay?"

"Mmm-hmm."

I fling the moist washcloth on the other side of the bed, while I excitedly get busy...jerking my dick. I don't need her to guzzle on my Johnson; I'm already worked up.

I notice that Evette is grinding against the bed sheets. I guess she's trying to reach a climax by putting some friction on her clit. Being thoughtful, I slip a hand beneath her as I'm jacking off. I clip her stubby little clit between my knuckles, pinching it as hard as I can.

Evette's got a loud mouth on her. She screams for the whole 'hood to hear as she releases a little puddle of slimy girl-cum.

Howling my head off, I bust right along with her.

Obviously, I'm not the only freak in this relationship. Evette is sneaky with it, but I realize that she's just as freaky as I am.

I didn't plan to, but I might be falling for this nutt-ass broad after all.

If Evette plays her cards right, there just might be a future for us.

CHAPTER 17

Brick usually listened to rap music. On his way to work this morning, he felt like screaming out in pain and rage. Times like this he only wanted to hear the oldies. The kind of music that his stepfather, Mr. Rodney, used to play while getting his drink on. Mr. Rodney would throw back some cheap liquor, close his eyes, and nod his head with understanding while listening to the wails and musical moans of Bobby Womack, Al Green, or Otis Redding…old school cats like that.

With earpods in place, Brick's shoulders bobbed to music as he walked from his car to the work site, where the rest of the crew was starting to set up equipment. Teddy Pendergrass was belting out "If You Don't Know Me By Now," and Brick was feeling every word. Thomasina should've realized that it was his deep, deep love for Misty that had compelled him to try to put her out of her misery. But she was pushing him away, hating on him. Treating him like he was some random stranger…like she didn't know him at all.

Ready to put in a hard day's work, Brick's hands were itching to get on the drill. Breaking up some concrete and tearing up some shit could relieve some stress.

He planned to use his half-hour break to fill out the paperwork for the loan.

Cliff, the supervisor, was giving out instructions to some of the guys. The minute he saw Brick, he stopped talking and began walking briskly toward him.

Sensing that something was amiss, Brick slowed his stride. He pulled the earpods out. "Whassup, Cliff?"

"You got trouble, Brick. I don't know what's it's about, but a detective from the Philadelphia Police Department was here looking for you. Said he wants to ask you a few questions. Did you get yourself into some trouble?" Cliff's brows were furrowed with concern.

"Uh, not that I know of."

Cliff handed Brick a card. "He left his card; wants you to give him a call."

Brick examined the card that was embossed with the city seal. "Yeah, okay. Look, I'm feeling kinda sick."

"If you need a few days off to handle this thing, then take some sick time."

"That'll work. Put me down for two sick days."

"You're a hard worker, Brick. A good man. I hope this isn't a serious problem," Cliff said.

"Nah, nothing serious. I think I know why the detective wanted to see me…" Brick laughed uncomfortably. "Seriously, it ain't about nothing. I'll be back on the job day after tomorrow," Brick replied, wishing that his words were true. If Thomasina had sent the cops after him, it could only mean one thing: Misty was dead. And Brick was now a suspect in a homicide.

He stuffed the card in his pocket and turned around.

Inside his car, Brick let his tears fall. He shed tears for losing the love of the only woman that had ever loved him unconditionally. Thomasina had taken a big gamble on a dumb, young dude like him. He'd promised to never let her down. And look at what he'd done. Broken her heart into pieces.

He cried for his innocent son. He'd hoped to break the cycle, but just like him, his boy was also going to grow up without a father.

And he shed tears for Misty. Love her or hate her, she had been a whirlwind of vibrant life. Gone too soon. *Rest in peace, Misty baby. I tried. I did the best that I could for you.*

ဆာ

Anya discovered a twenty-dollar bill tucked beneath her pillow. Pocket money from Brick. *Aw, how sweet,* she thought, touched by his thoughtfulness. The hotel and food was more than enough hospitality. The hard exterior was only one aspect of Brick's personality. His mean streak was reserved strictly for those who pissed him off. Brick obviously had a soft heart, and Anya intended to earn a place on his good side.

Sick of wearing the scarf, she worked on her hair, styling it as best she could with a palmful of gel. She put the iron and ironing board that the hotel provided to good use, ironing out the wrinkled clothing she'd gotten from the Salvation Army. She wanted to look her best if she stumbled upon her father.

A little blush and some lip gloss and she was good to go. Feeling fresh and exhilarated, Anya was out the door.

With a portion of the twenty dollars, she bought a SEPTA day-pass and began combing the city streets and parks, searching for her father. She'd been trying to find him for weeks, but with hundreds of homeless people living on the streets, locating her father was a daunting task.

At an off-ramp near the Vine Street Expressway, Anya held out a ten-year-old photo of her father. "Have you seen this man?" Anya questioned a haggard white woman.

"Oh, yeah. That's—"

"You've seen him?" Anya said hopefully.

"Yes, that's my son. That's Bobby. I haven't seen him in a long time." The woman placed the photo against her heart, crinkling it up as she hugged it dearly. "I miss my Bobby. Thank you for bringing me his picture," she told Anya.

Realizing the woman was mentally unstable, and that she might have to fight her to get the picture back, Anya resorted to trickery. "Your son looks just like you. Same nose and mouth. But his eyes…"

"He has his father's eyes," the woman said bitterly.

"Lemme see."

The woman released the photo from her bear hug, and Anya snatched it from her grimy fingertips.

The homeless woman became infuriated—thrashing and cussing up a storm. "Motherfucker, give me Bobby. You, bitch! Give me my goddamn child back!"

The way she came after Anya, snarling and growling, teeth bared like an animal, one would have thought Anya had snatched a puppy from her litter.

Anya raced away, easily outrunning the undernourished woman. On the next block, she encountered a man sitting on top of a flattened cardboard on the sidewalk. His legs spread out in a V. High-water pants exposed legs that were crusty, scarred and scabbed over. As if he were invisible, people passed him by without so much as a glance.

Anya drifted over to a man. Bending at the waist, she said, "Hello, I'm looking for my father. Have you seen him…you know, like…during your travels?" Once again, she held out the old photo of her father. She was a little upset that the picture was now crumpled from the crazy lady's body lock.

"That's your daddy?" the man asked in a voice that was coarse from liquor, or perhaps his scratchy tone was a result of an illness brought on by years of living out in the elements.

Anya nodded briskly. "Yes, that's my father. His name is Herbert. Do you recognize him?"

"Never set eyes on 'em," the man said gruffly. "Pretty thing like you shouldn't have to search for a deadbeat dad. Forget about him; I'll be your daddy." His tongue slipped out, suggestively licking lips that were cracked and dry. In an obscene gesture, he gripped his crotch and winked.

Disgusted, Anya moved on, continuing her search in alleyways, parking lots, subway concourses—all of the known haunts of the homeless. At a gas station, she encountered a young couple carrying all their worldly goods, strapped to their bodies in backpacks.

The nation was in a sorry state. The young homeless were a demographic that was becoming alarmingly prevalent. People had little sympathy for the young and able-bodied homeless, believing that their predicament was the result of laziness or drug use.

But Anya knew from her own harrowing experience that the loss of shelter could happen to anyone. The homeless couple was pumping gas, trying to earn a few bucks toward their daily survival. She showed them her father's picture. A bad odor emitted from the pair. It was the smell of gasoline and tuna fish—an odd and unpleasant mixture of scents. Anya had to hold her breath while they scrutinized the photo. The young couple shook their heads. "Never saw him before," the young man said.

"There's an organization that travels around the city offering shelter to people living on the streets. They try to gather names and other information from people that are willing to cooperate," said the woman.

"Do you know the name of the organization?" Anya asked.

"Beats me. Something with the word 'Homeless' in the title. I bet you can find them on the Internet. I hear they have a database of information on street people, including photos."

Her search had not been an entire waste. Feeling more hopeful than ever, Anya thanked the couple. She wondered why they hadn't accepted help from the organization. Maybe they didn't want to disclose their identities. There were a million reasons why some people were without food and shelter.

She concluded her day's journey at the public library on the Parkway, where she'd hoped to be able to use one of the computers and find out more about the organization that identified street people.

Anya left the library in disappointment when she was told that their computers were down.

Outside the library, she was immediately accosted by sad-faced, gaunt, forgotten people who were begging for loose change. This was the reality of the homeless.

On second thought, the notion that there was a database of information about street people seemed rather farfetched. Tomorrow, she'd backtrack to some of the places she'd already visited when she'd first arrived in Philly. Places like Needle Park in the Kensington section of the city, where many of the homeless congregated. She was likely to get more information from personally combing the streets than she'd get on the Internet.

Survival on the mean streets was like living in a jungle. There were an astonishing number of crimes against the homeless. People moved around when areas became too dangerous or when weather conditions destroyed or caused their makeshift shelter to become uninhabitable.

Anya was afraid that if and when she ever found her father, he'd be crazy as hell; unable to recognize her. It was so scary to think that her father may have forgotten he'd ever had a daughter. But her worst fear was that she was too late—that her father was dead.

ℰℛ

Brick had paid for two days when he checked in. More money down the drain. He shook his head, thinking about all the money he'd been wasting on hotel rooms. And this time, he'd checked in using his real name. Stupid!

I should've used an alias when I checked into that joint. I gotta bounce; it's too easy for the cops to find me if I stay there. I'ma shoot through the spot real quick; get my shit and tell shawty, deuces. She seems like a nice girl, and I feel bad for having to run out on her. But I ain't got no choice. It's time for us to part ways.

Speeding to the hotel, Brick zoomed through yellow lights, only tapping lightly on the brakes whenever he approached a stop sign.

CHAPTER 18

I can't keep my mind off the strippers that I wanna get with.

It's not the way I planned it. I'm not having a big welcome home party at a strip club with all my homies drinking and getting lap dances.

Being stuck in this house with Evette is getting on my nerves. Don't get me wrong; I like that she goes along with all my freakish ideas. She cooks, cleans. I believe she'd even give me a tongue bath, if I let her.

I shouldn't complain because I'm treated like a king in this piece. But Evette's money situation isn't up-to-par. After she bought me some clothes and gave me pocket money, she's pretty much tapped out until her next payday.

In the meantime, a nigga needs to buy weed on a daily basis. I like to chill at the corner bar, and hang out with my new friends— Blake and Munch—a couple of West Philly dudes I met at the barbershop a few days ago.

Munch is a bulky nigga. He's built solid—not chiseled like me. Blake is a light-skinned, curly-headed, pretty boy. Lean frame. Blake ain't nothing but a featherweight, but he thinks he's God's gift to women.

So far, both Blake and Munch have been cool with me, sharing their weed and liquor. But how long can I keep freeloading off these dudes? If Evette wants to keep me interested, she should be figuring out a way to get her money right. She's gon' have to step it up, and do better by her man.

I didn't tell Blake and Munch too much about my past, but they do know I just got out of the pen. I didn't tell them I did a long stretch. If I give out that kind of information, they're liable to start snooping into my past.

When I admitted I've never been to a strip club, they both fell out laughing, thinking it was hilarious.

It's not my style to deliberately make myself a laughing stock. There's a method to my madness. If I confessed about never seeing or touching a stripper, they'd volunteer to take me to a strip club and even treat me to some lap dances.

So here I am, wearing the new sneakers and new clothes Evette bought me, waiting for Blake to roll up in his Chevy. The whole time I was locked up, I always envisioned myself riding around in a Benz, a Beemer, or an Escalade…something fly and luxurious. But what the fuck. Riding in a Chevy is better than riding the bus.

Everybody from my old 'hood is frontin' on me. It's all good, though. I'ma be up one of these days.

The car horn honks and I run out of the crib. I lock the door with the set of keys Evette gave me. Shit, I'm liable to put her ass out now that I got my own house keys.

"Get in the back, Munch," Blake says when I approach the car. Munch doesn't hesitate. He gets right out and hops in the back.

I'm riding shotgun while my man, Blake, is steering with his knees while he rolls up a blunt. Hanging with these niggas, I'ma have to develop a taste for tobacco leaves; they don't fuck with rolling paper at all.

Blake passes me the blunt. Power 99 is blasting from the speakers and I'm smoking, enjoying the city sights…feeling nice.

"Yo, that ain't your personal; pass that blunt back here," Munch says from the back.

"My bad." I turn to pass the blunt to Munch.

"Hell, no. Don't let that nigga put his mouth on my weed," Blake intervenes.

Now I'm in a quandary. I'm holding the blunt in mid-air, not knowing what to do.

"Man, why you always drawlin'?" Munch asks.

"Hmph! We both know where your mouth been."

"The same place your mouth been."

I shrug my shoulders and help myself to another puff, figuring I'll keep on smoking until these niggas come to some kind of conclusion.

"That's bullshit. Nigga, I told you last week, I'm not smoking behind you no more."

"You smoked behind me last night, so why you frontin'?" Munch argues.

"I must have been so high that I forgot about my new rules," Blake suggested.

"You frontin' for Kaymar."

"I'm not frontin' for nobody. I'm keeping it one hunnit."

Now, I'm high as a kite and curious about what they're talking about. "What's wrong with his mouth? Why can't he smoke some of this shit?"

"Because this nigga's nasty."

"No, I'm not," Munch grumbles half-heartedly.

Blake reaches for the blunt, so I have to give it up. He puffs and turns around and blows a cloud of smoke in Munch's direction. "Get high off that," Blake says, laughing.

"That ain't even funny," Munch complains.

"I'ma tell you what's not funny," Blake says in a serious tone. "It's not funny when people all over Philly know all about your bad habit."

I'm wondering if Munch is a heroin addict. And did he get

something off a dirty needle? "Yo, somebody needs to tell me something," I blurt out. "No disrespect, Munch, but I don't wanna smoke behind you either, if you got that monster!"

"I ain't got no HIV."

"Oh, okay," I mutter, feeling relieved.

"Tell him whatchu got," Blake prods.

"I ain't got nothing!"

"Yeah, aye. Tell him what you had."

"It ain't his business."

"What did he have?" I ask, urgently. These two niggas is crazy. Both of 'em are starting to remind me of the backwoods lunatics you see in horror films.

"Munch got his name from munching on a whole lot of different pussies—"

"Say whaaat?" I turn all the way around and gawk at Munch.

"Not a *whole lot* of different ones," Munch says to his defense.

"Eating three or four strange pussies a day is a *whole lot*. Nasty ass!"

"You don't think it's nasty when I'm doing it for you."

Huh! I look from Munch to Blake, thinking these weirdo niggas are really on that shit! I'm seriously considering bailing out of this car. Fuck the strippers. I'll check them out on my own dime. I can go to the strip club by myself as soon as Evette gets paid.

Blake passes me the blunt, but now I'm leery about his and Munch's homo activities, and I refuse to take it. "Nah, I don't want no more. I'm good," I tell him.

"Man, don't listen to Munch. He don't do nothing he don't wanna do."

I lift an eyebrow. "Y'all homos?"

"Hell, no!" Blake explodes into laughter. "I bring Munch along whenever I need him to handle the foreplay on the bitches I be fucking. That's how we get down."

I'm still confused, but extremely intrigued. "What does Munch do?" I crane my neck and give Munch another questioning look. His expression is rather sheepish, but I also see a trace of pride. Now, I'm finally getting the full picture. Munch is a little slow. Mentally delayed. And I don't know why Blake is even fucking with the bull, but I don't roll with niggas that used to ride the little school bus.

"Munch has a bad pussy-eating habit. He's addicted. You know what I'm saying?"

"Nah, whatchu mean?" I respond.

"I mean, Munch gotta eat pussy all the time. He craves it."

I peep Munch again, and that twisted son of a bitch is in the backseat smiling and nodding his head about his nasty addiction.

"Munch is my man from ever since we were kids. So I look out for him. Every now and then, I run across an extra freaky bitch, and I convince her to let Munch give her some oral before I fuck her. By the time he's done slurping on that pussy, my dick gon' slide right in!"

CHAPTER 19

N ow my interest is piqued. My wheels are spinning. I don't know how I feel about Munch and Blake's arrangement, but the idea is stirring something inside me. I decide to ask some more questions. "So what does Munch get out of the arrangement? Does he get sloppy seconds after you smash?"

Blake frowns and shakes his head. "Munch don't care about fucking."

"While Blake is smashing, I jack off," Munch volunteers.

Blake nods his head. "See, I told you, man. Munch and I ain't into any homo behavior. The problem that I have with Munch is that he done went buck wild with his oral actions. Women all over the city are passing his number around. On the weekends, when the clubs let out, bitches be hitting Munch up like crazy. All of 'em wanting they pussies ate before they call it a night. And Munch don't even make the bitches come to him. He goes out of his way…hooking up with females in the parking lot of the club they just left. One night he gobbled up three pussies out of one car, and four pussies out of another."

"Umph!" I thought I was twisted, but I ain't never heard of no shit like this.

"And Munch don't get nothing out of the deal. He don't charge the bitches… He don't even jack his shit off. Just eating one stank pussy after another. After them hoes cum, they drive off and leave him with a hard dick and no satisfaction."

Munch is awfully quiet; he's not defending himself at all. So I feel compelled to ask Munch about his mental status. Once again, I turn and look in the back seat of the car.

"Yo, I ain't passing judgment on you, bro'," I say to Munch. "But why you letting hoes take advantage of you like that?"

"Ain't nobody taking advantage of me. I'm satisfying my oral fixation. Simple as that."

"Going around eating pussy is crazy, man. You got to be a little slow. You know…half a school bus kind of slow. Are you a lil' bit retarded?"

"Ain't nothing slow about me," Munch says with an attitude.

"Munch is an intelligent mufucka," Blake pipes in. "But he letting his addiction rule his life. Now he done caught a venereal disease in his mouth." Blake tosses a blameful look at Munch.

I grimace. Both these niggas are weirdoes.

"I got treated for that. My mouth is clean as the board of health," Munch brags.

"So what! You gotta be careful where you put your mouth, man."

Munch rolls his eyes. "Nigga, stop frontin'. Don't act like you don't eat pussy."

"Yeah, I do. Ain't nothing wrong with giving oral. But not all the time. Man, all I'm saying is that you need to cut back. That's all I'm saying."

"Aye. I can do that."

By the time we get to the strip club, my shit is harder than concrete inside my pants. Here it is, broad daylight outside, yet it's dimly lit in the strip club, giving it an after midnight kind of vibe. These bitches up in here are running around flaunting naked tits and asses. I ain't never seen nothing like this before.

I got a strong sex drive. Truth. You can't bring me in a place like this and expect me to be satisfied with merely looking.

"Why they showing tits and asses, but their pussies is all covered up?" I ask Blake.

"No nudity," he explains. "Pick the shawty you want to give you a lap dance, and I'll pay her a lil' extra to let you rub on her pussy."

"Man, I don't wanna rub nothing. I wanna fuck. And not just one stripper. I wanna fuck all of 'em." My voice comes out louder than I anticipated.

"Whoa, my nigga. You sound crazy."

"I'm just saying, man…this is like window shopping without no money. It's real frustrating. I didn't come out of the crib to get worked up for nothing."

Blake nodded in understanding. "Some of these chicks will let you pay to play, but not until they finish their shift. They don't fuck right here inside the club."

I'm getting very aggravated. My dick is bricked and I can't use it on none of these bitches. This is fucked up!

A dark-skinned shawty with a nice donk switches past me. "Yo, chocolate ass, come over here and let me wax you," I blurt, rubbing on my dick. The girl turns her nose up and keeps it moving.

"Relax, man. Don't be insulting the strippers. I'ma treat you to a lap dance to calm you down." He beckons a stripper with a cute little butt. "Give my man a dance," he tells her. "Treat him extra special, aye?"

The stripper smiles and positions herself in my lap. As soon as she starts swiveling around, I immediately ejaculate. But she can't feel the moisture through my jeans. She keeps on working that ass and my Johnson rises to the occasion, again.

By the time the song is over, I bust twice.

I go to the bathroom and clean up as best I can with paper

towels. When I come out, Munch is getting a lap dance from a white chick and Blake is focused on his cell. Looking down, he's tapping on the screen and smiling.

I don't like the way people act nowadays. Everybody's always fucking with their cell phones. All this text messaging and shit is getting out of control.

"So how'd you like your first experience at the strip club?" Blake asks as he puts his phone inside his pocket.

"It was cool, man. Thanks," I say as I cut my eye at this chocolate shawty with the extra big ass. I wanna get a dance from her next. I wanna cum on that chocolate ass.

"Me and Munch are about to be out. You staying here or do you want me to drop you off at your crib," Blake says.

"We just got here!" I'm shocked that Blake is ready to bounce. I'll stay if he lets me hold some money, but I can't afford lap dances at ten dollars a pop.

"I know, man, but me and Munch gotta go holla at this chick up in the Northeast."

"You're taking Munch with you?" I frown, recalling what he said about Munch and his nasty ways.

"Yeah, man. That's how we do. We cleared up our misunderstanding. Munch is cool. He went solo for a while and he paid the price. That bull knows I look out for him. He got that habit, but I know how to keep him in check. When Munch fucks with who I fuck with, he ain't gotta worry about picking up any diseases."

I nod my head in understanding, but my mind is running a mile a minute. See, I wanna get involved in the freak shit they're into, but I don't wanna sound like I'm begging. I could use a nigga like Munch at my crib. But something tells me that Blake isn't willing to loan Munch out.

I'ma have to figure out a way to lure Munch over to the crib without Blake finding out.

CHAPTER 20

Shawty wasn't anywhere to be found when Brick got back to the hotel. Good! He could tell that she was growing attached to him. He was on the run now, and the only way to travel was solo. Brick was relieved he didn't have to see the disappointment on her face when he told her it was time to cut the cord.

There were only a few items to scoop up; everything else was stuffed inside the duffle bag. From the bathroom counter, he gathered his razors, shaving cream, toothpaste, deodorant, and other odds and ends. Next he surveyed the bedroom to make sure he didn't leave anything behind.

On his way out, he spotted a pen and pad that was stamped with the hotel's logo. Thinking about what to write, he squinted up at the ceiling. He was going to start off with an apology for leaving Anya hanging, but decided to keep the message short and to the point. *The crib is paid for. You can stay here 'til checkout time tomorrow. Take care of yourself. Brick*

He tore the sheet of paper off the pad and placed it on top of the remote, which Anya was sure to grab when she returned.

Stirring outside the door told him that shawty was back. Damn! Brick balled up the note and tossed it in the waste bin. He'd have to deliver the news in person.

Anya broke into a surprised smile when she saw Brick. "Hey! I thought you were at work."

She'd taken off the bandana. Her hair was short-cropped and slicked back with gel. Cute. And her face was even prettier than he'd realized. Shawty shouldn't have any trouble finding a man. Brick hoped she'd raise her standards and get herself a good man—with some balls. Not another punk-ass, wannabe pimp, like Cash Money.

Feeling guilty, Brick wouldn't meet her eyes. "Yo, I'm outta here. The room is paid for until tomorrow. Checkout time is eleven. Stay outta trouble." Brick hefted the heavy duffle bag over his shoulder, and crossed the room.

"Why are you leaving? I thought you said I could chill with you for a while."

"Change of plans."

"Do you want to talk about it?"

Brick was instantly annoyed. "I don't owe you no explanation about nothing. I got problems, and I can't have you tagging along. You're a nice girl and everything, but the way I see it, you're unnecessary baggage."

"I know you're on some kind of mission—trying to touch Smash Hitz." She shook her head. "That's the major league. Do you really think you can get close to someone of his stature?"

Brick frowned in irritation. "You know too much already. I don't like people in my business. Got me feeling uneasy." Brick's face darkened as he stepped toward her. "Take some advice, lil mama, stop running your mouth. Forget you ever met me."

"You can trust me, Brick."

"I don't trust anyone."

"Last night, I was thinking about my problems and from the little that I know about yours…I think we can help each other."

Brick looked at her like she was crazy. "What can you do for me?"

"I can finance your trip to Miami."

Brick gave a humorless laugh. "Yeah, right. You're one step away from the women's shelter, but you want me to believe you have enough money to get me to Miami?"

"I really can," Anya argued. "Not right now, but—"

"Not right now is exactly what I thought," Brick said sarcastically. He gazed at her with disdain. She was desperately grasping at straws. Lying and coming at Brick like he was on some kinda sucka shit.

Brick was actually relieved Anya had let down her guard, showing her true self. He no longer felt sorry for her. With a clear conscience, he could roll out.

"You should call that shelter, and make some arrangements for yourself," Brick said in a cold tone, and then sauntered toward the door.

"When my mother got killed…" Anya paused.

Brick stared at her, waiting for her to finish the sentence.

Anya's eyes began to water, and her body trembled. "There was a lawsuit. My father was awarded a lot of money. My father. He…he…"

"He what?" Brick said impatiently.

"Started messing with drugs. He blew all the money. Lost everything. Sent me away," Anya said, talking fast. Brick tried to make sense of her words, but her staccato bursts of information didn't make sense or add up. From what he gathered, seemed like she was telling him that her pops blew some lawsuit money, and lost everything.

She didn't have a pot to piss in, so where was she going with this? She damn sure didn't have enough dough to finance his mission.

Brick gave Anya a long look. It seemed like she was falling apart. Shaking and carrying on…unable to speak in a complete sentence. *Shawty might be missing a screw or two.*

"You need to chill out. For real." He shook his head in disgust. "Why you tryna play me?"

"I wasn't. I get upset when I think about what happened to my mother."

Brick wrapped his hand around the doorknob. *I thought she said that she didn't even remember her mother. Shawty got issues.*

Forcing patience into his voice, he said, "Maybe you need to talk it out with a professional. Look, shawty, I'm outta here. And you're lucky that I'm not kicking you out. The way you acting makes me think twice about leaving you here. Something could spark a bad memory…cause you to black out and start tearing up shit. If you tear up a bunch of shit, the hotel's gon' come at me—try to hit me with some vandalism charges. I got enough on my plate; I don't need any more problems." Brick rubbed his forehead, wearily.

"I'm not crazy. I don't go around damaging property. I wouldn't do anything like that," she said, tears sliding down her face.

"Aye, cool. Have a good life." Brick turned the knob, opened the door.

Anya grabbed his arm. "Please don't leave me. I need you."

Brick felt all his resolve melting away. There was something in her voice, a pitiful note of panic that resonated within in. Many times in his life, he'd begged someone not to leave him…pleaded not to be kicked out. Starting with his mother. Then his foster parents. Then Misty. And now, Thomasina.

Brick knew all too well the pain and the fear of being all alone in this world.

"Aye. We gon' ride this out together. But you gotta stop crying. Please." Brick reached out to wipe her face.

Anya tumbled into his arms.

Comforting her, Brick held her close, his hand unconsciously stroking the middle of her back.

"I need you, Brick. Need you to make love to me."

He stilled the movement of his hand. "Come on, shawty; it's not even like that between us."

"My name is Anya—not shawty."

"Anya, no offense, but I'm not tryna go there with you. "

She wiggled out of his embrace. "Why not?" The lush curve of her lips twisted with defiance. She pulled her top over her head, removing it before Brick could stop her.

Stripped down to a black bra and a short skirt, Anya was more than appealing. Her bra was basic black. Nothing lacey…no pushup cups. But that black against her caramel skin was seductive as hell.

Yet Brick was able to maintain his composure. "You're at a weak point, shawty…I mean, Anya."

"You don't find me attractive?"

"That's not the problem. You're a pretty girl. But, I'm not tryna get into any emotional entanglements."

"Entanglements?" She scoffed. "There're no strings attached." She reached for his hands. "Touch me." Her dark eyes challenged him, lured him to move closer.

She took his hands and guided them to her hot skin. Her body felt delicate beneath his touch. So fragile, he feared that she'd easily break if he didn't handle her carefully.

"Hold me. I need you so much." The look in Anya's eyes was hypnotic, pulling him in like a magnet.

Brick linked his arms around her waist, pulling her closer while telling himself that he would hold her—console her—for only a moment.

The past few days had been emotionally charged…draining him. Having a woman in his arms was surprisingly soothing. He could feel his resolve weakening. "This ain't right," he murmured, fighting with his own urges. Anya was a pretty girl, but she wasn't the woman he wanted. Thomasina still had a place in his

heart. And so did Misty. He loved both mother and daughter…
in different ways. He was bereaved—in deep mourning over the
loss of both of them.

"Life threw us together," Anya said softly. "Let it happen,
Brick. We need each other. Don't fight it."

As his hands began to roam her body, wandering beneath her
skirt, Brick's mind was telling him to get his shit together and get
the hell out of the hotel room. But Anya felt so soft and sensual,
her body was purring for him. A temptation that was hard to resist.

Before common sense took over, he scooped her up in his
arms, striding toward the bedroom, his gait long and rapid, his
jaw clenched as if to control his savage urges.

CHAPTER 21

In the bedroom, Brick was barely out of his clothes. He must've been taking too long because Anya was all over him, tugging on his shirt, covering his back and his neck with her lips. Her passion was palpable as she covered his upper body with her heated kisses. Hot sparks that burned and tingled raced against his skin. He murmured…moaned. He was close to groaning out loud, but he sealed off his impassioned sounds by clamping his lips onto hers, his tongue stroking deeply into mouth, licking and tasting with primal intensity.

Anya circled her arms around his neck, fastening their bodies together. Brick's fingers were busy, unclasping the snaps of her bra. Urgently, his hands worked their way around to her front, massaging her breasts until her nipples tightened and pushed against his fingertips.

Brick pacified each hardened knot with puckered lips that sucked softly and gently licked.

"Fuck me," Anya pleaded, no longer able to restrain her raw, carnal hunger.

His boots were still on his feet, his jeans and briefs hung at the middle of his thighs. Giving her what she wanted, and taking what he needed, Brick entered Anya. His thickly muscled body rose and fell as he spiraled into her depths. Her skin was hot with desire, sending off a whiff that was arousing and intoxicating.

Anya's female scent, uniquely her own, incited a dry thirst that only a sip of her nectar could quench. He pulled out, leaving her gasping, leaving her pussy moist and puckered with need.

He repositioned her so that her flower petals were flush against his mouth.

But one taste was not enough; Brick hadn't realized how much he hungered and yearned for a woman's flavor.

With Anya's legs secured around his neck, Brick drank from her fountain of pleasure until Anya reached a screaming climax.

Now it was his turn. Swiftly, he rid himself of his boots and clothing. Naked, Brick stood over Anya. His powerfully muscled body was moist with perspiration. His heart pounded with desire. Instead of jumping in the pussy the way he wanted to, he remained standing, admiring and taking in the triangle of loveliness between her legs.

Anya spread her thighs for him. Her eyes, bright with desire, urged him to join her.

Transfixed, Brick gazed at Anya's naked beauty, his palm fisted around his massive dick. Petite and achingly beautiful, Anya suddenly reminded him of his first love...Misty.

Bending slightly, his stomach was laced with tight muscles. As his dick hardened in his hand, his powerful biceps bulged and flexed. He squeezed tightly, fisting his dick as if to subdue the growing throbbing. A sudden sting of tears burned his eyes. In a confused state of mind, Brick was dizzied by the combination of anguish and lust.

Blindly, he lunged for Anya. Feeling and sniffing his way to her luscious feminine part. He roughly pulled her legs apart, fitting the head of his dick between the petals, pushing into the snug interior, panting and desperate to plant himself deeply inside.

"Do you know how bad I've been wanting you? How hard it

was to sleep by myself with you in the next room? How could you torture me like that…denying me the pleasure of this thick, pretty dick."

"You got it, now, baby. It's all yours," he said in a thickened baritone.

"I don't want you to think about that other woman right now. Concentrate on me," she coaxed. "In this moment, it's all about you and me. Pretend I'm your woman… and you're my man. Take this pussy, Brick. Own it. Treat it like it's really yours!"

Anya's lustful words incited Brick to release a strong, masculine groan.

Brick thrust into her. "Oh, shit," he blurted as he drove himself unmercifully deep. He thrust in and out at a feverish pace. He was fast-fucking and unable to slow his stroke. "This is how I treat my pussy," he growled, as he plunged and pummeled without tenderness.

"Beat it up, baby! Your pussy loves to be punished!" Anya shouted. Her crude words intensified Brick's pleasure.

Goddamn, this chick is talking mad shit! I can't hold back much longer.

Uncaring if he split her in two, Brick widened Anya's legs as far apart as he could stretch them. Going in for the kill, Brick pumped dick until the friction scorched his skin. He felt blood rushing through his veins. He was close to cumming.

Anya seemed to suddenly vibrate. He looked down and realized she was shaking violently beneath him. Her pussy spasmed around his dick. She whimpered and cried out his name as she climaxed again.

And this time, with a great roar, Brick joined her.

ဆုဆ

"I don't usually lose control of myself like that...did I hurt you?" Brick asked Anya as they lay together in bed.

She shook her head. "The only way you can hurt me is when you leave me. Notice that I said *when* you leave me...not *if*."

Brick propped himself up and stared at her in surprise. "I'm not tryna hurt you. But you did say that there wouldn't be any strings attached."

"I know. Can't help it if I caught feelings."

"Damn," he muttered.

She stroked the vein on his muscular arm. "Yesterday, you had on a wedding band. Today, you don't. I don't know what your situation is, but my intuition tells me you're very much in love with your wife."

He let out a long sigh. "It's true. I love her, but I took the ring off because the marriage is over. My wife wants a divorce."

"Do you want a divorce?"

"No. But there's nothing that I can do to change her mind."

Anya looked off in thought and frowned. "How'd she ask for a divorce...I mean, isn't she in coma?"

"Misty's in a coma. She's my wife's daughter."

"Her daughter?"

"Yeah, it's a long story." Brick dropped his gaze as he pictured poor Misty lying in the hospital, caught between this world and the next. "Things don't look too promising for Misty; she's not gon' make it," he confessed, leaving out his involvement in her current condition.

"I'm sorry to hear that."

"She used to be my girl...we were together since we were kids."

"How'd you wind up marrying her mother?"

"It's real complicated; hard to explain."

"Try. I'm a good listener." She caressed his arm again, coaxing him to talk.

"When things began to fall apart between Misty and me, her mother, Thomasina, was there for me. I fell for her."

"Because she reminded you of Misty?"

Brick smiled. "Nah, Misty and her mother are nothing alike. Totally different personalities and they don't physically resemble each other at all. The reason I fell for Thomasina had nothing to do with Misty.

"At first it was only sex." He laughed a little. "And I dug her maturity. Then I think I fell in love with her because she loved me. She treated me good; you know what I'm saying? I had a hard life. Nobody ever cared about me or showed me love the way Thomasina did."

"Not even Misty."

Brick smiled sardonically. "I guess she did. In her own way."

"Are you still in love with Misty?"

Brick paused. He let out a sigh. "I'll always love Misty. She's got a place right here...forever." He touched his heart.

"Well, I'm not asking for forever, Brick. All I want is right now," Anya said sincerely.

"Right now is all I can give you, baby. Somebody tried to take Misty out. I don't know who. But whoever it was, they fucked her up real bad. Misty wasn't perfect, but she didn't deserve to be beaten beyond recognition....paralyzed...her body shriveled."

"Damn. That's horrible," Anya said.

"I can't rest. I won't have any peace until I get revenge."

"Let me help you."

"I know you mean well, but all you're doing is distracting me."

"How?"

He looked over at his crumpled clothes on the floor and chuckled. "Do you even have to ask that?"

"I'm not trying to be your girlfriend. But we're adults. And having sex is what adults do."

"So, you wanna be my fuck buddy? That's all?"

"I wouldn't put it that way."

"How would you put it?"

"I wanna be your friend."

"That's cool."

"Your confidante," Anya added, her voice taking on a softer tone.

She touched herself, parting the lips that glistened with Brick's lust. "And I want this to be your personal pussy. The hole you cum in when life gets to be too much."

Brick should've been out of the hotel over an hour ago, and yet he was still lingering in bed. Anya's words stirred and aroused him; had him seeking out the pleasure between her legs once again.

CHAPTER 22

"Do you realize how much your lawyer cost us?" my mother hisses in the phone. She's been griping about my legal fees ever since I got popped. After ten years, I know that bill has to be paid in full.

"Mom, all I'm asking is for you to let me hold a couple hundred. I'll pay you back."

"Kaymar, listen to me and listen to me good. I put a second mortgage on this house to pay for your legal defense, and that's the only reason why you're walking around free today. Theodore's family had to use the public defender, and he's locked up for life."

"I know, Mom," I say irritably. I hate it when she keeps pounding in my head what she did for me. Shit, she's my mother. Parents are supposed to look out for their kids.

"Mom, just let me hold a hundred," I ask, reluctantly bringing down the amount of money I want.

"I'm not letting you hold one measly dollar. Boy, what's wrong with you? You should be trying to pay me back all those thousands of dollars I wasted on your defense."

"Wasted?" I repeat, offended.

"That's right. If I had it to do all over, I'd let you sit in jail and pay for what you did to that poor woman."

"I ain't do nothing. You heard what my lawyer told the jury. I was a minor... following the lead of an eighteen-year-old adult."

"Theodore is slow. Everybody in our neighborhood knows you talked him into doing that crime. You're wicked, Kaymar, and I can't be bothered with you anymore. I have to make peace with Jesus and you need to do the same."

"Mom!"

"Don't call here again, Kaymar. You're a grown man now and I'm not responsible for you."

My mother hangs up on me. I stand in disbelief as I listen to the dial tone. Red hot fury shoots through my system. I look around Evette's outdated kitchen. The wallpaper is decorated with roosters, and that shit is starting to really irk me.

Evette is at work, and therefore out of the reach of my wrath. I have to release my rage on something, so I go on a rampage inside the fucked-up kitchen. I use the receiver of the old-fashioned wall phone to bash a hole in the kitchen wall. In the midst of the act, I convince myself I'm killing roosters. I have to kill something after the callous way that my mom has dissed me.

I hang the phone up and then begin to knock stuff off the counters: the toaster, salt and pepper shakers, napkin holder...all that shit. Then I hurl a teakettle against the canisters, toppling them like bowling pins. I karate kick a dent in the refrigerator. I pull a wooden cabinet door off the hinges; break dishes and glasses. I dump forks and spoons out of the drawer and onto the floor.

After I finish trashing the kitchen, I stumble into the living room, preparing to wreak havoc in here. But I'm stopped by the ringing phone.

Figuring my mother has had a change of heart, I run back to the kitchen. I know she loves me. No mother will allow her son to suffer if she can help it. The phone is lopsided on the wall, and I'm relieved it's still working. I lift the receiver off the hook.

"Hello!" I say breathlessly.

"Yo, man. What's good?" It's Blake on the other end of the phone. I'm very disappointed.

"Whatchu been up to?" he asks.

"Ain't shit," I reply with a sigh.

"I'm chillin' at the crib, watching this flick, but it's kind of boring…"

Is this nigga for real? Why would he call me to tell me about his boring day? I'm not feeling this shit at all, so my eyes wander around the kitchen. I get a small amount of satisfaction as I observe the damage I've done. The calendar on the wall is miraculously in place. I notice the red circle I put around Evette's next payday. It's in two days. Yes! I'm somewhat uplifted by the fact I'll have some money soon.

"Munch is bored, too," Blake continued.

I should cuss Blake out. This nigga done rang my phone, interfering with my rampage, and he ain't got nothing to talk about.

"So I called this broad named Tillie to see if she wants to get down with me and Munch. She's all for it but she wants to bring along one of her girlfriends. Two chicks are too many for me."

"Say what?" I'm surprised Blake would admit to something like that.

"Me and my girl was at it for hours last night," he explains. "I can't fuck two bitches after all the work I put in last night," Blake says with a chuckle.

"Oh, aye."

"You interested in taking up some of the slack? Wanna join the party?"

"Do I? You ain't gotta ask me twice. Where's the hookup spot? Your crib or Munch's?"

"See, that's the problem. Munch's mom stayed home from work today, so we can't go over there. And my sister got the exterminator over here, fumigating the place. That boarder of yours… the chick that stays with you, she won't be home 'til after five, so I figured we could bring the party to your spot."

I got Blake and Munch believing that Evette's a chick renting a room from me. I don't admit this is her crib or that we're in a relationship.

"Y'all can party over here. It's cool with me." My bad mood is improving. "What time are y'all swinging by?" I ask because I need some time to straighten up the mess I made in the kitchen.

"Half-hour…maybe an hour."

"Okay. See you when you get here."

Suddenly, my world has brightened. I'm straightening up the kitchen, sweeping up glass, wiping down shit, and I got the nerve to be whistling as I work.

Forty-five minutes later, Blake and Munch are at the door, carrying two six-packs of beer. The two females they brought are as different as night and day. One girl is pretty enough to be on TV. Her light brown hair is styled in a wrap. Parted down the middle, showing dark roots. She has beautiful brown eyes, real wide and expressive. Her sparkly lip gloss is getting me in the mood for kissing. I could easily romance this chick before I start drilling.

The other one is so butt ugly she looks like a Halloween mask. Her nose is so flat, it's a wonder she can even breathe. But I shrug it off. Pussy is pussy. I'm prepared to lay pipe in either one of these hoes. It don't even matter which one. I'll do both of them, if Blake can't hold up his end.

"This is Kaymar," Blake says, introducing me to the females. "Fawn and Tillie." Both chicks are wearing short skirts, I notice.

"Mmm. Kaymar is hot. Built nice with those muscles. He can get it," says the flat-nose chick named Tillie. Not only does her nose look like she's gone a few rounds in the boxing ring with Floyd Mayweather, but she also has a severe case of acne.

She starts giggling. The ugly chick would be the one to put in first dibs, but what the fuck? Like I said, pussy is pussy.

"We gon' find out if Kaymar is all talk or if he can really put in some work," Blake says with a slight edge to his voice. "That nigga is always bragging about his fuck game…we gon' finally find out."

I look around a little uneasily. My fuck game has not been up to par lately, but I don't think it's my fault I can't last long. I cum quick because Evette's pussy is uninspiring.

I notice Munch is sitting on the couch, leaning forward like he's ready to pounce. He's not saying anything. He's quietly sipping beer and licking his lips as he stares at the two girls. He doesn't appear very happy about our little setup with these chicks. Munch looks hostile and on edge.

"What's up with Munch?" I ask Blake in a whisper.

"That nigga's hype. He's been sniffing glue, getting himself prepared."

I start to ask why he has to sniff glue, but fuck it. What the hell do I care? I absently rub my dick as I gaze at Fawn. She smiles at me and I no longer want to be a part of this freak scene. Fuck these niggas. I want Fawn all to myself.

My thoughts are distracted by a rustling sound. I jerk my head over to the couch and I'm shocked to see Munch's face buried in a piece of cloth. When he lifts his head up, he has a fierce look in his eyes.

"What's wrong with him?" Fawn draws close to Tillie.

"Girl, that's how he gets. You gon' love it. Munch has a serious tongue game."

"I don't wanna find out. He looks crazy; I changed my mind,"

Fawn states with a frown. Munch has his crazy-eyed focus on her, and she's trying to get behind her friend, Tillie.

There's a loud explosion when Munch suddenly kicks the coffee table over and starts crawling around in a circle like a dog chasing his tail. Both Tillie and Fawn are screaming and freaking out. If I had a piece on me, Munch would be one dead mufucka.

I scowl at Blake. "Man, what's up with your nigga?"

"Yo, Munch. Get a grip. You're fucking up the party, man!" Blake yells. But Munch acts like he can't hear him. He's crawling all crazy, using one hand like it's a paw or a hoof, scratching on the carpet…looking similar to a bull, preparing to charge.

"Blake, man! Get control of that glue-sniffing asshole." I've had enough of this circus. I want everybody to get the fuck out. Munch is giving me plenty of reason to eighty-six him and all of these nut-asses.

Everyone except Fawn. She can stay; I have plans for us.

"Did you bring the shit?" Blake asks Tillie in a desperate voice.

"Yeah." Tillie pulls open her big purse and starts digging.

My eyes nearly pop out my head when she pulls out a studded collar with a looped handle. She hands the collar to Blake. In a flash, Blake wrestles with Munch until he somehow gets the collar around Munch's neck.

CHAPTER 23

B rick gave Anya the money to rent a motel room. Keeping a low profile, Brick stayed in the car while Anya checked them in, using her identification. Clean but small, the motel located in Lower Bucks County offered few amenities. With his cash on hand running perilously low, Brick could only afford cheap lodging.

It was in Brick's nature to be a provider, to take care of the people that depended on him. Anya didn't seem to mind the downgrade. Outside the bedroom, she was easygoing. A sweet girl. Easy to please and easy to get along with.

But she was a beast in bed. Anya's sex game was off the chain. She was becoming a pleasurable distraction, and Brick couldn't allow good pussy to take him off his square.

Touching Smash Hitz was going to take a little longer than he'd anticipated. At present, he had to worry about every day survival. If he didn't earn some income soon, he and Anya would both be tossed out on the streets. And Brick couldn't let that happen. She was depending on him, and he wouldn't let her down.

It occurred to him to get a gun and stick up some drug boys, but he couldn't do that. From his own drug-slinging days, he knew that there was a price to pay when a hustler came up short, and Brick didn't want to jam up a young bull for a little bit of pocket change. Only ballers that were handling weight made long paper, and getting to the big boys would take a lot of effort and planning.

Brick didn't have time for that. He needed a quick come-up, and he could think of only one way to accomplish that.

Anya used most of her time searching for her father, but being in Bucks County was a disadvantage. Right now, she was sitting in the Internet access station in a quick-copy shop near the motel.

While Brick was putting together a money scheme, Anya was pouring through a database of homeless people, hoping to locate her father. Brick couldn't say that he wished her luck. At least, not at the moment. As skimpy as his pockets were, one more mouth to feed was pushing it.

ഔൽ

To make sure he couldn't be traced by his fingerprints, Brick pulled on a pair of latex gloves. Wearing a sleeveless, hooded sweatshirt, sunglasses, and a ball cap pulled down low, Brick pulled open the door to a small bank that was tucked away behind a strip mall. He'd been casing the place since arriving in Bucks County, and he liked the fact there wasn't a security guard on the premises.

Robbing mufuckas or hitting ATMs used to be a way of life back when Brick and Misty were in their teens. He believed he'd lost his heart for criminal activities, but in a bold and desperate move, Brick rushed inside the bank. Hand inside his pocket, he gripped his cell phone, giving the impression he was concealing a weapon.

As he rushed toward the teller, stunned customers scattered, creating a clear path for Brick.

Brick grabbed a male customer who was in the middle of a transaction by the back of his collar, and yanked him out of his way. Brick didn't open his mouth. Silently he pushed a printed note toward the terrified teller. The note clearly stated that Brick had a gun, and he wanted all the cash in her drawer.

Hastily, the shaken teller gave him a bag of money.

Brick exited the bank and made a run for it. No good Samaritans chased him. No cops pursued him. He hopped a fence in the bank's parking lot, pulled off the hoodie and ditched it, and then sprinted two blocks until he reached his car parked in a residential neighborhood.

Behind the wheel, his chest heaved and he gasped for breath. He'd run only a short distance, but his chest was on fire. With construction work and weightlifting, Brick's body was ripped and cut, but he obviously needed to get in some cardio exercises if he planned to continue racing away from crime scenes on foot.

During the drive back to the motel, his eyes roved anxiously from the rearview mirror to the bag of money in the backseat. So far, so good. There were no squad cars tailing him and no exploding dye packs popping off inside the bag. But then again, maybe dye packs exploded silently. Hell if he knew how that shit worked.

Nobody could identify him...all they could say was that a big black man had robbed the bank and left on foot, but still, he needed to keep it moving, and get the hell out of Bucks County.

But he couldn't leave town just yet. He had to go back to the motel and get his personal items. Nothing he possessed had any real value, but the photographs of his son were irreplaceable. Taking a huge risk, Brick went back to the motel. Once inside, he glanced out the window every few minutes, checking to see if the cops were lurking outside.

With nervous hands, he counted the money. Only twelve thousand. Damn! He'd expected a bank job to bring in a lot more than that. Still, he was relieved the money was not covered with red dye.

From his duffle bag, he pulled out a couple of items, and then changed from dark pants and boots to a pair of cargo shorts and sneakers.

Bucks County was a wrap. It was time to move on. Brick was ready for Miami, but he needed some more information from that lil' punk, Cash Money.

One last glance around the room, and he noticed Anya's red-print overnight bag. Brick's heart dropped. He didn't want to hurt Anya, but it was time to make a clean break from her. He'd leave her a stack and then move on to Miami with a clear con-science.

Anya could do much better than him—a troubled man on the run for attempted murder…and now a bank robbery. He couldn't contribute anything positive to Anya's life. Leaving her behind would be an act of kindness.

But Brick realized Anya wouldn't take it that way. She'd feel rejected. Brick imagined her hurt and disappointment when she discovered he'd ducked out on her. She deserved an explanation. Instead of leaving her overnight bag behind, he tossed it in the trunk alongside his duffle bag.

While driving, one hand steered, the other roved over the screen of his cell phone, placing his call to Anya on speaker. It would be real dumb to get pulled over for driving around with a cell phone up to his ear.

"You still researching stuff on the computer?" he asked when Anya picked up.

"Yeah, I'm done. Was just getting ready to log off."

"There's a change in plans…" Brick hesitated briefly. "I'm… uh…on the move. Understand what I'm saying?"

"No. What do you mean, you're on the move?"

"We have to get out of Bucks County...go our separate ways. It's not safe for you to be with me."

"Brick..." She spoke his name pleadingly.

"I'm on the run, Anya. And I don't want to drag you any deeper into my situation."

"This is so sudden. What happened?"

"Things changed; that's all I can say. I'm not gon' leave you hanging, though. I got something for you."

"But—"

"Meet me outside the copy center in five minutes," Brick said firmly.

"All right." There was acceptance in Anya's voice, and Brick was relieved.

ळ⃝ભ

As soon as Anya got in the car, Brick pulled off.

Offended, Anya tsked through her teeth. "Oh, my goodness. Are you in that big of a rush to get rid of me?"

"It's not you. I got law enforcement on my ass. I got shit to take care of...for Misty. Until Smash Hitz and that tranny get bodied, I can't be out here fucking around and getting caught."

"Why are you ditching me? I told you that I'm willing to help you."

"You don't need to get involved in my problems. Stay focused on looking for your pop. And after you get that resolved, I want you to find yourself a good man."

"I'm not looking for a man."

"A pretty girl like you should be thinking about sharing a future with a nice dude. I'm bad news, baby—I'm all fucked up!"

"No, you're not."

"You're better off without me. Real talk. I'ma give you enough bread to hold you until you get yourself together, aye? I want you to get yourself an apartment, and stop all this moving around. You deserve better."

"If you say so." Anya's tone was snippy.

"I'm sorry, Anya. I really am. But I'm tryna look out for you. So where do you want me to drop you off? I can give you enough money to stay in a nice hotel until you find something permanent."

"A nice hotel is the farthest thing from my mind. You're not the only one that's out for revenge. Wanna know what I discovered today?" Anya said angrily.

Brick cut an eye at her. "You found your pop?"

"No. I found out one of the men that brutally murdered my mother is out of jail. He's free as a fucking bird…walking the streets right now." She stopped talking and murmured something under her breath. She dropped her head and Brick realized that she was crying.

"It's okay…" His voice trailed off. He nodded sympathetically, at a loss for words.

"It's not okay. I'm consumed with hatred. Just like you." She looked up at Brick with tears streaming. "Fuck getting me an apartment. If you really want to do something for me—something that's meaningful—then get me a piece. I need a gun, Brick. I'm gonna personally put a bullet between that killer's eyes."

Anya's mouth tightened. Her eyes, no longer filled with tears, were icy cold. Turning her head, she stared out of the window. Every few moments, a deep, shuddering breath expressed her quiet rage.

Brick kept driving. He had a much better understanding of why Anya became so violently passionate when they were in bed. It was the only way she could express her pent-up rage.

He rubbed Anya's shoulder with one hand and steered with the other. His reassuring hand had no effect on Anya. She didn't revert back to her usual sweet self. She sat motionless. Staring out the window, intent on committing murder.

Making a split-second decision, he proceeded to cross the Tacony Palmyra Bridge.

"We're going to Jersey?" she asked without emotion.

"It's close enough to Philly to handle business, but far enough away to be a good hideout spot."

"What about the gun?"

"I'll make some calls. I gotchu. I'll take care of it."

They had an understanding now. A nonverbal agreement. They were rolling together. Neither was concerned about the danger. They both possessed a thirst that could not be quenched until blood was spilled.

CHAPTER 24

O n his hands and knees, Munch is growling and pulling, but Blake yanks him over to Tillie. At this point, Fawn is standing near the front door with her hands over her mouth. There's a mixture of shock and excitement shining in her pretty brown eyes.

Munch rears up and knocks Tillie into a chair. Standing on his knees, he holds her down with his forearms. Tillie isn't fighting back at all. Her short skirt is hitched up. She's got her legs cocked open, and she ain't wearing any panties. The bitch came prepared.

Munch is a big freak. The way he's chowing down on that girl's pussy is bananas! I have never seen any shit like this. He's growling, sucking, and licking—slurping. The way this nigga is gobbling up pussy, I'd be surprised if that ho, Tillie, has any pussy left to share with Blake and me.

After about five minutes of watching Munch, I realize he has no intention of stopping. I turn to Blake. "I thought he was supposed to be getting her ready for you?"

"He is," Blake says. Blake is looking real comfortable with the situation, and he's not even holding the handle of the collar anymore. He's letting Munch freestyle on that coochie.

"How long is he gon' be at it?" I ask, disgruntled. Shit, I want my turn to smash.

Blake shrugs. "I think he sniffed too much glue. If I try to pull him off, he might bite her."

"So! Let him bite her. He's taking too long." I cut an eye at Fawn and she seems mesmerized by what's happening in the living room. Munch has turned into some kind of pussy-eating animal. Fawn is watching as her girlfriend, Tillie is lying back, busting one nutt after another.

Meanwhile, Blake and me huddle together, both silently coming to terms with the fact that Munch is not going to stop and we may possibly have to share Fawn.

"I don't do sloppy seconds!" The words fly angrily out of my mouth.

"Man, I'm the one that brought you in on this. Fuck if I'm going behind you," Blake declares.

I turn to Fawn. "Who do you wanna get with first?" I'm confident she's feeling me as much as I'm feeling her, so I stand there, smirking.

Fawn looks from me to Blake. "Umm…Umm."

Umm! What the fuck!

"I think… I'm gonna pick…" She keeps pausing and hesitating, acting like she can't make up her mind.

You could have knocked me over with a fuckin' feather when she points to Munch, and says, "I wanna wait for him."

Blake is as stunned as I am. I keep a straight face, but Blake turns beet red. I guess Pretty Boy never had a chick choose Munch over him.

"Aye. I got shit to do." Blake plays it off like he's real busy. He checks the screen of his phone. "My baby mom is blowing up my phone. Tell Munch I'll swing back to pick him up in a couple of hours."

"Hold up, Blake. How you gon' walk out and leave Munch in my crib? I'm not fucking with him and that dog collar. I refuse to get bit, tryna pull him off shawty. Worse comes to worst, I'ma let him eat that bitch alive," I say with a surly attitude.

Blake holds up the cloth Munch had been sniffing on. "He can't keep going without this. He'll be more manageable when it wears off."

"What about me?" Fawn inquires. "Is he gonna do me after he finishes with Tillie?"

Blake looks at Fawn like she's scum. "I don't know, bitch. Ask him!"

"Who you calling a bitch? I don't know why you coming at me like that," Fawn complains.

Blake grabs one of the six-packs and slams the door on his way out.

Munch and Tillie are in their own world. The living room has a thick, musky odor. I don't actually know how a whorehouse smells because I've never been inside one, but I bet it has the same scent lingering in the air right now.

I give Fawn a suggestive look. She smiles, which makes me feel confident I can change her mind about waiting for Munch.

"While they're busy, why don't we get into something?"

"Get into what?" she asks, her eyes gleaming. I realize she wants me to give her some head. I'm actually considering it. But on some real shit...I ain't never done that before. Not to a female.

I can't take my eyes off Fawn's glittery lips. For some odd reason, I feel compelled to kiss her. I haven't kissed a girl since I was a teenager. I wanted to save myself for the right one, but life is too short to wait for the right girl.

I take Fawn by the hand and pull her into my arms. She feels small and delicate. I press my lips against hers. I'm feeling a little awkward at first, but then my tongue takes over, starts sliding inside her mouth, licking her tongue. She's making little sounds in her throat. My breathing is heavy as hell, and my Johnson is getting activated.

My joint is acting crazy. It's discombobulated and bunched up all crazy and uncomfortably in the front of my pants. I want to take it out of confinement—give it some freedom. I also want to coerce Fawn into fondling my dick. Real sneaky like, I slip one arm from around her, and I allow my free hand to journey down to my crotch. The moment I touch my zipper, I hear movement. I crack an eye open and here comes that fuckin' Munch! He's crawling all zigzag and crazy...heading in our direction.

Something's wrong with this nut-ass bull. I'm sick of all this crawling around on the floor. It's nerve-wracking. The shit is getting old. And the way he's crawling now is more disturbing than before. His movements are no longer fast and furious. He's crawling in a slow and crooked way...like an old dog that needs to be put down.

I let go of Fawn and reluctantly break the kiss. I glower at Munch's retarded ass. Damn, can't he see I'm tryna get my mack on?

No doubt about it, Munch is cock-blocking, and he don't give a fuck. Greedy bastard. I feel like putting a muzzle on this mufucka. If he wants to act like a mangy dog, then he needs to be treated like one.

The sluggish and wobbly way he's crawling looks so fucked up, I have to shift my eyes away from him. He's disgusting. But a noise draws my attention back to Munch.

"Watch where you going, man!" I yell as Munch bangs into the TV stand and then a floor lamp, nearly knocking it over. If I didn't know any better, I'd think Munch is drunk from all of that pussy juice he's been guzzling.

I can't believe the timing of this dude. Why he gotta come over here fucking with us? I was *this* close to persuading Fawn to play with my dick. I might've been able to get her to suck it.

Fawn pulls away from me and gazes down at Munch. He's

brushing against her leg. I swear to God, I'ma smack Munch upside his head with a rolled-up newspaper if he rears up and starts humping on Fawn's leg.

When Fawn bends a little and brushes the side of his face with the back of her hand, I realize I might have to switch chicks. I turn around so I can check out Tillie. See if she's worth fucking. But that broad is sprawled out in the chair, sleep. Or maybe she's unconscious. Or dead.

For somebody who'd been acting terrified of Munch, Fawn is now extremely bold. She grabs the handle of Munch's collar and guides him to the couch. She lets go of the handle and starts pulling up her skirt. Before she can sit down, Munch has his face buried in her pussy. I notice his pussy-eating pace has changed. He's slowly gliding his tongue up and down, between her pussy lips. I can tell he's really enjoying it by the way he's turning his head from side to side, making sure he's licking that coochie from every possible angle.

Fawn slides down to the couch and wraps her legs around Munch's neck. I walk over to the couch to get a closer view. I want to be in close proximity, with my dick in my hand, as soon as Munch finishes eating.

I squeeze my Johnson as I observe Munch alternate sucking Fawn's clit and lapping between her cunt lips. This is fascinating. Got me swiftly hand-stroking. I'm not gon' front, this freaky shit has me horny as a mufucka.

I've been watching porn on cable since I got out of the joint. At first I was caught up, but now that crap seems corny compared to watching the real deal. Yeah, I love this scene.

"Eat all that pussy up," I encourage Munch.

Fawn moans louder after I add my two cents' worth. My dick is straining under the pressure of all this freakiness.

I grab the loop of his collar and yank it. "Yo, that's enough, Munch. Save me some of that. Let me get in there." I got my dick in my hand, tryna force it between his lips and into her pussy. But Munch won't stop. He's still lapping; his tongue accidentally flicks against my dick as he savors her juices.

That nigga's slippery tongue sends a couple of electrical jolts up my spine, and now I'm backing away. I'm not with any homo activities. I'm not in jail, anymore.

So I'm beating my meat to the rhythm of Fawn's melodic moaning. Munch is mercilessly lashing her pussy with his tongue.

Blood is rushing through my veins. I'm getting dangerously close to poppin' off a geyser of dick juice. A spur-of-the-moment decision has me walking fast toward flat-nosed Tillie. She's still sprawled out, but I don't care. I give her pimply face a hard blast of hot jism.

Startled, Tillie jumps out of her sleep. She sits upright, flailing her arms and struggling for breath. She snorts, gurgles, gasps, and pants. If you ask me, she's overreacting. She's basically carrying on like she's a victim of drowning.

CHAPTER 25

"What happened in the kitchen?" Evette wants to know when she gets home from work.

"I was mad about something," I mutter as I aim the remote at the TV.

"You put a giant hole in the wall and you dented the fridge!" she exclaims. "What happened to the dishes?"

"I broke 'em," I say, dryly.

"Why?"

"I didn't break all the dishes. There's a few left," I mumble without interest.

"Kaymar! Even the Aunt Jemima cookie jar is cracked. That belonged to my great aunt; it's an antique!"

"Yo, Evette. Stop all that complaining, and let me watch TV in peace."

"I'm sorry, baby. I'm just trying to understand—"

"Ain't nothing to understand. I'm in here starving, and you're worrying about a few lousy dishes and a dumb-ass cookie jar."

Evette comes in the living room. "What are you in the mood for? I can heat you up some spaghetti."

I roll my eyes. "Man, I don't want that crap. How many nights in a row are you gon' keep feeding me leftovers?"

"Baby, listen, the only thing in the freezer is pork chops and ribs."

"Throw that shit out! How many times do I have to tell you that I don't fuck with pork?"

I'm feeling extra surly because Fawn wouldn't give me her number. There's something about that chick. I dig her. But she's playing hard to get. Talking about I can get in touch with her through her friend, Tillie. That's bullshit and she knows it. Tillie can't stand me. Ol' bitch acting like a little bit of protein almost killed her. On some real shit, my dick sauce probably helped her bumpy skin condition.

"Money is low," Evette says. "But I can probably squeeze out enough to buy you a cheesesteak."

"That'll work," I say, cheerfully. "Make sure they put some fried onions, sweet peppers, and ketchup on it."

"Okay. I can eat the leftover spaghetti or I can fry some pork chops for myself," Evette says, thinking out loud. She's still standing in the living room, and her presence is irking the shit out of me.

"Aye, get to stepping, Evette. Go get your future husband some grub!"

Evette laughs as she slings the strap of her purse over her shoulder. She crosses the room and gives me a kiss on the cheek. She knows I don't play that kissing on the lips shit.

Once Evette is out of the house, I go in the kitchen, grab the house phone, and call Blake. "Yo, I need to get in touch with that chick, Tillie."

"Man, I'm with my baby mom. Hit me up later. We'll discuss it when I have some privacy."

Blake disconnects. I don't want to discuss anything. I just want the broad's number. Shit, I'm not on Blake's timeline, so I dig out a scrap of paper with Munch's phone number. I've never called that fool before, but I'm desperate.

His mom answers. I'm annoyed because I called Munch's cell; I wasn't expecting to have to go through his mom. "Can I speak to Munch?" I ask in a respectful voice.

"Who is this?" she asks, irritably.

"This is Kaymar."

"I don't know who you are, Kaymar. But you need to know the rules. In this house, my son's name is Owen. I don't know how he picked up that horrible nickname, but I don't acknowledge it. In the future, don't call my son's phone asking for anyone named Munch."

Damn, Munch's mom got a lot of mouth on her! She needs her ass whooped. "Oh, my bad, can I speak to Owen?"

"Hold on." She sounds real pissed off when she tells her son that he has a phone call. I tap my foot impatiently as I wait for Munch to pick up the phone.

When he finally takes my call, he sounds out of it, like he just woke up. "Yo, Munch," I say in a cheerful tone. "I need Tillie's number. Do you have it?"

"Tillie?"

"Yeah, the chick you brought to the crib with Fawn." I wanna say, 'the bitch whose pussy you gobbled until she passed out.'

"Oh, yeah? I just woke up. My head's a lil' fuzzy. But, um… why do you want Tillie's number? Didn't I hear you tell Fawn you want to get with her?"

"Yeah, but she said I have to go through Tillie."

"Fawn left her number with me. She told me to give it to you."

"No shit?" My face lights up like a Christmas tree.

"Yeah, man. She said she wants to try you out."

"That's whassup."

"So, when are you tryna see her? I can't get out tonight; my mom got a long list of shit for me to do. But I can help you with

Fawn tomorrow. You know…get her in the mood, so she'll be ready for you."

"Nah, I'm good, man. I don't need your help."

"Aye," he says. From his tone, I sense Munch doesn't think I can satisfy Fawn without him starting her off with his special skills.

"So what's the number?" I ask, irritably.

As Munch rattles off Fawn's phone number, I quickly scribble it down on a napkin. I'm cheesing like I hit the jackpot. I wanna ask him why his mom picked up his cell, but fuck it…that's Munch's problem.

I have to hurry up and make this call to Fawn before Evette gets back from the deli. Evette gon' have to get me a cell. It's ridiculous to have to sneak around like a criminal fucking with this house phone.

I call Fawn and she picks up on the first ring. I ask if we can hook up tomorrow, during the day. I don't tell her about Evette; I don't wanna say anything that might chase her away. She agrees to swing by around eleven. If my money was right, I'd take Fawn to a nice hotel. Or out to lunch. I don't know what it is about this chick, but she got my dome spinning.

"Is Munch gon' be at your house?" she asks.

"No, it's a private party. Just me and you."

"Oh."

"Is something wrong?"

"I'ma be up front with you because I don't wanna waste your time or mine."

"Whatchu saying?"

"I'm saying, I can get a fuck off anybody. But after the way Munch put it on me, I can't settle for below-average oral sex."

Damn, Fawn is blunt; no beating around the bush with this

chick. I scratch my head, not sure about how I should respond to her question. I've never eaten pussy before, and I don't plan on starting. At least not in the near future. She has me in a tight spot.

"The way you're hesitating makes me think we need Munch to get it poppin'. I'll try you out after he gets me in the mood," Fawn states. There's no shame in her game. These new breeds of females demand what they want. Fawn acts like she doesn't wanna give up any pussy unless I can eat pussy to her satisfaction. I'm not comfortable with her requirements.

On some real shit, I don't know how to eat pussy. But I'm so attracted to Fawn, I'm too scared to admit it. I don't want to blow my chance to get up in that hot box. I'm gon' have to string her along.

"Nah, we don't need Munch; I gotchu," I say in a voice I hope sounds convincing.

"You sure? Don't make me come all the way to West Philly only to find out your oral performance is whack."

"You'll see," I boast. "My head game is tight!"

"I'll be the judge of that."

I laugh. Fawn has a pleasing way about her. She can easily get a smile out of me.

"By the way. My pussy is addictive. The average nigga can't get enough of it," Fawn tells me. Then she does this cute, playful little giggle.

Teasing her back, I say, "Munch sucked on your friend's pussy much longer than he licked on yours. I think your friend must be the one with the good stuff."

"Trust. This pussy of mine ain't nothing to play with."

"Yeah, aye, shawty. We'll see about that."

I pace for a good five minutes after I finish talking with Fawn.

I'm excited about her coming to see me tomorrow, but I'm also nervous about going down on her. I don't know if I can do it. I've watched enough porn to know the basics of pussy-eating. And I had a bird's-eye view of Munch lapping up her juices. But seeing it and doing it are two different things.

I might need another lesson before I'm ready to take the plunge. Maybe I should let Munch come over and start Fawn off. I can probably fake it by licking around her coochie a little bit after he does all the heavy lapping. But then again, I don't want to put my mouth on anything Munch has been slurping on. That saliva-dripping mufucka is a regular at the free health clinic. I'm not tryna catch hoofing-mouth disease.

I'm sitting on the couch, deep in thought, when Evette comes home with my cheesesteak. Evette goes into the kitchen and places it on one of the few plates left after the fit I threw this morning.

She brings my food to me in the living room. Sets the plate in front of me, with a tall glass of Pepsi. She likes playing house and doing domesticated shit. It makes her feel good about herself. On some real shit, though…she could've handed me my grub the minute she walked through the door. A nigga is hungry and don't need a plate.

Evette watches me bite into the cheesesteak. She's wearing a proud, lopsided smile, as if she prepared the food with her own hands.

"I'm just gon' warm up that spaghetti for myself. I'm too tired to fry those pork chops," she says, absently.

I murmur a sound, letting her know I hear her, but I'm too busy killing the cheesesteak to get involved in a discussion about what she's gon' fix herself to eat.

She goes back into the kitchen, leaving me in peace. As I'm tearing up my Philly cheesesteak and guzzling down Pepsi, I'm feeling concerned. I don't think I can bullshit my way through a pussy-eating session. I may have to seriously consider letting Munch come over tomorrow. But I'm not gon' eat behind his dirty ass. Hell, no!

Munch can handle the first half. When he gets Fawn close to the edge, I'll take over and lay some pipe. After I finish deep stroking that bitch, I don't wanna hear shit except, 'Thank you, Kaymar!'

CHAPTER 26

The place was nothing fancy. A family-oriented motel with a swimming pool. The room was basic, equipped with a small fridge, a coffee pot, and a microwave—merely a place to rest their heads.

Brick sat in a chair, searching through his contact list. He wanted to get in touch with Tayshaun from the projects, but it wasn't easy because Tayshaun, also known as Taye, changed his number every two weeks. Taye sold everything: drugs, electronics, weapons, cars, and even concert tickets…you name it and Tayshaun sold it. If he didn't have it on hand, he could get it. Brick was interested in purchasing something from the arsenal of illegal weapons Taye possessed.

Anya stared out the window, gazing at the pool area, listening to the sounds of water splashing and the sounds of childish squeals and laughter. An unwelcome flashback of happy times with her parents on vacation in New Jersey blazed across her mind. She could clearly envision her mother relaxing by the pool and reading a novel while she and her father splashed around in the water.

The swimming pool below the window sparked another powerful memory. Anya's parents walking the boardwalk holding hands while Anya sat upon her father's shoulders.

Instead of brightening her mood, she was haunted by the memory. Cruelly reminded of how much she'd lost.

She turned away from the window, pulled the curtain closed. She walked over to Brick. He felt her eyes on him. He could feel her sorrow as he busied himself, sending out texts to people who could possibly put him in touch with Tayshaun.

Brick continued handling business, his fingers tapping on the screen. Respecting Anya's somber mood, he felt no desire to fill the silence with unnecessary small talk. She'd told him what she wanted and he was doing his best to get it for her.

"My mother was stoned to death—that's how she died," Anya said.

Brick's fingers stilled. Holding his cell, he looked up at Anya, scowling in confusion. "Was she on vacation somewhere? Did it happen over in Iraq…Afghanistan?"

Anya winced. She drew her hand to her mouth and absently gnawed at her fingernail. Until this moment, he hadn't noticed Anya biting her fingernails.

"No, it didn't happen in a Middle Eastern country; it happened in America. My mother was stoned to death in Philadelphia. One of her killers got a life sentence; the other got ten to twenty."

Brick continued to scowl at Anya quizzically.

"My mother never got justice. And while those two killers get a cot and three hot meals a day, my father ends up homeless—a bum, living on the streets.

She looked Brick in the eye. "Ain't that some shit? A woman endured a brutal death by stoning in modern times in an urban city, yet one of the killers is walking around free!"

"Come again? I assumed she got shot…you know, during a robbery."

Anya let out a bitter laugh. "No, she was stoned to death in Tacony Creek Park in Philly." She grew quiet again. Drew in a deep breath and released it.

Brick set his phone down, prepared to give his undivided attention. Or hold her in his arms if she required comforting. Whatever she needed, he was there for her.

"My mother was from Trinidad. She didn't have any blood relatives in the States. What I remember most about her was that she worked hard. Went from a cleaning woman to a registered nurse. She worked the third shift at a health care facility. Being the supervisor, she got to work every night a half-hour early. My dad usually drove her, but sometimes she drove herself. Whenever she drove, she always parked in the underground lot on the premises, believing she was completely safe.

"But one night, two teenage boys were looking to jack somebody's car. When my mother parked and opened her car door, they were hiding in the shadows, and ordered her at gunpoint to get back inside the car. She was abducted inside her employer's parking lot.

Brick frowned. "Why didn't they just take the car?"

"I've asked myself the same question a million times. Why didn't they just take the car?" Anya shrugged helplessly. "When the prosecution asked the same question, the sixteen-year-old blamed the older boy, stating it was his decision to make my mother drive out of the garage to a remote location."

"Why?"

"So they could rape and rob her." Anya emitted a soft whimper of despair.

"Wow, baby. I'm really sorry to hear this."

She held up a hand, indicating she wasn't finished…she needed to continue. She cleared her throat. "No one ever told me exactly what happened to my mother. My grandmother, my father, my aunt Minerva; everyone hid the truth from me."

"They were trying to protect you."

"Well, I read every news article that pertained to the crime on the Internet."

"Damn," Brick murmured.

"I read the complete court transcript online. I know every aspect of my mother's fear. Her pain. I've read every pleading word she spoke to those two murderers. They made her drive to a remote area and then they raped her. Both of them raped her in the back seat of her car. When they were finished, they took her purse, her car keys, and her clothes. Then they ordered her to get out of the car. She did what they said, but those animals..." Anya couldn't go on. She broke down and wept.

"It's okay. Let it out, baby. I gotchu," Brick said as he circled his strong arms around her.

Anya pulled out of his grasp and went in the bathroom and closed the door. She was in there for a good five minutes. Crying. Wailing. The mournful sobs changed to sniffling. Then Brick heard Anya blowing her nose. He heard the sound of running water. And then she opened the door. The tear stains had been washed away, but her red-rimmed eyes could not conceal her pain.

Composed, Anya sat down. She cleared her throat and continued, "They called it a random killing. How do you have that kind of rage toward someone who has never done anything to you— someone you've never set eyes on before?

"My mother's nude body was found at Tacony Creek Park under the Olney Tabor Bridge. The autopsy report said she died of blunt trauma to the head, but her whole body was stoned. After they killed her, those killers drove around in my mother's car for two days. Two days!

"She did everything they told her to do until they insisted that she walk out of the park naked. She didn't care about the wallet, her car or anything. All she asked them for was something to cover up with.

"One of 'em hit her with a small stone, telling her to start walking toward the creek. At that point, she did. She started walking away from the car, naked. They hit her with another stone, telling her to speed it up. She began running. And they chased her, hitting her with bigger stones. Rocks. Stoning her until she couldn't run anymore. Until she dropped. And they kept on hitting her. She was crying, begging them not to kill her. Telling them she had a child. The transcripts say one of the rapists told her to bow her head and say some prayers. She was praying when he bashed her in the back of the head with a rock. Though she was probably dead, they didn't stop. They turned my mother over and bludgeoned her face."

Brick expected Anya to break down again, but she was eerily calm.

"I don't know which one dealt the killing blow, but as far as I'm concerned, they both deserve to die."

"Maybe the young bull was following blindly behind the older dude," Brick suggested.

Anya's face grew taut. Her eyes were black dots of fury. "At sixteen, he knew right from wrong. He didn't do anything *blindly*. He fully participated in rape, sodomy, and a heinous murder. That wasn't your everyday carjacking, turned accidental homicide. My mother was degraded, taunted, and tortured." Anya dropped her head again, as if too overwrought to go on.

"It's all in the court transcripts," she said, dropping her gaze. "The sixteen-year-old and the older boy described the crime in the exact same way. But each said that he was coerced by the other. It doesn't matter who coerced whom. They're equally to blame." She looked up, staring deeply into Brick's eyes, revealing the depth of her agony.

Brick saw himself in Anya's eyes. Her eyes mirrored his pain. She was a woman who could not rest until she'd exacted revenge.

And there was nothing Brick could say or do to convince Anya to move on and let it go.

"The last time I saw my mother, you know what she said to me—she said, 'See you in the morning, Sweet Cakes.' But I never saw her again. Not even in the casket. It was a closed-casket funeral, and I recently found out by reading the news reports, that the mortician couldn't fix my mother's battered face."

Brick recalled that his mother had told him something similar the last time he'd seen her. She said she'd see him in a few days, but she disappeared without a trace. Leaving him in the hands of child abusers.

Bringing Brick back to the present, Anya said, "They bashed in her skull. And then they turned her over and bashed in her face, thinking they could conceal her identity. How do you exert that much hatred and aggression toward an innocent person?"

Brick shook his head. "I don't know. Two psychopaths. That's the only explanation I can think of."

"Well, I'm a psychopath now," Anya said. "The sixteen-year-old is grown. And I'm comin' for him. In the transcript, Kaymar is accused of pulling my mother's hair, and telling her, 'Your mouth is too dry, bitch. I wanna see some slobber running down my dick.'"

A groan escaped Brick's throat. It was hard hearing what had been done to Anya's mother. He felt every bit of her rage and anguish. Whenever he imagined Misty on the ground and helpless and getting hit with a tire iron, his blood ran cold.

"I'ma look that killa in the eye while he's sucking on the end of a pistol," Anya said with her jaw clenched. "And before I cock the hammer, I'ma tell that depraved bastard I wanna see some slobber on the barrel."

CHAPTER 27

Sometimes I get the willies when Evette touches me. I don't know what she's doing to me, but today she has the magic touch. The shit feels good.

I'm laying with my back to her, and she's running her fingernails softly down my back…giving me the shivers. Causing my dick to bob up and down.

Growing bolder, she places a kiss on the back of my neck.

I tense up. Evette knows better than to be putting her crooked lips anywhere except on my dick. I have rules about kissing and any kind of romantic gestures.

"Cut it out," I warn her as she sneaks in a couple more sloppy kisses.

"I'm sorry, Kaymar. I couldn't help it. You're so gorgeous. Like a work of art. It's hard keeping my lips off your body."

I don't have a comeback because her words sound so sensual, they take me off-guard.

"I just wanna kiss every inch of you. Can I? Please, Kaymar?"

I'm still at a loss for words, and Evette takes my silence as permission to put her messed-up mouth on my body again. This time, she presses her lips against my shoulder blade.

I wince, surprised at how good her lips feel. Her mouth moves lightly across my broad back and settles on my other shoulder blade. A moan escapes my lips when I feel the cool moisture from her tongue.

She's licking me now. Like a cat. She's got me shuddering and reaching for my dick.

But nah, I ain't going out like this. I flip over, and now I'm lying flat on my stomach, doing my best to keep my dick restrained. I don't wanna pop off and waste a good nutt. I start Evette off every morning with a thick cum shake. I doubt if her day would go right if she didn't get her morning ration.

I'm struggling and straining to keep from busting, tryna let Evette enjoy herself for a few more minutes before I grab her by the hair and pull her head back. The more worked up I am, the rougher I get with her.

Evette doesn't mind the rough treatment. She likes it. I have a routine in the morning. It kills me to hold back as I push past lips and tonsils to get where I gotta go. When my dick is embedded in the back of her throat, making her gag, that's when I relieve myself.

Except for the days that I use my nutt to heal the whelp marks I put on her ass, we've been sticking to this routine like clock-work. I don't know why she feels the need to switch up the game right now with all this mushy kissing.

Licking and purring, Evette glides her tongue down the middle of my back. I'm mad that this bullshit feels so fucking good. She got me squinting and flinching as if her tongue is a high-voltage taser gun.

I kind of know where she's going with this. And she's taking shit too far. *Aye, aye,* I yell in my head, but I don't say anything.

"I know you don't like me to get overly affectionate, Kaymar, but would it be okay if I kiss you on your butt?"

Hell, yeah! I think to myself, but I don't say anything. Mum's the word; the cat's got my tongue. I ain't verbally agreeing to a damn thing. *Do ya thing, ma, but don't expect me to cosign on nothing.*

She kisses both butt cheeks, murmuring, "I've been waiting for you to let me kiss your hard, muscular ass, Kaymar."

Her warm breath on my ass tickles and arouses me.

Getting greedy, she separates my butt cheeks. A strangled groan rises in my throat. Helping her out, I lift up a little. Now she has total ass access.

Hot jolts zing through my system as her tongue dips deeply.

"Goddamn!" I shout as her tongue slips and slides deep inside, teasing me as she circles my anus with the tip of her tongue. Now I'm starting to lose it, grinding hard, and acting like I done found a wet pussy hole in the mattress.

She's driving me crazy and I can't take any more of this! I'm ready to explode.

I shake her off of me and then pounce on her. "You tryna make me your bitch or something?" I growl in anger.

Her eyes are wide with fear. "No, I wanted to try a new way to please you."

I smack her face. Not real hard because I don't wanna send her off to work with my handprint on her mug. "Talk that shit to somebody that don't know you."

Her good eye fills with tears. The droopy eye is dry.

"I told you, I'm not with all that kissing and affection."

"I know; that's why I was trying something different."

"Well, I don't like it. You were acting too tender and romantic. We gon' do this my way. Understand what I'm saying?"

Evette nods dumbly; she has no idea what I have in mind.

I pick up a pillow and toss it at her. "Put that under your head and lay still."

She's wearing a terrified look as she obeys me. I ain't paying that scared look on her face a bit of attention; I know she's faking the fear factor. I can guarantee you that if I stick a finger in her pussy, it'll be soaking wet, bubbling over with excitement.

"I call the shots in this relationship. If you wanna lick ass, you gon' do it my way."

"All right," she says, nodding. So I straddle her and then shimmy upward. Squatting over her face, I separate my own ass cheeks, and align my butt hole with her mouth. My nutt sack is dangling on top of the bridge of her nose. Meanwhile, I'm sliding my dick up and down her forehead, right between her eyes.

Once again, Evette is a quick study. I don't have to give her any guidance. I'm literally sitting on her mouth with my ass cheeks spread open, and she's giving me a thorough tongue job. The shit she's doing feels real raunchy and erotic. Her lizard tongue is darting all fast and crazy. *Whew! Goddamn!* She's got me losing control and squirting out cum.

Amazingly, my nutt isn't squandered. I smile with pride when I peep the high-protein shampoo that's saturating the front of Evette's hairline.

෨෬

Munch came through about an hour ago. We've been sitting in the crib, smoking weed and kicking it while we're waiting for Fawn. I been calling her every fifteen minutes, but she's not picking up. I look over at Munch and shake my head. He picks up his cell from the coffee table and taps on it, sending her a text message.

"Where's she at?" Munch says, somewhat irritated as he sets his phone on the coffee table. "I'ma try again in a few minutes."

When he first got here, we were laughing and joking around; the mood was upbeat. Now we're both tense and solemn, realizing Fawn has played us.

"That bitch is fucking with us; she ain't coming," I say.

"Nope. It don't look like it," Munch agrees.

Rejection hurts. Feels like I've been stabbed in the heart. I was really feeling Fawn. I was willing to go out on a limb for that slut. Agreeing to share her with Munch wasn't an easy decision.

I intended to show Fawn a lot more of my tender side today. I planned to hold her in my arms and kiss her lips while Munch took care of the sexual needs between her legs.

I was so concerned about showing Fawn a nice time, I refused to allow Munch to sniff glue. That nigga is on chill. I got him nice and mellow. I let him smoke up most of my weed so he won't rip up Fawn's pussy. I figure she'll appreciate having her cunt sucked softly and licked with a gentle tongue stroke.

But it don't pay to be nice to bitches; they take kindness for weakness every damn time.

"Whatchu got in your fridge? I'm getting hungry," Munch says.

"Nothing, man. Evette ain't going shopping for food until tomorrow." I kick it like Evette is the housekeeper slash boarder. I keep the nature of our relationship on the low.

"Y'all ain't got any snacks… potato chips…a bag of pretzels."

"Nah. We down to bare bones in this crib." I fail to explain that I used the last cash Evette had to buy the weed his ass is smoking up and enjoying.

"Wow, I could go for a hoagie or cheesesteak right about now."

"I know, right? Why don't you call the deli and order us some grub?"

"I can't, man. I'm broke."

I sigh. The best part of this fucked-up day was giving Evette that early morning shampoo. I find myself looking forward to her coming home. Fuck Fawn! I gotta bitch at home that's willing to do whatever it takes to satisfy my sex drive. She ain't selfish like Fawn. I can't even remember the last time Evette had a climax. In this relationship, it ain't about satisfying Evette's needs. She's the kind of female that gets her pleasure from knowing her man's all right.

CHAPTER 28

Anya woke up in bed alone. Her first thought was that Brick had deserted her. Last night he'd promised to put his Miami plans on hold and help her get the scumbag that murdered her mother. But maybe her situation was too intense for him…more than he'd bargained for.

Her sense of panic was alleviated when she saw the text he'd sent. Brick had gone to Philly to handle some business. He said he'd be back around noon to take her to lunch. Immense relief washed over her. She was falling for Brick. He was sensitive and sexy. The combination made him so easy to love.

Their relationship was a temporary situation. Brick had made that clear. Still, Anya was determined to make the best of every day that she and Brick shared. During this temporary love affair, she was not going to hold back from showering him with all the love stored in her heart. If he only gave her a mere fraction of the love she planned to give him, she'd be able to walk away without any feelings of regret.

She thought about what she'd wear on her lunch date with Brick and sighed. Anya had been rotating the same three outfits all summer. It was a shame that some desperate and immoral person had broken into her room at the youth hostel where she was staying when she first arrived in Philly. Her money and possessions had been stolen. With no means to pay her weekly rent, Anya had been cast out into the streets.

She could have called her aunt and gotten airfare back to Indiana, but that would have defeated her purpose. Instead, she met a boy named Troy at a seedy hotel. Troy, who went by the name Cash Money. She called him C.

From the moment that she told him about her inheritance, Cash Money stuck to her like glue. He looked out for her. Found ways to pay the rent in the hotel. And when they had absolutely no money or food, he would take her to his mother's house for meals.

The difference between Cash Money and Brick was that Brick was helping her without expecting anything in return.

Merely thinking about Brick put a smile on her lips. It would be nice to put on something new and pretty for their lunch date. With the money Brick had given her, she could buy something fly, but she hadn't noticed any malls within walking distance of the motel.

Making the best of what she had to work with, Anya ironed her cut-off shorts and top. Giving herself a feminine touch, she painted her fingernails and toenails in multiple colors: turquoise, pink, and a bright yellow to fit her sunny mood.

At noon, she met Brick in the parking lot. To her surprise, he was driving a different car.

"Where's your car?" she asked as she slid in the passenger seat. The car he was driving was nothing spectacular. It was actually a downgrade from his previous car.

"I had to get rid of it."

"Oh." She didn't press him for details. He'd tell her whatever he felt she needed to know.

Brick patted the steering wheel fondly. "This baby don't look like much, but she'll get us wherever we need to go."

"Did you hook up with your friend?" Anya was curious about the gun Brick said he'd be able to get for her.

"Yeah, my man in Philly handled the car transaction. He can't get you that piece right now, but he'll have something in a few days."

"Okay, that's cool." A part of Anya felt instant relief. If she had the gun in her possession, she'd feel compelled to embark on the search for Kaymar Crawford. She was grateful to have a little extra time to chill with Brick. Constantly thinking about retribution put a drain on her spirit.

She promised herself that until she had the weapon in her hand, she'd keep her mind off of revenge and savor every moment with Brick.

"Is there anywhere special you'd like to eat? The sky is the limit," Brick said, teasingly.

"With these old clothes, I'm not dressed for anywhere special," Anya replied.

Brick gave her a look that told her she was crazy. "You're special, and you look good in anything you put on."

"Stop playing."

"I'm speaking the truth."

"You're sweet. Thank you, Brick," she murmured.

"For what?"

"For making me happy. I can feel myself glowing when you're around."

Brick smiled, but didn't say anything. Anya understood that he didn't want to give her false hope. But fuck it. She was caught up, and didn't mind showing it.

"How about that restaurant. You ever eat there?" He pointed to The Cheesecake Factory, which was on the other side of the road.

"Oh, yeah, I love that place. The food's good and the cheese-cake is to die for."

"I'm sold," Brick said as he made a turn at the next light. A few minutes later, they were parking in the lot.

Though Brick was only about four or five years older than Anya, he seemed much older. Carried himself like a mature man. In his presence, Anya felt cared for and protected. As they entered the restaurant, two energetic kids ran ahead of their parents and almost collided into Anya. The way Brick pulled her close to him was so endearing. It was a small gesture, but it meant a lot to Anya.

There was a forty-minute wait. Brick asked her if she wanted to go somewhere with a shorter wait. "No, I'm good," Anya said with her nose practically pressed against the glass case displaying the vast variety of cheesecake. "So many choices, but I think I'm going to try the key lime. What about you?" she asked Brick.

"Whatever you're getting. I trust your taste," he said. "Oh, I left something important in the car. Be right back." Brick squeezed her shoulder reassuringly, as if he sensed that every time he left her, she feared he wouldn't come back.

"Here you go," Brick said, handing Anya an iPad. "I bought this off of my man. Figured you was feenin' to get online."

She covered her mouth to smother a squeal but her eyes bulged with surprised pleasure. "Thank you."

"Now you won't have to search for your pop using a public computer."

Anya looked at Brick and pointed her finger. "You are so lucky that we're in a family restaurant." She shook her head. "Umph, umph, umph."

He laughed uneasily. "What are you talking about?"

She licked her lips. "I'm just saying. If I could do what I wanted right now…" She shook her head ominously. "I'd pop that zipper in your pants, slide that thing outta them briefs, and I'd do you right."

"Whoa!" Brick looked shocked by Anya's brashness. Frowning, Brick turned his head from side to side, looking around the foyer area.

"I'm sorry. I didn't mean to embarrass you. I don't think any-one heard me," Anya reassured him.

"I'm not thinking about these people. You talking dirty...got me looking around, tryna scope out a private area."

Anya giggled.

"I'm serious. There's gotta be a cubby hole around this joint somewhere." He looked around again. "I'm not particular...are you?"

"Hell, no," Anya replied, smiling.

"I'm about to yank yo' lil' sexy ass into the bathroom. But I'm tryna be civilized about it. I need to call the manager!"

Anya's eyes danced with excitement "What do you wanna say to the manager?"

"I'ma be like, 'Excuse me, sir. Do y'all got a closet we could use real quick? Me and my girl are having an emergency. We need to handle something while we're waiting for our table.'"

"You so crazy. I didn't know you had a sense of humor."

"I'm not being funny...I'm dead serious. You talking trash, and now you gon' have to back up your words." Brick proceeded toward the hostess.

Anya gasped. "Brick!"

He ignored her. "Can I speak to the manager?"

The hostess's trained smile remained in place. "Is there a prob-lem, sir?"

Mortified, Anya rushed forward and tugged on Brick's arm. "There's no problem. We were just wondering how much longer we have to wait."

The hostess nodded in understanding. "Oh, you're in luck. Your table is ready. Follow me, please."

Walking behind the waitress, Anya whispered to Brick. "I'm gonna get you for embarrassing me like that."

"I got extra paper! I was gon' grease the manager bull's palm and see if he could give us his office or something."

Covering her mouth, Anya giggled again.

After they were seated, the hostess gave them their menus and left.

Anya leaned forward. "You can't be serious. Stop messing with my head, Brick. I can't tell if you're being straight up or if you're messing with me." She searched Brick's face.

Brick picked up a menu and opened up. With his face concealed behind the menu, he said, "Say some more shit out in public that gets my dick hard, and you'll find whether I'm playing or not."

Her heart fluttered and her coochie puckered at the same time. She picked up her menu and perused it, while stealing glances at Brick. She couldn't have found a better companion. The fine-ass man on the other side of the table was not only sweet and considerate. Brick had some freak in him! Anya was intrigued by the sexual possibilities that they could explore together.

Testing Brick, she slid her foot out of her sandal. With her toes pointed, she stretched out her leg beneath the table and rubbed her foot against Brick's crotch.

With his eyes fixed on the menu, Brick took Anya by surprise when he grasped her foot. He looked down at her multi-colored toenails. "These joints look better than the cheesecake on the menu. I'ma have to sample this one, this one, and this one," he said, playfully wiggling her toes.

When he maneuvered his bulky body in a position that appeared as if he were about to get under the table, Anya yelped and snatched her foot out of his grasp.

"You gon' stop playing with me, aye?" Brick said with a devilish smile.

"Okay!" Anya said, nodding briskly.

CHAPTER 29

Munch got tired of waiting around for Fawn. He got up outta here and went home to get something to eat. He said he might be back after he eats lunch. It was on the tip of my tongue to ask him to bring me a plate when he comes back through.

As mean as Munch's mom is, she'd probably bust him in the head if he tried to take some food out of her house.

Munch is a twenty-eight-year-old mama's boy. That nigga is scared to death of his mother. I wouldn't be surprised if his mom takes a strap to that ass.

There's nothing for me to do except smoke weed and watch TV. My stomach growls and I realize I'm starving like Marvin. I suck my teeth in disgust. Evette might be handling herself in the bedroom, but she's doing a piss poor job of keeping food in this house.

Munch's mom is loud, rude, and mean as a snake, but I gotta give her props…she keeps her boy well-fed. She should come over and give Evette's dumb ass some lessons.

Those earlier feelings of warmth toward Evette are slowly turning to resentment. I'ma handsome, dark-skinned nigga. I got a six-pack. My ebony body is ripped and defined from front to back.

Evette is a fuggly ho…tore up from the floor up, and she knows it. That bitch should be working two or three jobs if that's what's required to take care of me. I've been dealing with this low-budget broad because I was right out the joint, but I can see that I'm gon' have to get me a better bitch. Somebody that can afford to buy me weed and feed me whatever I want to eat. All this waiting for payday bullshit is starting to wear on my nerves.

My stomach is turning inside out and I'm thinking angry thoughts when the doorbell suddenly rings. I jump up, hoping Munch snuck some food out of his mother's kitchen.

I swing the door open and, to my surprise, Fawn is standing there. "Hey, lover, sorry I'm late," she says. Her honey-colored hair is parted on the side, showing those dark roots that look so sexy on her. It's curled on the top…hard for me to describe, but it's styled in a sort of upsweep 'do. She looks even prettier than I remember.

"I'm glad you made it," I say, sounding real smooth, but my heart is pounding away. I give her a long look and nod my head. "You looking good in them jeans."

"Get a good look because I don't plan to have 'em on for long."

I laugh. Fawn is the complete package. Beautiful, banging body, and a lot of confidence. She seems like the type of chick that likes to call the shots.

"Yesterday was wild," Fawn says. "I never experienced anything like that." She looks around. "Where's your friend? He sent me a text saying he was here with you."

"Oh, yeah…he was, but he went home for a few minutes. He'll be back."

"I don't have a lot of time. I'm on the clock. I dropped a client off for a medical appointment, but I have to pick her up in an hour."

"Oh." I scratch my head, hoping to quickly figure something

out. "I'ma call Munch and see what's taking him so long," I say as I turn toward the kitchen.

Fawn grabs my wrist. "I already tried him out; now I want to experience you." Her voice is very seductive. She's working on the button of her jeans, and I'm starting to sweat.

"Look, I'm not gon' front; I never ate no pussy before." I look down in embarrassment. "But we can do something else," I mutter softly.

"Aw, that's so cute," she serenades. "After the way you were bragging yesterday, I should feel some kind of way."

"I know. I know, but I learn fast."

She laughs and her laughter sounds like a pretty song. "I can tell by the way you kissed me yesterday, that you're the romantic type. If I had more time, Kaymar, we could take it to the bedroom...fuck and suck each other until we're delirious. But I can't stay long, sweetie."

"I understand," I say, looking down at the floor. She has me feeling like a shy little boy.

"Well, let's make good use of the time we have together." Fawn holds out her arms. I ease into her embrace, my mouth seeking her lips. She only gives me a quick kiss. "Kaymar, I can't get into all of this...I'm kinda in a rush."

"My bad."

She kicks her sandals off and begins to wiggle out of her tight jeans. I unsnap my pants, preparing to fuck the shit out of Fawn.

"No! Leave your clothes on," she orders as she strips off her thong. Suddenly, I'm mesmerized. All that thick, curly pussy hair is turning me on.

"I'ma guide you through it, Kaymar," she says as she presses her hand upon my shoulder, gesturing for me to stoop down.

I feel like I'm in a trance as I obey this broad's command. I'm down on my knees, staring at her pussy. Going on instinct, I grip her hips and bring that pussy flush against my face. I don't need any instructions because Fawn is leaking cunt juice and I'm lapping it up and loving it.

I pull away briefly. "If I knew pussy tasted like strawberries, I would've been eating it a long time ago," I tell her, and I'm speaking from the heart. Pussy is good!

"Not all pussy tastes like this, sweetie. I got that good stuff," she says and pushes my face between her thighs.

My dick is rock hard but I ignore it as Fawn fucks my face. She's not allowing me to lick her anymore. She clutching my head and banging her pussy against my face all crazy, rattling my brains around.

I pull my head back. "Yo, Fawn. Slow down, shawty. I'm tryna eat your box out, but you're acting crazy." I'm a little irritated because I want to taste some more of her sweet flavor. I stand up and reach for her hand. "Come on, let's take this shit to the couch. This is my first time and everything, but I got the hang of eating pussy now. I want you lying down with your legs spread wide open, so I can work my tongue right."

Looking indecisive, Fawn looks over at the couch and then back at me. "Okay, but let's do it my way for a few more minutes, and then we can switch it up."

Reluctantly, I lower myself back down in front of this crazy broad's hairy pussy. I don't even get a good look before she's grabbing my head and humping my face real hard, once again.

I don't like this, but I go along with it. Then something happens. Fawn stops thrusting, but she's whimpering and moaning. Her entire body is shaking and vibrating like she's been electrocuted.

When she finally stops moving, she goes limps and begins to slide down the door. I rise up, and catch her before she falls.

The nutt she just busted is drizzling out of her pussy, enticing me. Cradling her in my arms, I walk fast as I carry Fawn to the couch. I don't know what's come over me. I can't blame my behavior merely on being hungry, because on some real shit, I'd turn down a cheesesteak for the sweet drippings between Fawn's legs.

Once I'm situated in the right position, I try to suck the guts out of Fawn. I like the stringy, sliminess of her cum. I could eat her pussy drops for breakfast, lunch, and dinner. After a while, her pussy juice starts to lose some of its flavor as well as the slippery texture.

She pats my head. "That's it, Kaymar. Stop! Ain't no more. You cleaned me out, baby," she says with a satisfied smile.

"But I'm not finished." I feel desperate.

Fawn sits up and closes her legs tight. "I have to pick up my client."

"How you gon' leave me like this?" I feel anger rising up in me.

"I told you I couldn't stay long." She gets up and walks over to where her jeans are pooled on the floor.

It's hard to describe how I feel. Sad…heartsick. Forlorn. "Baby, please. Don't put them jeans on." I'm about ready to run over and tackle Fawn's ass.

She steps into her jeans. "Lemme explain something, Kaymar…" She pauses and pats her crotch. "You can lick this cat all day long, but if I'm not aroused, the flavor is not going to taste the same."

"What do I have to do to get you aroused?"

She shrugs. "I have to go; I'm running late."

"Just tell me." My voice cracks because I'm getting frustrated.

"I warned you. I told you that this pussy ain't nothing to play with." Fawn gestures toward her crotch and laughs.

I can't laugh along with her because I don't find what she's saying funny.

"After you drop your client off, can you come back through?" I sound like a sucker, and I'm shocked at myself. This ain't even me. I don't beg bitches for a muthafuckin' thing. Why am I standing up here, pleading with this broad to let me eat some more of her pussy? But I can't help myself. They say you should be careful about the company you keep. I'm wondering if hanging with that pussy-addict, Munch, has started to rub off on me.

Fawn sighs. "I'm running late; I'll give you a call later."

The way I'm feeling, I'd like to handcuff this bitch, yank them jeans off of her and burn 'em—force her to have to stay with me until I'm ready to let her go.

But I say, "Aye, I'll be waiting for your call." I'm all broke up inside as I watch her turn around, taking that sweet pussy away from me—walking it out the door.

CHAPTER 30

Days go by and I don't hear a word from Fawn. At first I was moping around, but now I'm pretty much over that ho. Whatever spell she had on me is starting to wear off.

It's two-dollar drink night at this little hole in the wall joint a few blocks from the crib. Evette got paid, and I finally got some money in my pockets. My paper is not as long as I'd like, but I create a big-ass knot by covering a bunch of ones with a few twenty-dollar bills.

I'm chilling with Munch and pretty boy, Blake. For some reason, Pretty Boy ain't getting any play. It's my night tonight; every bitch in this dip has her eye on me.

I'm not even tryna holla at none of 'em. I'm playing it cool… sending two-dollar drinks to the chosen few. The rest of these bitches can suck my nutts! They can keep sashaying past me and batting their eyelashes all they want, but I ain't buying them shit. I'm invested in the hoes already drinking off me…and before this night is over, they gon' pay up.

Two-dollar drink night isn't the welcome home fantasy I imagined, but for now, this is the closest I can get to my dream of ballin'.

Desperate for attention, this real thirsty chick sends me a drink. I don't even look at her or thank her. I throw the liquor back and chase it down with big swig of Heineken.

Munch's seat has been empty for quite awhile. His ass is the bathroom, allegedly taking a leak. But I'd bet good money that Munch is hemmed up in a stall, licking the lining out of some broad's coochie.

Ordinarily, Blake would be checking on Munch, making sure the bull don't eat nothing he didn't give his stamp of approval on. But Blake has been having a texting war with his baby mama for the past half-hour. He's too distracted to keep tabs on Munch.

As the night progresses, chicks get bolder. They're taking turns sitting next to me and striking up a conversation. I'm barely responding to these chicks. After the hell that bitch Fawn put me through, I'm not making it easy for none of these hoes. When one of 'em figures out what I want to hear, then I'll start talking.

Blake puts his cell phone away. Finished battling with his baby mama, he's now running game on this super tall chick, trying to line up his pussy for the night. The chick he's talking to doesn't appeal to me. She's real tall, like a basketball player. Big ol' mannish hands and everything. I wonder if she's a tranny. I laugh to myself. It would serve Pretty Boy right if he ended up with a man in his bed.

I turn back to the chick that's sitting in Munch's seat. Her name is Detina.

"My girlfriend wants to know if you want to come back to her place tonight," Detina asks.

"It depends," I say in cool-ass way.

"Depends on what?

"On whether I can get into a ménage with both of y'all."

Detina glances away in embarrassment. Her laughter sounds both nervous and excited. She picks up her drink and guzzles it down. She's acting like she's shook by my proposition, but I wasn't born yesterday. This cunt knows good and well she's with it. She just don't wanna seem overly eager to get in the middle of a dick and pussy sandwich.

"Okay, I don't mind," she finally concedes.

"What about your girlfriend. Is she with it?"

"I can't speak for her."

"Well, go talk to shawty. Find out where her head is at."

"Wait, I need a moment." This chick, Detina, gestures to the barmaid to bring her another drink. On my tab! The nerve of this cunt whore! I'ma break her face if she can't convince her friend to agree to a threesome.

The barmaid gives her a fresh drink, and she immediately starts sipping. "I can't believe I'm considering doing something so freaky," Detina says.

Next to me, Pretty Boy's cell phone goes off; the ringtone is loud and startling. He takes the call, and then nudges me. As he's handing me his phone, he says in a malicious voice, "You playing Big Willie tonight, but you still ain't got your own cell phone."

Detina bursts out laughing. I'm embarrassed and furious. I'm ready to fuck up Pretty Boy for putting me on blast. Detina deserves to be bitch-slapped for laughing so loud after having two or three drinks on me.

"It's Fawn," Blake says.

Anger instantly melts. *My baby's on the phone?*

Leaving Detina sitting alone at the bar, I walk away with Blake's phone in my hand. I keep walking until I'm outside. A call from my baby requires complete privacy.

"Hello."

"I know you're mad, but get over it. I miss you and I wanna see you tonight." Fawn doesn't bullshit around. This chick gets straight to the point.

"Damn, can't I get an apology for the way you left me waiting around for your phone call?"

"I'm sorry, Kaymar. Can I make it up to you?"

"How?"

"I have something for you," she says in a teasing, singsong voice.

"Oh, yeah, whatchu got for me?" I should be cussing this bitch out instead of allowing her to persuade me.

"I'll give you a hint. What I have tastes like strawberries."

"Damn, you got my mouth watering. How long will it take you to get to my crib?"

"Give me forty-five minutes. I already have my car keys in my hands. I'ma hop on 95; I'll be there in around forty-five minutes."

We hang up. For a few moments, I'm standing there smiling and unconsciously licking my lips. I'm on some sucker shit. I check myself and wipe my mouth with the back of my hand.

I have no idea what I'm gonna say to Evette. But whatever I come up with, she better go along with it.

Inside the bar, I find Blake and give him his phone. I still don't see Munch. Bitches are probably in the bathroom taking numbers. I honestly don't understand why he likes to eat a bunch of anonymous pussy, but I can't judge the man.

"Oh, there you are." Detina gives me the thumbs-up sign. "It's all good. My friend, Shay, said we can all chill at her spot."

I look toward the end of the bar and the shawty named Shay smiles and waves at me.

"Yo, jot down your number on a napkin. Something came up. I'ma have to holla at you and shawty some other time."

Detina glares at me. I don't blame her. I'm mad at my damn self for turning down an opportunity to get into a ménage.

"Are you serious?" Detina turns up the corner of her lip.

"It's an emergency."

"Mmm-hmm," she murmurs with a hand on her hip.

"Yo, seriously. My baby mom just went in labor," I tell her, unable to think of any other emergency.

I hurry out of the bar. The crib is not that far, so I take off running...hauling ass so I can quickly explain the situation to Evette before Fawn gets there.

ഗൗ

"You know I haven't dealt with that many females. I still got a lot of wild oats to sow," I explain to Evette.

"Okay, I realize that," Evette says, pacing in the bedroom. "But..."

"Look, I'm tryna be a man about this. I could do my dirt in the streets, but I'm not. How many men would be honest enough to do their extracurricular fucking right here under your nose? Can't I get some credit for keeping it real?"

Evette opens her mouth to say something, but then changes her mind. I run it down like a courtroom lawyer, and she can't think of a word to say in her defense.

"Evette, get a move on! Make the bed up real quick before you go in the spare bedroom!" I yell at her.

She stands there looking pitiful. "I mean...I understand what you're saying. Being in prison for that long time, I realize you missed out on a lot of living. But I just think we should've discussed it together. Made a joint decision about you bringing a girl home."

"What's your problem? You act like I'm bringing home my future wife. You're the woman I'm planning to marry. Are you really that insecure over a jumpoff?" I look at Evette like she's crazy. My mouth is hanging open and I'm blinking all crazy with my eyes poppin' out of my head.

She hesitates for a moment and then shakes her head hesitantly. She's scared. She doesn't want to push me over the edge, but I can tell she's not convinced it's a good idea for me to let shawty come to the crib.

Time is ticking. I have to quickly persuade Evette to get on board with this. I soften my approach. "You need to trust me. Do you honestly believe I'd mess up what we been building for two years?"

"Why do you need another woman?"

"For sex."

"But I give you all the sex you need. I do it all. Anything you ask for." Her voice is whiny, getting on my nerves. She's starting to piss me off. I realize talking soft and tender isn't getting through to her; now I'm about to go ham on this broad.

"I'ma twenty-six-year-old man!" I holler at the top of my lungs. I pound on my chest like King Kong. My loud mouth and the booming on my chest are scaring the shit out of Evette, making her twitch and jump.

"You tryna rob me of my youth," I say loudly, trying to get my point across.

"No, I'm not. I just don't know what else I can do to satisfy you."

"It ain't all about you, Evette." I grab my head, groaning real loud. I'm acting like I'm so frustrated, I can't take another second of her selfishness. "I'm too young to be tied down to one woman. I'm tryna be honest with you, Evette. But if you can't deal with an honest nigga, then it's time for me to get up outta here."

I ain't got no place to go, so I'm taking a big chance in calling her bluff.

Her lips quiver. I'm relieved to see she's breaking down. "I appreciate that you're being honest," she says. "I'm surprised; that's all. You don't have to go nowhere. I don't want you to leave me over something like this. We'll work it out."

I turn my mouth down in a bitter frown. I shake my head in disgust. Evette looks down in shame. Without hollering at her, I'm quietly getting my point across. Letting her know that I'm really disappointed she would risk me packing up and leaving over her insecurities of me dipping my dick into some extra pussy.

"How long do you need to see other females?" Evette asks, as she slowly accepts it's my way or the highway.

"Until I sow all my wild oats," I snap. "I'm all man, baby. If you want a faggot, go get yourself one!"

"I know you're all man. I'm just saying…." She scratches her head. "We're supposed to be getting married; I was going to ask you about going to get the license."

"Nah. I ain't getting no license yet. The wedding is still on, but we're gon' have to delay it until I can get the desire to fuck other broads out of my system."

Evette sniffles; it's an ugly, annoying sound. If she thinks I'm going to hug her and console her, she's nuttier than I thought.

"Cut that sniffling out," I tell her. "You knew what it was when you first started writing me. I been in the joint since I was sixteen. A young boy doesn't know anything about women. You gon' have to pump the brakes on this marriage shit and wait for me to live a little and fuck a lot!" I say the last few words with my mouth twisted in malice because Evette is irking me by sniffling and crying.

"But I've been waiting for so long, and you promised me—"

"Fuck what I promised you. I'm not jumping into marriage before I find out what other pussies feel like."

She winces.

"Yo, I thought this was my crib, too."

"It is!"

"Well, if I you can't deal with me bringing my female company home, there ain't any point in me staying here." I walk to the closet, move around some clothes. Then I yank a shirt off the hanger, giving the impression I'm about to start packing.

"It's okay, Kaymar. I get it. I really do. I'm being selfish. You should have all the extra women you need until you get it all out of your system," Evette blurts in desperation.

"That's what I want to hear. Now you're talking like you have some sense. If it's one thing I can't stand, it's an insecure, jealous chick."

"I'll learn to deal with my insecurities, Kaymar."

I've been told more than once that I look extra handsome when I smile. So I flash her one of my best smiles. "That's good to hear. If you can handle me sexing another female right here in the crib, it'll make our relationship stronger. Dig what I'm saying?"

She shrugs uncertainly. "I hope so."

"Marriage is a sacred union, Evette. I don't want to get married and then end up resenting you because I feel like I'm missing out. The majority of married men cheat. But I want to be a faithful husband. Understand what I'm saying? Would you rather I cheat in your face while we're single, or do it behind your back after we're married?"

She walks over to the bed and pulls off the top sheet. "I prefer that you cheat in my face, Kaymar," Evette admits in a sorrowful tone.

Yes! I'm so happy, I wanna hug Evette.

While Evette is straightening up the bed, I notice a stain on the bottom sheet. It's not all that noticeable, but I don't wanna put another woman in a bed that has a cum stain left over from when I was jacking my dick watching porn.

"Yo, hold up. Don't throw the covers over these joints. There's a cum stain from this morning."

"We didn't do anything this morning," Evette says dumbly.

I shake my head. Seems like she deliberately acts dumb just to get on my nerves. "Man, change the damn sheets. Oh, and get those fluffy pillows out. Spread them shits all over the bed. Make it look real nice and cozy for my company."

Evette gives me a hurt look when I tell her that I want the fancy pillows on the bed. Impatiently, I flick Evette on the ass. I don't smack her ass real hard, the way I do when I'm making a sexual gesture. That two-finger flick I just gave her generates a sharp sting—lets her know I'm not fucking around.

"Get your ass in gear, Evette. My company will be here any minute."

CHAPTER 31

D riving a different whip, Brick was able to slip into his old neighborhood undetected. Hoping to catch a glimpse of Thomasina and his son, he parked in the lot of the Superfresh on Fifty-Sixth Street. It was Tuesday, and if Thomasina was back to her usual routine, she'd be doing her weekly grocery shopping today.

Like clockwork, she came out of the market at ten-fifteen with Little Baron sitting in the cart. She pushed the cart over to her car, opened the trunk, and started loading it with bags. With one less mouth to feed, there weren't as many bags as she used to bring out of the store.

It took all of Brick's willpower not to run over to Thomasina's car, lift his son out of the cart, and cover his face with kisses. Under the circumstances, all he could do was watch from afar. Using binoculars, he got a good look at his son. *My lil' man is lookin' real husky. Getting big in only a few weeks.* He watched as Thomasina lifted Little Baron out of the cart. Before putting him in his car seat, she reflexively kissed his cheek. A smile curved Brick's lips. Despite his absence, his son was well cared for and loved.

He kissed his fingers and blew a kiss in his son's direction. *Here's one from Daddy. I love you, son.*

Brick was banned from his boy's life, and rightfully so. He

couldn't blame Thomasina for doing what she thought was best for their child. Still Brick believed with all of his heart that the day would come when he and his boy would be reunited. It might be years from now, but that day was surely going to come.

Thomasina drove out of the lot and turned right. She never missed a day going to the hospital to see Misty, but at least he knew of her whereabouts right now.

He picked up his cell phone and called Anya. "It's cool. Her mom's not at the hospital. Go on up to her room; try to get in at least a five-minute visit. And make sure you tell her what I said."

"I gotchu," Anya said and then disconnected.

Knowing that Anya had his back, Brick exited the parking lot with a sense of relief.

Brick waited a few moments and then exited, making a left. He had an appointment with Tayshaun to see what was up with the fake ID he promised to have ready this morning. And he also needed to find out what was up with the gun and the other weapons he'd made a deposit on. There was a delay in getting Anya the gun she wanted because Taye insisted on putting all the weapons in the same order. The killing tools that Brick had ordered from Taye were taking a lot longer than expected.

Anya's method of revenge seemed too delicate. A bullet between a nigga's eyes seemed too humane in Brick's opinion. God help Brick's victim...that mufucka, bitch or whoever was going to experience a lot of pain. It would be slow and torturous. He was gon' make the mufucka wish for death exactly like Misty had. And this time Brick would make no mistakes. Misty's assailant would not be left lingering between life and death. He or she was going to get a one-way ticket to hell—but they wouldn't be taking the express. Nah, they had to take the slow route. Slow and bloody.

Brick drove to the projects, but Tayshaun wasn't around and

no one had seen him. A ten-thirty appointment didn't mean a thing to a nigga like Tayshaun. *'Hood niggas be on their own time-frame!*

He was pissed that he had to hang around waiting for Tayshaun to come through. Killing two birds with one stone, Brick decided to get rid of his frustration while improving his running stamina.

He drove to Valley Green in Germantown and hit the trails. Running up steep inclines had perspiration pouring off his body. His mind was no longer on the sorrow of losing his wife and child. He wasn't pissed with Taye and his CP-time shenanigans. He wasn't worrying about how he'd manage to infiltrate Smash Hitz organization nor was he pondering the many ways that he wanted to murder the man and his bitch-ass, tranny lover.

His mind was empty of all thoughts. Running was meditative. The sounds of his feet pounding against the ground soothed his troubled spirit.

৪৩০৪

At Brick's request, Anya had been calling the hospital daily to check Misty's status. Brick told her that he didn't want to bump into his wife at the hospital, and so he sent Anya to visit Misty, requesting that she give Misty a message from him. Anya didn't like the smell of hospitals. She didn't like visiting sick people. But she'd do anything for Brick. As far as she was concerned, Brick was her man. Even if his feelings weren't as strong as hers...she was all in. Committed. She didn't mind throwing that "L" word around because for her it was real. It had to be love. What else would make a woman come out of her comfort zone and go put in time with her man's ex. A woman that couldn't talk back...a woman that was half-dead and in a coma?

Wearing a sundress, shades, and looking respectable, Anya breezed past the nurses' station. None of the staff even looked up or questioned who she was visiting. She slipped into room 507 and covered her mouth to smother a gasp.

Misty looked like a skeleton. She was surrounded by tubes and machines. The sight of her frail body and deformed face caused Anya to wince. She had to choke back tears, even though she had never known Misty.

This isn't living. She looks dead! Why would the medical profession allow someone to go on like this? The medical profession should be ashamed to be so cruel as to prolong this girl's misery.

Anya pulled a chair up close to the bed.

"Hi, Misty." She waited a few beats, expecting Misty to open her mouth and say something. "Um…you don't know me. My name is Anya. I'm a friend of Brick's. Well, I'm more than a friend, if you know what I mean. Just in case you can hear me, I wanted to give you a message from Brick. He said he's sorry the plan didn't work." Anya went silent momentarily and observed Misty…trying to ascertain if there was any intelligent life inside her. But she saw no indication of life. There was nothing more than a corpse lying in the bed. *Poor thing.* Anya swallowed and then cleared her throat.

She felt a little foolish talking to someone she didn't know personally—someone barely alive—but it wasn't about Anya's feelings. She was there for Brick. Being his eyes and ears. His mouthpiece. Visiting his precious Misty since he couldn't be there himself.

"Brick said he hopes you found Shane. He said, 'tell him, whassup.'"

As if reacting to Shane's name, Misty's hand twitched. Anya reared back in surprise. Had she imagined Misty response? Anya's eyes darted from Misty's hand to the door, hoping no one had popped in. She'd be beyond humiliated if anyone heard what she was saying. No doubt, she'd be considered insane.

Anya rubbed the top of Misty's fisted hand, telling herself she was doing it for Brick. Doing what he'd do if he were allowed in the room with Misty.

Finally, she stood. She bent over Misty and whispered in her ear, "Brick says to tell you he loves you. Always has; always will."

It took a lot to share that part of Brick's message. But Anya wouldn't be comfortable with herself if she selfishly left out Brick's parting remarks.

She walked to the door, stopped, and looked back at Misty. "I don't know what went wrong between you and Brick, but you were a lucky to have a man like him in love with you."

Anya left the room and hurried to the elevator. Inside the elevator, she released a long breath. If possible, she loved Brick more than ever. No other man would ever measure up to his sensitivity and his strength, the way he was able to put those he loved before himself.

CHAPTER 32

I've been seeing Fawn regularly for a minute now. She claims I'm moving too fast, but this dirty bitch got me sprung and I can't help myself. I don't know what it is about her. She's a slut…no doubt about that. I heard when she's not with me, she's out there fucking everything that moves.

The reason I dig her so much is the sex. The first night she came over, I didn't wanna embarrass myself by cumming too quick, so I spent the whole night sucking on her pussy. I wouldn't even let her suck on my Johnson for fear she'd find out about my cum-quick problem.

I don't put my business out there with everybody, so I didn't tell Pretty Boy Blake about my situation. But I confided in Munch. Munch is a cool ass mufucka. He's crazy, but you can talk to that nigga. So I told him about my issue. And that nigga came through. He put me on with this potion that you get from Chinatown. I didn't think it would really work, but what the fuck, I was willing to give it a try.

I told Evette to go grab me a bottle on her lunch break. She brought it home and I'll be damn… That Chinese love potion bullshit really works. It's got ginseng and some other shit in it. It's nasty as hell, but it gets the job done.

Now I'm fucking like a porn star. Banging the headboard against the wall… mattress springs squealing, the bed is rocking.

Fawn be screaming and shit when I give her a good dick down. This shit is bananas. While I'm laying pipe, she's clawing my back up and screaming my name. This is the kind of good fucking I dreamed about all those years I spent in the pen.

Sometimes I hear Evette sobbing in the next room while I'm plundering inside Fawn's coochie. Fawn makes so much noise, she can't hear Evette's mournful sounds. But I do. Hearing her cry her heart out while I'm fucking another bitch brings out the freak in me. The louder Evette sobs, the harder I bang Fawn.

Times like this, I love my life. This shit is bananas. I got a full-time freak and part-time slut.

My world could be even better if Fawn would cooperate with me.

See, I wanna take it to the next level with Fawn. Move her in here and fuck and suck that good, slutty pussy every day and every night. But Fawn won't listen. She's hard-headed and refuses to get serious. That bitch is coming and going outta this crib as she pleases. She's making me mad and driving me crazy.

But it's all good. I got a plan. Come hell or high water, I'ma turn that ho into a housewife.

ಇಂದ

This morning, I wake up to the sound of Evette knocking on the bedroom door. It's odd for Evette to try to get in the bedroom when I have company, so I pat the side of the bed that Fawn was lying on...you know...to cover her up if she's exposed. But she's not here. Her side of the bed is empty.

Evette taps on the door again.

"You can come in," I say in a sleepy voice.

Evette comes in wearing a bathrobe and one of her corny nightgowns. Fawn keeps it sexy in the lingerie department, so I stopped caring about Evette's grandma gear.

"Where's Fawn? In the bathroom?" I ask, hopefully. I like waking up with my shawty lying next to me. But Fawn is independent. She'll hop up in the middle of the night and roll out without saying a word.

"She left. She said she'll call you later."

"Damn!" I sit up. I'm feeling irritated that Fawn keeps pulling this shit. It aggravates me that she slips out without even saying, 'I'll see you later, nigga.' Her behavior is so suspicious that I asked her if she's got some dick on the side, but she claims I'm the only one she's dealing with at the moment.

At the moment! That kind of talk made me wonder if she was planning on giving my pussy to somebody else in the future.

Fawn quickly corrected me. "My pussy doesn't belong to you or any other mufucka. My pussy belongs to me and me only." She's strong-willed and feisty. That's what I like about her. But I still wish I could have a little more control over her.

Evette can tell that Fawn's got me sprung, but she keeps her mouth shut and stays in her lane.

Fawn comes through about two or three times a week. On the nights she's here, I demand my space and make Evette sleep in the spare bedroom. Actually, in my quest to keep Fawn from getting suspicious about Evette and me, I made Evette move all her clothes and personal items into the spare bedroom.

I'm still fucking with Evette, but what we do is kept real low-key.

Fawn thinks that Evette and me are nothing but roommates. In fact, I told Fawn I own this spot. I told her it was left to me by my great uncle, but being that I'm out of work, I rent out a room to Evette.

In Fawn's mind, Evette ain't nothing more than a boarder.

Evette doesn't make any waves when Fawn's around because she hoping my relationship with Fawn is only phase.

But keeping it real… I'm all in with Fawn. She's the one I really want to marry. I want her to have my babies.

Fawn has a thing for candles. She's got a collection of 'em spread all over the top of the bureau. Evette picks up the newest edition and pulls off the cap. She sniffs it and wrinkles her nose. "I don't like this one."

"Yo, put that candle down. Stop fucking with Fawn's shit. Don't nobody care what you like." I'm mad because Fawn left, but I'm taking it out on Evette. "Whassup, anyway? Why you in here waking me up all early in the morning?"

"Can I lie in the bed with you for a few minutes before I get dressed for work?" she asks, using her pitiful voice, tryna get me to feel sorry for her.

"Damn! Can't a nigga get some sleep?" I sigh real loud. But her pitiful act is working. Ever since Fawn entered the picture, I've been neglecting Evette.

I decide to go easy on Evette and have a heart. "Aye, come on. You can snuggle up. But only for a few minutes." Evette got two write-ups on the job. One more and she'll get suspended. We can't afford for her pay to be cut any worse than it already is.

She knows what it is when she crawls her ass in bed with me. She is well aware that there's not enough time for me to feed her my special morning nutt shake that revs up her day. There's so much ginseng in my system, I don't cum quick anymore. It takes a good twenty or thirty minutes before I pop off.

My thick and delicious nutt shakes are the reason why Evette is only one write-up from getting suspended.

I'm on some new shit, anyway. Something I peeped in a porn flick. It's so freaky that I can't control how fast I cum. I'm back to being a two-minute man when I indulge in this freaky morning sex trick.

"Are your underarms shaved?" I whisper in a husky voice.

She nods; she can tell by my voice that I'm ready to get my freak on.

Evette opens the drawer of the nightstand on Fawn's side of the bed and pulls out a small container of lubrication. Ordinarily, she wouldn't be allowed to be rustling through Fawn's personal items, but today is an exception.

Evette squeezes out a generous amount of lube into the palm of my cupped hand.

Now she's on her back with her arm stretched upward, giving me access to her underarm. I spread the gook all over her smooth, cleanly shaven armpit, and my Johnson is jumping in anticipation.

"Sit up." I growl the command.

She sits up, and gets in position with her arm pressed tightly to her side.

I'm on my knees, with my back pressed against the headboard. I steady myself by gripping one of her shoulders. Kneeling behind her, I stick my Johnson into the lubed-up space between her upper arm and her armpit. I'm sliding my joint in and out. Evette's armpit is gooked up and making squishy sounds like a hot pussy.

Seeing the head of my dick protruding from her armpit...seeing it brushing against the side of her titty is about to take me over the edge.

But I hold off. Evette is wiggling around and panting. I know her coochie is feening, so I slip my middle finger into her juicy snatch. "Here you go, baby. Fuck on that."

Now we're both fucking. I'm tearing up her armpit and Evette is humping and working her pussy muscles like she's tryna break off my finger.

As soon as I feel the gush of a pussy eruption, I go ahead and release.

Afterward, I fall on top of her. We're both breathing hard. She's lying on her back, shuddering from the big nutt I just gave her. With my chest against hers, our hearts thump together. It's a tender moment for Evette and me.

"You're my freak in the sheets," I whisper tenderly. "Real talk, baby. I ain't never gon' let you go nowhere."

"Are we still getting married?" she asks timidly.

"No doubt." I kiss her on the side of her neck. I'm getting more and more affectionate with her as time goes by. Who knows, the day may come when I'm tongue-kissing her in the mouth. Evette's my bitch. Ride or die. I mean…she's still ugly and everything, but I'm getting used to the way she looks. Her looks don't bother me as bad as they used to.

"How much longer are you gonna keep Fawn around?"

Now she done pushed me too far. The tender moment is over. I sit up and look at her with one eye squinted because I'm mad. "Ain't no timeframe with none of my jumpoffs. Don't be clocking my relationships."

"The only jumpoff that I know about is Fawn. You're supposed to be open and honest, but you don't bring any other women around."

"Fall back, Evette," I chastise. "Sowing wild oats doesn't mean that I'ma act like a male ho. I only want one jumpoff at a time. When the relationship with Fawn runs its course, I'll get me another one. Understand what I'm saying?"

"But what about us? I was hoping that after you and Fawn break up, we could finally start making our wedding plans."

"Why you still on that? I thought we had an agreement that I could fuck a lot of broads to make up for all the time I lost in the joint? I said I'm gon' marry you, eventually. But if you keep harping on the subject, you gon' end up pushing me away. Is that what you want?"

"No."

"Aye. Let shit run its course. I can't predict the future. Who knows…I might be ready to take that trip down the aisle after me and Fawn call it quits. I don't know. You just gotta ride it out. Wait and see. Feel me?"

"Okay, Kaymar. I just hope that I'm not being stupid."

"Baby, ain't nothing stupid about a woman that will bend over backwards for her future husband."

Those words bring a quick smile to her lips.

"If it wasn't for the fact that time is ticking, I'd do some more freaky shit to you. I want you to come straight home from work tonight, aye? No going out with your girlfriends after work. I want you to bring my kitty straight home." I stroke her coochie.

"I will." She's blushing and smiling like a little kid. This chick loves it when I pay her any amount of attention.

She better have all the fun she can while it lasts. I don't know how she's gon' handle it when I get Fawn pregnant.

For that matter, I wonder how Fawn's gonna feel about it. My man, Munch, has been checking on some fertility potions in Chinatown. They're out of stock at the moment, but the shit will be in next week.

Fawn's a dime piece; she's soft and feminine. But her problem is that she thinks like a dude. She's starting to make a habit outta dippin' out of the crib before I even wake up. I don't like it and I'm a settle Fawn's wild ass down.

It'll be interesting to see whose gon' be running shit after she starts pushing out my seed. A bitch can't keep running the streets if you keep her barefoot and pregnant.

CHAPTER 33

"Are you sure she flinched?" Brick asked after Anya told him about Misty's response to Shane's name.

"I thought I was imagining it myself, but she moved. Her hand twitched, like she wanted me to know she could hear me."

Brick gripped his head, anguished. "Damn, I don't know how to feel about that. I want her to be peaceful in heaven or some-where in between. And as long as she's with Shane, I know she's happy. But if she heard you...that mean's she's still stuck in her body. She wanted to be free. Misty hated being stuck!"

Distressed, Brick pressed his fingers to his temples and rubbed. He looked so tormented, Anya wanted to say something to allevi-ate his pain.

"When I was in the room with Misty, I told her what you said about always loving her. It seemed like the corner of her mouth lifted up a little...like she was tryna smile."

"For real?" His troubled eyes instantly brightened.

"I can't be certain, but that's how it appeared to me."

Brick nodded. Anya watched as his facial muscles relaxed, and was pleased to see his mood shifting from agitated to peaceful.

"Any word on that gun?" Anya asked.

"Nah, that nigga ain't come through yet. Don't sweat it, though. Aye? My word is bond. I gotchu, baby."

She gave him a quick smile. "I know you do."

"So whassup with your pops? Find out anything?"

"No. Nothing online. I've been still taking his picture around asking people if they know him. Man, people lie so much. Have me out there following false leads. I've been to so many shelters, I can't even count 'em, but it's like he doesn't even exist." Anya dropped her eyes. "It really hurts...not knowing if he's dead or alive."

"What does your heart tell you?" Brick asked.

Anya looked up. She shrugged. "Nothing. I don't feel any kind of connection. My dad is probably dead."

"Don't give up, Anya. When my mom disappeared, I was too young to search for her. By the time I got older, I heard she OD'd. I have to tell myself it's true. For what other reason would a mother abandon her child?"

"I don't know, Brick. For the longest, I was so angry with my father for even touching that stuff when he should've been concerned about raising me."

"I feel you. I felt the same anger toward my mom. But she's been gone so long, I don't remember much about her. I do forgive her, though. And I hope my son will forgive me because the choice I made that forced me out of his life had nothing to do with the love I have for him."

Brick looked distraught; Anya instantly moved closer. The two embraced. "We're two hurt people, Brick," she whispered. "I'm so glad you're in my life. I don't know what I'd do without you."

"You're a sweet girl, Anya." He touched her face, ran his fingers through her short, newly permed hair. "At first I was only helping you out, but my feelings have changed; I need you, too."

"Really? Are you just saying that to make me feel good?"

"Nah. I don't play with people's emotions. I dig you. Whatever it is we're doing...it feels good."

"What we're doing is being good to each other, at a time when we both need it the most."

Brick didn't say anything. He held her closer. "You feel so small in my arms. So soft. Yet you're such a strong woman."

"I try to be strong."

"For a young female, you've been though a lot…and you haven't fallen apart."

"I can't. I won't let myself."

"It seems like every time I trust a woman, I end up getting hurt. But that's not gonna stop me. If I give up on trust, then I might as well give up on myself."

"Do you trust me?" Anya asked.

"I know it's crazy, because I've only known you for a short time. But from what you've been showing me…the way you make me feel…" He paused and placed her hand over his chest. "I trust you completely."

"What's crazy is, I hated you when I first saw you, and now that hate has turned to love. Yeah, I said it. I love you, Brick."

"Baby, I'd be lying if I repeated what you just said. But my feelings are strong."

"It's just a word, Brick. A word I wanted to share with you. You don't have to say you love me. I feel your love when you're inside me. It may not be what you felt for Misty or her mother, but I'm satisfied with the way you love me."

As she spoke, Anya caressed Brick's chest, paying particular attention to his nipples, enjoying the pleasant feel as the tiny bumps hardened at her touch. She could feel the hum of Brick's sexual arousal. Imagining his balls, full and sexually flushed, she positioned her hand between his legs and stroked his crotch. "Get out of those pants. I wanna lick your balls and sip your pre-cum. Then I want to feel your—"

Before Anya could finish her sentence, Brick's tee shirt was flung on the floor. She helped him out of his pants, kissing his chest, lowering her body to the area that was tense with desire. It was an automatic reflex to reach for Brick's burgeoning erection, but she fought off the urge to touch him with her hands.

"You want me to touch your dick, don't you?"

"Yeah, baby. Stroke my shit." Brick breathed heavily.

"No, your dick is big and long. It can travel to me if it really wants me."

"You know I want you."

"Show me."

On her knees, Anya craved to press her face into Brick's bulging crotch, but she forced herself to be patient. With a few inches of distance between them, Anya waited with her hands pressed to her sides.

Even as his dick burst through the slit in his briefs, Anya continued to keep her hands to her side. With her mouth parted, she waited for his hot meat to find its way inside her mouth.

"Ugh!" Brick groaned when the head of his dick thumped against Anya's lips. "Mmm," he murmured in relief as his dick stretched out and urgently penetrated Anya's ready mouth.

She captured the head of his dick, sucking gently, rolling her tongue over the tiny opening, moaning softly as she tasted the sweet and sour drippings that leaked from the tiny opening in the center of the bulbous crown of his dick.

She pushed his dick out of her mouth. "Take your drawers off. I wanna forget about the long hot day I've had. I wanna feel your hard body all over me. I want your thick inches to erase every bad memory from my mind. Can you do that, for me, Brick?"

As Brick rushed out of his briefs, Anya started stripping out of her sundress, trying to unzip it herself.

"Lemme help you get outta that dress, baby," Brick said.

He reached for the zipper. Anya's fingers played idly through the hairs that covered Brick's groin, and then began stroking his phallus, caressing his balls…stimulating him to the point of distraction. Instead of unzipping the dress, Brick ripped the fabric from Anya's body.

His mouth went to her bare bosom, devouring the small mounds. While Brick sucked her titties, Anya fondled his balls. Brick shivered; he grabbed her hand. "I thought you weren't going to touch me."

Anya laughed. "I forgot. It's hard to resist touching you." She squeezed his balls a little harder.

"Still breaking the rules. Okay, I tried to warn you. Now you have to be punished."

"Huh? What are you talking about?"

"Don't talk and don't move. Just do what I say."

"O…okay," she said tentatively.

"Put your foot up on the chair."

Anya walked over to the chair that was next to the bed and hesitantly lifted her foot to the cushion.

Brick came behind her and wrapped his arms around her. "I'ma about to punish your pussy and you can't take your foot down off the chair. You can't slump over, either. You gotta stand up straight and take it. Think you can handle that punishment?"

"Mmm-hmm," she said, dreamily.

Brick was behind her; Anya couldn't see his face. The breathy sound of his voice, the feeling of his fingers brushing against her skin was extremely arousing.

Anya's flesh tingled in anticipation as she waited for the punishment to begin. She had no idea what he was going to do to her pussy, but she was excited by the mystery.

From behind, his hands fastened onto her hips. His hot mouth seared the back of her neck. Anya drew in a breath...eagerly waiting to be punished.

A brawny large hand slid around and caressed her pussy, probing with a tenderness that contradicted the massive size of the finger that assessed the amount of pussy moisture that had accumulated. When Brick knelt between her trembling thighs, Anya could only assume her pussy was ripe and ready to be reprimanded.

With one foot on the floor and the other on the chair, Anya's pussy lips were stretched open as wide as a gaping mouth.

Crouched on the floor, Brick attached his mouth to her open pussy and sucked while she jerked and shivered, struggling to stand up straight.

As if his suckling lips weren't punishment enough, Brick's tongue joined in on the chastisement, lashing and whipping her clit and inner lips, making Anya moan and writhe...and cry out.

"Stop, Brick! Oh, my God...I can't anymore! That's enough!" she pleaded, shaking, her knees threatening to give out as Brick's able tongue dug in deeper.

Brick withdrew his lips from her wet pussy. "I don't think it's enough. You can take some more."

"No, I can't. For real, baby. You gotta stop. Please. Don't punish me anymore. I'm sorry. Okay, I'm really sorry. "

"I'll decide when you've had enough. From now on, Anya, every time you break the rules...this is gon' be your punishment." Brick sealed his lips around her pussy, alternately sucking with his lips and fucking her pussy with his stiffened tongue.

Unable to bear another tongue lash, Anya wobbled and then collapsed. Brick caught her and brought her gently down to the floor with him. Positioning her private part above his face, Brick held Anya firmly. "Don't move," he told her.

With Anya's legs parted, her knees supported on his shoulders, Brick thrashed and flogged the dark pink crevice with his strong tongue. Even when he felt her shuddering from a powerful climax, even when he tasted the tart juices that splashed and splattered, Brick didn't stop. He thoroughly punished Anya until he licked clean every drop of her silken passion.

CHAPTER 34

The flavor of Fawn's pussy is constantly changing. I know she's fucking around on me, but when I'm sucking her sweetness, it don't even matter. I mean…I could be eating out some dude's old-ass nutt, the way this bitch is out there whoring around.

But like I said, I don't care about anything when my tongue is gliding into all this sticky, hot liquid caramel. Mmm. Fawn's pussy is the bomb.

It's a shame Munch was high on that shit back when he dabbled in Fawn's juices. That nigga can't remember what she tastes like. Fuck it! That's too damn bad. Fawn is off the market. Aye, well keeping it real, she's a stank ho when she's not with me, but when she's under my jurisdiction, ain't no other dicks or tongues going anywhere near her pussy.

I'm always teasing Munch about how he ate the best poontang in the city and don't even remember. Munch be like, "Come on, man; lemme get at that one more time. You got me real curious." And I be like, "Nah, mufucka, you had your chance and you blew it…that's what you get for fucking with that glue."

The way I brag about Fawn's tasty drippings, I got that nigga feenin'. Begging for just a lil' taste of my baby's good gushy. But he ain't getting none.

I got game, though. Every time I need a favor from Munch, I

tell him that I'ma let him holla at Fawn. It works like a charm. He be running errands for me and everything.

Munch would cum all over himself if he knew Fawn's freaky ass has been hinting that she wants to get with him, too. But I ain't with it.

Fawn be deliberately tryna get under my skin when she says, 'Whassup with Munch?'

The next time she plays with me like that, I'ma crack her ass. Finger flick them butt cheeks, the way I do Evette. I wonder how Fawn would feel if I started spanking that ass, and leaving letters on it. I don't think she could take it. Everything ain't for everybody. Ass-spanking is strictly for Evette. That's one of the many freaky ways that we connect.

I show Fawn the softer side of my freakishness. But shit, if she keeps fucking me over the way she's been doing, she gon' see a side that she might not like.

Neither one of them bitches knows how violent I can really get. They think it's all peaches and cream. That's what I want them to think. I fooled my therapist while I was in the joint. Made him believe those stupid exercises he told me to use for my aggressive tendencies had gotten rid of all my urges. I still get violent urges. I just know how to deal with my urges. I know how to distract myself with something perverted. That's where Evette comes in. She has no idea that with her cooperation, I'm able to get out most of my aggression.

But if that bitch Fawn don't give me a seed, somebody's gon' get hurt.

෨෬

"Is your period late?" I ask Fawn when I finally finish licking out her drippings.

"Why you worried about my damn period?" she asks, shaking her head. "I don't know what's going on inside your head. You worry me sometimes, Kaymar," she says as she recovers from a shuddering climax.

"I'm just saying. I don't use any protection. You said you don't take birth control pills because they make you nauseous. I'm only asking out of concern. I don't wanna fuck around and knock you up."

"It's my body; if I'm not worried, you shouldn't care either." She pulled me down on top of her. "You know how we do. Give me some dick. I'm ready for you to ride me for the next fifteen minutes. Then I gotta roll."

I don't appreciate what Fawn said. She's making a jab; letting me know that my stroke lasts for exactly fifteen minutes. I don't know whassup with that concoction from Chinatown, but it's not working the way it used to.

In the short amount of time that I've been dealing with Fawn, I done put more nutts up in that pussy than I can count. The bitch ain't pregnant yet.

I'm tryna bless her with my seed, but her pussy is rebellious. If I can't slow her down with childbirth, then I don't have any other choice but to take more forceful action. As much as I love this no-good cunt, I might have to start whoopin' Fawn's ass the same way I do Evette. Maybe worse.

Where does he hang out? Who are his friends?

his neighborhood. He'd only been out for a short time, someone

CHAPTER 35

A nya took his computer-printed picture from her purse and gazed at it through narrowed eyes that were filled with loathing. Though a decade had passed since this mugshot was taken, she figured that he couldn't have changed too drastically in ten years. She'd recognize him in an instant.

She'd had his home address before she'd left Indiana. Found it on the Internet. Even though she didn't have a gun yet, it was taking all of her willpower not to go to his house and throw acid in his face.

How would she be able to quietly follow and keep tabs on Kaymar Crawford when the mere thought of him caused her to shake with rage? She wondered how she'd react when they finally came face to face. She'd probably scream and curse, and try to scratch his eyes out before putting a bullet in his head.

Any day now, she'd have that gun in her hand. She needed to start plotting on how she was going to lure the killer to a private place where they could spend some quality time.

Where does he hang out? Who are his friends?

It would appear suspicious if she started asking about him in his neighborhood. He'd only been out for a short time. Someone might alert him that inquiries were being made. She wouldn't get the opportunity to hit with a surprise attack if his friends were able to describe her.

Anya had wanted to handle Kaymar Crawford on her own, but she realized that she needed Brick's help. His guidance.

Fact checking was necessary before she got Brick involved. Using her iPad, she did another online search for Kaymar Crawford. This time she searched the Philadelphia Sex Offender's registry. Voila! There he was. Kaymar had an updated address in West Philadelphia.

This was a game changer. Brick grew up in West Philadelphia. He knew every inch of the area. Brick would be able to quickly find out the killer's favorite places, be it the basketball court, a neighborhood park, the corner bar...wherever. Brick would find him.

And if the creep was hiding inside his crib, Anya knew that Brick would find a way to lure him out. He'd toss a grenade in that piece—blow it up. He'd smoke that killer out, if he had to.

ജ‌ൗ

The display of sparkling weaponry Tayshaun spread out was impressive. No one would imagine a rundown crib in a housing project was a stash spot for such a high-tech arsenal.

There was every kind of firearm imaginable. An assortment of handguns, assault rifles, knives, and explosives. Tayshaun had survival weapons Brick had never imagined using, like the turbo crossbow with brass inserted arrows and the high-powered sling-shot with steel ball bearings.

"What this? It looks like some James Bond shit." Brick picked up a futuristic-looking gun.

"That's a digital revolver, man. It comes with a custom wrist-watch. The watch sends a wireless arming signal to the gun. It won't fire without the watch. That baby costs fifteen stacks."

Brick put the gun down. It was out of his price range, and too high-tech.

Brick studied the selection of guns and picked up a lightweight .22 revolver.

Tayshaun frowned. "Whatchu gon do with that? That gun ain't got no power."

"It's a gift for a friend," Brick replied.

"Most females like to carry semi-automatics nowadays."

Brick didn't say anything. Tayshaun was fishing for information. He perused the weapons and noticed a cell phone mixed in. "You selling cell phones, too?"

Tayshaun laughed. "That's a stun gun. 4.5 million volts. Good decoy, right?"

Impressed, Brick nodded. "Yeah, I want that piece."

Brick was hype. He felt like a kid in a candy store. He wanted everything on the table, but his budget only allowed for a select few killing tools.

"You got it." Tayshaun placed the fake cell phone next to the revolver.

"Check out this two-toned nine-millimeter. Chicks say this piece is sexy."

Brick gazed at the pistol briefly. But it was the collection of shiny blades that really drew his attention. Knives, swords, axes, and hatchets. This was the kind of shit that got his adrenaline pumping. He couldn't take his eyes off of a long, beautiful sword. Damn, he wanted that joint just for the hell of it, but how would he look walking around with a sword. That's the kind of shit niggas getting long paper like to display on their walls. People don't take swords out on killing missions.

Brick pointed to an Asian-style knife with a ferocious curved blade. "What's this called?"

"Don't get me to lying, man. Do I look like a ninja? I just sell this shit to people that are into knife-fighting." Tayshaun looked at his watch. "We gotta speed up this transaction. Did you bring the rest of that paper you owe on that ID?"

"Yeah. I gotchu."

"Aye, then pick out the rest of the shit you want; I gotta keep it moving."

Brick made his selections. As an afterthought, he threw in the high-powered slingshot.

"You hunt?" Tayshaun asked, nodding toward the slingshot.

"Nah, man. I like this joint. Keeping it as a personal toy." Brick put all of his new possessions inside his duffle bag. Smiling, he headed for the front door.

Tayshaun met Brick's smile with a serious expression. "Yo, man, I tell this to all my customers… If you get jammed up with any of that shit, you're on your own; I can't help you. Understand what I'm saying?" Making his point further, Tayshaun gesticulated excessively. "You don't know me; I don't know you. We ain't never met! You dig? So don't come back around here, and don't send nobody to see me, 'cause I don't fuck with everybody!"

"Chill out, Taye. You getting all worked up and paranoid for nothing. You know I ain't no snitch."

"I'm just saying, man. Making sure we got an understanding."

Tayshaun cracked open the door, and stuck his head out. His eyes suspiciously scanned outside before opening the door wide enough for Brick to exit.

Brick had dropped a small fortune on the ID and the weapons. At two hundred dollars each, the battle hatchet and the small pack ax were the cheapest items in his new collection of killing tools.

Back in Jersey, Brick stopped at a liquor store and picked up a bottle of champagne. The next stop was a bakery, where he bought a small chocolate cake. Finally, the Party Store for a shiny bag and tissue paper.

Leaving his tools in the trunk, he entered the motel room with the gift bag, cake, and champagne.

"Happy Birthday, Anya," Brick greeted.

"How'd you know?"

"I have my ways." He'd actually seen the exact date stored in Cash Money's phone. Dude was waiting for Anya to collect that dough from her lawyer.

Anya's eyes surveyed the packages. "Is all that for me?"

"It sure is, birthday girl." He put the cake and champagne on the table, and handed Anya the gift bag.

"It's heavy."

"Look inside."

She pulled out the tissue paper and lifted the gun from the bag. "Wow." She stroked the barrel. "This is nice!"

"I thought you might prefer something lightweight. Easy to handle. The barrel is five and a half inches. You wanted a long barrel, right?"

"Yeah." She nodded her head thoughtfully.

"It's a .22. Small holes."

"That's perfect. Thank you, Brick."

Brick looked her in the eye. "Are you ready to do this?"

"Yeah. I've been waiting a long time." Nervously, Anya bit her bottom lip.

"What's wrong?"

"I've been thinking. After this is finished, I'm out of here. Relocating to Mexico. I spoke to my lawyer today, and he said it's going to take another ten to fourteen days for the money to clear."

"Baby, that's your money. You don't have to give me reports on that."

"I know. I'm just saying… I know that I slowed you down from handling your business—"

"No, you didn't. I still don't have all the info I need."

"Well, I want you to know I can help finance the trip to Miami, if you can wait a couple weeks."

"Nah, I'm good. I can't wait that long. After you handle your business, I'ma leave you with enough paper to hold you until your money comes through."

Anya bit down on her bottom lip, worriedly.

"What's wrong?"

"I don't think that I can handle it alone."

"I wasn't going to let you. I gotchu. I'm there. Where's the mufucka living?"

A look of relief washed over Anya. "Well, I thought he was staying at his parents' house on Olney Avenue, but I looked him up on the Sex Offender's Registry today, and I discovered he moved to West Philly. I did a Google search. The street he lives on is near Forty-sixth and Market."

"I know the area well. I'ma put some feelers out on ol' boy first thing tomorrow."

Brick picked up the ice bucket. "Going to the ice machine; be right back."

After he closed the door. Anya picked up the gun and stared at it, feeling a mixture of fear and exhilaration. And sorrow. What those two monsters had done to her mother was unspeakable. Imagining her mother's last hour on this earth caused Anya unbearable grief. *An eye for an eye, and I'm not backing down! Kaymar Crawford is as good as dead.*

CHAPTER 36

After celebrating her birthday with chocolate cake and a champagne toast, Anya and Brick lay in bed naked, watching a movie together.

Brick sat with his back supported by the headboard; Anya lounged in the space between his legs, her back pressed against his brawny chest. His arms circled her waist, Every so often, he nuzzled her neck, kissed her cheek before returning his attention to the TV that was mounted on the wall.

For Anya, this was the sweetest moment of her life. Basking in the comforting warmth of Brick's body heat, she closed her eyes. She felt completely secure. And loved.

"Are you falling asleep?" Brick asked.

"No. I'm enjoying the moment. This is the happiest I've been in a long time. I know it sounds corny, but I want this moment to last forever."

Brick murmured a sound. "I could restart the flick if you want to…you know…to extend the moment," Brick said with a chuckle.

"Aw, you're mean. Making fun of me because I'm a romanticist." Laughing, Anya twisted her body slightly so she could look at Brick, face-to-face.

"I was only messing with you. I'm about to really extend the moment. I want you to turn back around and close your eyes."

"Okay." Smiling, Anya obliged. She heard rustling as he reached beneath the pillow, and then blindfolded her with a necktie. "Oh, this is freaky."

"Shh. No talking." He put the rim of her glass to her lips. "Take a sip." He turned the glass up, careful not to spill any of the champagne. "Is it good?"

"Real good. It tastes different…it seems more sparkly with the blindfold on."

"Want some more?"

"Mmm-hmm."

"Let's change positions." Brick repositioned Anya, guiding her movements until she was seated with her back against the head-board. He sat next to her on the edge of the bed.

He picked up the glass. "Ready?"

She nodded. He gently brought the mouth of the glass to her lips. She took a deeper sip, and champagne trickled down her chin. Reflexively, her hand went up to wipe away the dribbling liquid.

Brick clasped her wrist. "I gotchu."

She could feel his face close to hers. She flinched when his tongue mopped the dribbling champagne from her chin. "Oh, Brick," she murmured.

"You like that?"

"Yes," she whispered hoarsely. Her senses were heightened. She could hear the sound of something swishing in the glass that Brick held. "What are you doing now?"

"No questions. Now be patient. Lemme do this."

Anya's flesh prickled in excitement as she braced herself to be doused with more champagne. But instead, Brick placed something close to her nostrils. "Sniff."

She inhaled deeply. "Mmm. What is it? Smells like fruit…with a hint of chocolate."

"Open up."

Anya parted her lips for him. Brick inserted the tip of something soft and moist. "Bite it," he said.

She bit into a chocolate-covered strawberry laced with champagne. Greedily, she pulled the remaining portion from his fingers and slowly chewed, moaning softly. "How'd you hide that from me?"

"Ah, you don't know about my stash spots."

Anya smiled as she chewed and swallowed.

"There's chocolate on your mouth, baby." Brick wiped her lips with the pad of his thumb. His touch was sexually charged. Her moist mouth parted. She imagined parting her vagina and inviting his dick inside.

Brick inserted a chocolate-smudged thumb into her mouth. Hungrily, Anya sucked his thumb until she'd cleaned it.

Thoroughly aroused, her chest rose and fell. She gave a soft gasp as the chilled champagne suddenly trickled over her breasts.

Brick tortured her aching nipples with the hot lash of his tongue.

"Fuck me, babe," Anya's voice was rough with need. She looked into his eyes, detecting a mixture of savage lust and a soft tenderness.

Brick laid her down upon the pillows, breathing deeply as he positioned himself on top of her. His chest pressed against hers. His lips covering her neck. The heat of his hard body made her whimper and writhe with need. The heavy masculine scent of his skin was unbearably arousing.

Rolling her hips, she invited him to enter her.

"You ready for me?"

"Oh, God, yes."

Bending slightly, he swiped her pussy with a finger, and brought her flavor to his lips. "Mmm, so sweet, baby," he mumbled, panting with need.

"Brick, I need you," she pleaded hoarsely. Arching her hips

while struggling to part her thighs wide, she urged him to plunge deeply.

Brick pressed his hand against her shoulder, and inserted small increments of dick...pushing in and then withdrawing, forcing Anya to accept his pace.

"Brick..."

"Not yet," he uttered, maintaining a slow and relentless drive until his dick was embedded to the hilt. She felt every thick vein, every straining inch of him. Crammed with his throbbing thickness, her muscles seized and clenched so tightly around his girth.

Anya writhed beneath him, her head thrashing as he rode her. Plunging and retreating, and leisurely building her arousal, Brick made the climb to climax a long-lasting and pleasurable journey.

She wrapped her legs around him, tethering him to her until a violent jolt coursed through her body. Her pussy spasmed as it sucked hard on the dick that filled her.

"You finished cumming, babe?" Brick purred with his mouth to her ear.

Caught up in the sweetest orgasm ever, Anya couldn't respond. The climax rocked her body, stealing her breath and depriving her of coherent speech. All she could do was moan blissfully.

When her thighs fell apart in complete exhaustion, Brick claimed his own pleasure. With an agonized groan, he shafted her harder, delivering deep, long strokes.

He claimed her good pussy. He praised it, remarking on the tight fit, the fragrant scent, and the tangy taste of it.

Guttural cries tore from Brick's throat, when at last, he spurted his seed deep within her womb. He collapsed on top of her, his face buried between her breasts. Chest heaving, breathing harshly as he struggled for air. A stallion winded from a long, hard ride.

CHAPTER 37

E vette is standing at the stove cooking my dinner. I'm sitting at the table, hungry as a mufucka and mad about everything. First of all, Fawn stood me up tonight and she's not picking up my calls. I'm antsy and cranky. My food should be on the table, not being whipped up on the spur of the moment.

"Why can't I get dinner on time?" I grumble.

"You told me you were cooking a candlelight dinner for you and Fawn."

"Do you see Fawn in this kitchen?" I look all around, with my eyes bugging.

"I know you're upset, Kaymar. Fawn doesn't treat you right. Maybe you're better off without her," Evette suggests.

I know she means well, but I get an instant attitude. "I hate it when you start flapping your lips, giving out advice I ain't ask for."

She bristles at the criticism. "I was only trying to make you feel better."

"If you want to make me feel better, get over here and do something constructive with your mouth."

Evette's feelings are hurt, but I don't care. Shit, I'm hurt, too. Fawn is doing me dirty; she's making a good man go bad.

Rolling my eyes and grumbling at the nerve at that smut bitch for treating me the way she does, I stand up pull and my pants down. I got my Johnson lying across my palm, and my shit is throbbing like it's as angry as I am.

"Get over here, Evette. Don't you see how bricked-up my shit is?"

"Okay, one minute," she says and hastily begins turning off the burners.

In a flash, she on her knees, where she belongs. I steer the head of my dick over to her mouth. She opens it, waiting to gobble up some dark meat. But I ain't ready to give it to her yet. "Close your damn mouth," I order.

She promptly obeys, closing her eyes at the same time.

I look over at the butter dish on the table. "Why you set this butter out on the table without any bread? What was I supposed to do with a stick of soft butter?"

She murmurs, prepared to respond. But I smack her lips with my dick, informing her that I'm doing all the talking.

I scoop up a handful of butter and smear it all over my Johnson. Shit is mushy. A different kind of feeling. I like it, though. I wanna jerk my dick off while it's greased up with butter, but I also want to share it with Evette.

First, I trace around the outside of her lips with the tip of my dick, drawing a greasy outline. Then I gloss up her bottom lip with the butter on my dick. She murmurs a sound, letting me know that she likes it. I coat her top lip next. Her mouth is all shiny like she's wearing a weird, yellow-tinted lip gloss.

"That looks good." I'm getting horny. And the hornier I get, the less concerned I am about Fawn.

"You hungry, Evette?" I whisper. She nods her head. "I know I am. But I'm not gon' be selfish like you are. I'ma feed you this buttery sausage. But you gotta lick all the butter off before I let you have it."

Her tongue comes out of her mouth, glides over my Johnson, licking off the butter. Lapping on my dick like she hasn't had a meal in a long time. I watch as her tongue swipes the length of my dick. I'm fully absorbed in the sight of butter on her face and on her tongue. I can hardly control the ejaculation that's bubbling in my balls and traveling down my dick. I curl my toes in ecstasy as Evette feasts on my thick, greasy meat. Amazingly, my entire hot sausage disappears inside her mouth.

In an act of wanton passion, I lock my hand around the back of her neck, digging my nails into her flesh as I flood her mouth with my butter-flavored jism.

Instead of feeling satisfied, I feel angrier than ever after I shoot my load. Every blue moon, I get burning mad after I cum. Don't ask me why. It's one of my quirks.

I'm feeling so disgusted, I take a swing at Evette. Avoiding my punch, she tumbles over and lands on her ass. Dodging a blow is a natural reflex, but Evette knows how we do…she was supposed to let me get some aggression out on her.

I look down at her. "I hate sluts. You disgust me!" I spit on her, imagining that I'm spitting on Fawn.

Spit, butter and cum are sliding down Evette's face.

"I gotta go for a walk or something. The way I'm feeling, I might hurt you real bad."

"Why, Kaymar? I didn't do anything."

"I don't know why. I only know that if I don't get out of here, I'ma start kicking you."

"Well then, kick me! If that's what it takes for you to spend some time with me, then do it. Kick me, Kaymar."

I shake my head. "Don't even tempt me. Aye? You wanna wind up with some broken ribs?"

"No."

"Aye, so don't be talking a bunch of shit. You have no idea what I'm capable of. So don't be tryna tempt me."

"I'm not trying to tempt you. I want to spend more time with you, but all you care about is Fawn."

"Don't bring up that slut's name. I gotta go out and get my

mind right," I say to Evette while she's pulling herself off the floor.

I run up the stairs and take a quick shower because there's butter drizzling into my pubic hairs and running down my inner thighs. Shit feels nasty.

ಬಂಜ

Freshly showered and wearing a change of clothes, I grab my container of that Chinese love potion and stick it in my pocket. A lot of the aggression has left me. Now I'm feeling pretty good.

Downstairs, I notice that Evette has wiped the butter, saliva, and cum off her face. She's back at the stove rattling pots and pans.

"I'll be back later," I say as a common courtesy. I really ain't gotta explain my comings and goings, but the memory of the vigorous way she sucked that butter off my dick is prompting me to treat her nice.

"Your dinner's almost ready. Do you want me to make you a plate and leave it in the microwave?"

"I'll eat when I get back in. I gotta get out of here for awhile— chase after some pussy. You know, fuck with some stray pussy so I can keep that slut, Fawn, off my mind."

"I understand," she says. The dismal look in her good eye expresses deep sorrow. Her sad expression tugs a little at my heartstring. "I got something good for you, later on. So wait for me in my room. Aye? Me and you gon' sleep together tonight. Get them sheets hot for your future husband, aye?" I pat her on the ass and wink, hinting at the deep burning that I'm going to put on her butt cheeks, followed by my healing ointment.

Evette brightens. She's wearing a smug expression as if giving her an ass whoopin' is better than slut-fucking. She got it twisted. I love Fawn's dirty drawers and her slutty pussy.

So I say, "But…um…if Fawn comes through while I'm out… you know the drill, grab up your shit and go sleep in the spare room." I smirk after bursting her bubble and letting her know what's good. Ain't nothing fake about me; I keeps shit one hundred!

Using the cell phone that Evette's broke ass finally bought me, I give Munch a call and ask him if he wants to go out and get into something.

"Whatchu feel like doing?" Munch asks.

"Hunting down some pussy; what else is there to do?"

He laughs. "I can dig it. You want me to see if Blake can get out?"

"Nah. That bull thinks he's God's gift to women."

"We need him for transportation," Munch explains.

"Can't you hold your mom's wheels tonight?"

"Nope. She's bitching about how I keep driving her car and don't put no gas in it. Said I can't drive her whip for two weeks."

"Two weeks! Man, just go in her purse and take the keys."

"You crazy? My mom don't play that shit. If I went in her pocketbook and took her keys, she'd whip my ass. I ain't lying. And on top of that, she probably would make me keep my ass in the house for at least two weeks. I'm serious, yo. My mom was in the military; she's strict!"

Munch's relationship with his mom is twisted as shit. A grown man scared to death of his mother. Crazy!

"Aye, well look, I got the number of this freak broad named Detina. She got a friend. I'ma call and see if they'll come and pick us up. I'll hit you back in a minute."

CHAPTER 38

I called Detina and after she fussed for a few minutes about me taking so long to call her, she agreed to scoop up her girl-friend and come pick me up. I didn't mention Munch because she was expecting a threesome. On some real shit, I don't know the rules for a threesome. I gotta get some more experience before I try that shit.

Anyway, I have my Chinese potion on me, so I'ma be stroking them bitches all night. While I'm fucking one…Munch can do his thing on the other.

Suddenly, I pictured the day I met Fawn. Munch went bananas that day. It was hard to control him. Suppose he flips out again?

I hit him up and tell him the good news…that two bitches are on their way to pick us up. Then I remember his wild ways. "Yo, Munch, I'm not tryna offend you but I gotta ask you some-thing—do you have one of those pit bull collars Blake used on you? I'm a little leery about you getting outta hand when we get with these bitches. You know how you can get."

"I'm not offended. I got a couple of them joints. Do you want me to bring the kind with the long leash or the loop handle?"

"Um…" I think about it. "You gon' be sniffing that shit?"

"Yeah, I already started," he says and lets out a soft growl.

"Umph. I might not be able to control you with the long leash, so bring the collar with the loop handle."

"Aye."

I'm excited about controlling Munch. Blake thinks he's the only one that can handle the man, but I know I can do it. I had three or four pit bulls back in the day. Ain't nothing to it. All you gotta do is yank on the collar and let the dog know that you're the master. I got this!

By the time Detina and her girlfriend pull up, Munch is buzzed. He has a gleaming crazed look in his eyes, making him appear to be a maniacal killer on the loose.

"Who is that?" Detina asks with her mug twisted up. "This is a ménage, not an orgy. Your friend can't come with us."

"This is my man, Munch. He's cool. Little buzzed right now. He just likes to watch. He won't bother you," I tell the girl.

Her girlfriend that's riding shotgun appears interested. "Let him come, Detina. I like the idea of an orgy. Come on, girl, stop being a stick in the mud."

Detina sighs. "All right. But that fool better not act as crazy as he looks."

The whole time I'm negotiating with the two bitches, Munch is standing around licking his lips. Sniffing.

"Why is he sniffing like that?" Detina asks.

"Coke," I say. If I tell her that the smell of pussy is fucking with his head, she might get scared and peel away, leaving me and Munch at the curb.

Detina introduces her friend, Shay. Shay has real big titties. Mmph. I'ma get lost between those big boobs.

By the time we get to Detina's crib, Munch is becoming un-hinged. Sniffing and snorting. Licking his lips and slobbering slightly. It's embarrassing because I didn't expect him to start showing his ass until the orgy was in full swing.

We aren't even in the living room and Munch is trying to get down on all fours.

"What the hell is wrong with him?" Detina demands.

"Where's the collar, man? Did you bring it?" I ask him. I'ma be a mad as a mufucka if Munch forgot that dog collar. This entire night will be shot to hell if I can't keep him under control.

"What kind of collar?" Shay asks.

"A dog collar," I say with desperation in my voice as I wrestle with Munch. He's breaking down, attempting to get on his hands and knees. He got me tussling with him. "Stand up, Munch!"

Munch is acting like a straight fool. It's a struggle trying to keep him in an upright position. If he gets down on his hands and knees without a collar, it's gon' be a wrap. This nigga gon' wanna eat all the pussy in the house and then some!

I pat his head, vainly trying to subdue him. But he's still acting rabid. I wish he'd calm down long enough for Detina to hand me that pit bull collar. He can show that doggish side of hisself all he wants, after I get him in a neck restraint.

On some real shit, fuck a looped collar, now I want the long chained kind of leash. I need to tie this mufucka to something so I can have some peace while I'm long-stroking these two pussies. Both these bitches want my dick and I wanna give it to 'em. After I'm finished…then Munch can do his thing.

"Didn't your ex have a pit bull?" Shay asks Detina.

"Yeah, but I had that crazy dog put to sleep when we broke up."

"I know, but don't you still have some of the dog's equipment around here?"

"I might. I'm not sure."

"Girl, go look."

"I don't know. I'm not comfortable with the way that dude is acting."

"Yo, Detina! Stop bullshitting and go get the leash and collar!" I yell. I can no longer keep Munch on his feet. As Detina rushes off to another room, he's sniffing under Shay's skirt.

"What's he want?" she asks.

"Can he sniff your pussy real quick? That'll keep him occupied. The fumes will calm him down while we're waiting on that collar."

As I say this, I'm wondering what effect the smell of pussy will actually have on Munch. Shit, for all I know, pussy fumes might make him crazier. Fuck it; it's worth a try. I'm sick of grappling with this big, sick in the head, mufucka.

Smiling like a naughty little girl, Shay lifts up her dress. Munch scampers over to her. She has on a white thong. Looks real sexy against her dark brown skin.

Munch doesn't even take the time to enjoy the visual of soft white fabric contrasted with ebony skin. Nah, this nigga is licking her crotch. Soiling the pretty satin material with his slobber.

I'm annoyed, but the freak in me is turned on by this shit. The girl, Shay, is moaning and grinding against Munch's face. Meanwhile, Munch is growling and trying to use his teeth to rip off the white thong. He succeeds in record time, unveiling Shay's chocolate pussy.

Detina is taking an extremely long time to come back with the collar. Watching Munch's long tongue swipes inside the deep crease of Shay's pussy is getting my dick rock hard. I feel compelled to beat my meat while Munch is drilling Shay's coochie with his tongue.

We're still in the hallway and all hell is breaking loose. My fisted hand is frenziedly working my pole. I'm audibly jacking off, taking brutal gasps as I spurt out a super-sized nutt. With my eyes glazed, I shake the last droplets of cum off the head of my dick. Coming to my full senses, I realize I've left a big puddle of cum on the shiny hardwood floor. I glance over at Munch and Shay. Munch has the bitch backed into a wall.

Shay's writhing and shrieking in delirium and Munch is growling a sound that I'm certain I've never heard before. Not from a beast or man. When I glance downward, I see that Munch has Shay's clit locked between his lips. He's shaking his head back and forth like a ferocious pit bull with its teeth locked on its prey. The long snarl that's emanating from the back of his throat sounds inhuman.

All bullshit aside, Munch should be discussing his issues with a shrink.

Detina finally comes out of the room, holding a leash and a collar.

Shay lets out an ear-piercing scream. I know that the bitch is cumming from Munch's lip lock, but Detina looks terrified and concerned for her friend's well-being.

"Oh, my God! Get him off of her! Make him stop!" Detina yells.

"I can't." I hold up my hands in a helpless gesture.

"Whatchu mean, you can't? Get that mufucka off my girlfriend!" Detina has her fist balled and she runs over to Munch like she's going to beat him in the head.

I grab her. Get her in a bear hold. "Yo, leave Munch alone. You might get bit if you try to pull him off that pussy. You gotta wait! Understand? Wait until that man is finished eating."

"But…but…look at Shay. She's out of it. She looks like she's finished," Detina states, nodding toward her friend. Shay is slumped and all I can see are the whites of her eyes.

But I know Munch. He's not finished eating. He's not gon' stop until he licks that pussy lining clean.

Detina is whimpering, sounding like she's about to cry. "This is horrible. How much longer is he gon' be on her like that?"

"Hard to say." I take her hand, as if to console her. But I really want to console myself so I press her hand against my awakening Johnson. "Don't worry about your friend. Munch won't hurt her. Whassup with you and me? We might as well get into some-thing. You 'bout ready to get this orgy poppin'?"

Detina snatches her hand off my boner, like I forced her to touch a hard turd or something. "I don't want you! I want some of what Shay is getting." She makes a whistling sound, desper-ately trying to draw Munch's attention away from Shay. Munch is too far gone to let go of the chocolate clit that he's working on.

Frustrated, Detina pulls her jeans down and swipes her pussy with her finger. "Here, boy," she calls. She looks at me with aggra-vation sparking her eyes. "He's not listening to me. Will he obey you?"

"Of course, I'm the one running this show," I say, sullenly.

"Well, call your friend. Sic him on me!"

CHAPTER 39

I barely got my dick wet. Those two cunts, Shay and Detina, are splayed out in the hallway, annihilated by Munch.

I got a little bit of pussy off of Shay, but she was so out of it, she was barely aware that my Johnson was lodged inside her hairy crevice. I left her a present, though. A tablespoon worth of cum. I usually bust a quarter cup, but I wasn't feeling aroused by that nearly comatose ho.

Both of them bitches had legs like Jell-O when I stood 'em up. They were acting like they were too out of it to drive Munch and me back to West Philly.

I wasn't tryna be stuck in Sharon Hill, Pennsylvania. Wasn't catching public transportation, either. Detina had me stranded and I feel like it was my right to snatch the car keys out of her pocketbook.

"That was a waste of time," I tell Munch as I drive back to our part of the world.

"What happened?" he asks, coming down from his high.

"You put them bitches to sleep."

"Both of 'em?"

"Yeah, nigga. Why you always tryna act like you don't remember nothing?"

"I don't."

"Bullshit."

"I'm serious."

"Nigga, pull down the visor and look at your face in the mirror."

Munch examines his reflection, running his finger over the sheen of vaginal juices that surrounds his mouth and covers his lips. He licks the right side of his top lip and then the left. "Mmm. Two different flavors."

"Yeah, nigga. Your greedy ass ate up both them bitches."

"I don't feel satisfied. Don't seem like I ate two pussies."

"You see the evidence, you greedy fool! Yo, man, on a different subject. I gotta ditch this car after I drop you off. If we ever run into those bitches again, act like you don't know nothing about the car."

"Aye. So what else we gon' get into tonight?"

"Nothing. You ruined my fun. I know better than to take you anywhere else with me. Better believe I'm not sharing any more pussy with you."

"Man, don't be like that. My bad; damn. I was under the influence. But I'm straight now, and I want some more pussy. I'm serious. I need some pussy real bad. I gotta get some more before I call it a night."

Munch keeps repeating how badly he needs to eat some more pussy, and he's working my nerves.

I tune Munch out. I try calling Fawn. I call her five times in a row, but she doesn't answer. As I drive in silence, I'm getting furious. Fawn has me out in the streets trolling around for pussy. Any other bitch would be happy to have a good man like me. All Fawn has to do is keep her hot ass at home with me. If she acts right, I won't stray.

It irks me to no end that Evette is the one lying in my bed, waiting for me. I don't want her; I want Fawn!

I can feel a violent rage slowly coming over me. A sinister thought enters my head. Now I know what I'ma do.

I'ma sic my dog on Evette. Scare the shit out of her. If she gets on my nerves bad enough, I'ma let him bite her!

I'm feeling better when I pull up in front of Munch's house, so I tell him, "Run in there and get that dog collar. I got something for you, man. But I can't give it to you unless you got on that collar. 'Nah mean?"

Munch is grinning. "Yeah, I understand. I'ma act right this time."

"Aye, run in the house and get it."

"Aye. Bet. Thanks, man. I promise!"

Munch hurries in his house while I wait in the car.

I leave Detina's car a couple blocks away from my crib. Although it's late at night, niggas is out. They roaming the 'hood like it's the middle of the day.

I have to admit, I'm embarrassed to be walking next to Munch while he's wearing the pit bull collar. I speed up ahead of him, making sure nobody thinks I'm associated with this nutt-ass bull.

Munch doesn't seem the least bit concerned that people are pointing and staring at him, and also giving him a wide berth. He's walking hard, licking his lips, and growling softly. Munch ain't thinking about nothing except tearing into a fresh batch of pussy.

I quicken my steps, putting a lot of distance between Munch and me. In case somebody decides to take a shot at his crazy-looking ass, I don't wanna be in the line of fire.

We get to the crib and I tell Munch to stay downstairs and be quiet until I'm ready for him. The only way Munch is gonna sit still is if he's occupied with that shit he likes to sniff. So I leave him downstairs inhaling on a piece of cloth.

I want to pull a sneak attack on Evette, so I creep up the stairs. A part of me is really hoping I'll find Fawn in the bed. If so, Munch can take his ass on outta here!

In the bedroom, I find Evette...not Fawn. My shoulders slouch in disappointment. Evette is lying on her stomach, buttocks fully exposed. Bitch fell asleep waiting for me to come home and light a fire to that ass.

But I don't feel like it. Takes too much effort. And I'm not angry anymore. I'm sad and disappointed. So sad, I can hardly keep myself from crying. If it weren't for Munch being downstairs, I'd be lying on the bed beside Evette, shedding tears.

Fawn! Where are you? I can't believe how much I miss that slut.

Filled with despair, I have to do something to get out of this overwhelming depression. I gaze at the deep crack of Evette's buttocks; I'm mesmerized.

I liberate my Johnson, and stroll over to the bedside table, and scrounge around until I find the tube of lubrication that Fawn keeps in the drawer. Handling Fawn's personal object makes my dick grow harder. It's throbbing in my hand as I rub lubrication over my heavily veined dick meat.

I'm fucking my hand now. I know Evette is awake, but she's faking like she's still asleep. I get on the bed and stretch open her butt cheeks as wide as I can.

"Mmph. That looks good. It's sexy in there," I murmur. Evette wriggles in response to my mumbled words of lust. "You awake?"

"Uh-huh."

"Hold your ass open while I beat my meat."

She reaches back and obliges—no questions asked.

I need to unwind and really enjoy myself, so I take my shirt and pants off, and come out of my drawers. I'm butt naked. Evette has that grandmom nightgown pulled up to her waist.

We're at the point in our relationship where we embrace everything about each other. She likes wearing grandma shit, so I don't try to change her. I like dabbling in freaky shit, and doling out small amounts of pain. I can be myself with Evette.

I crouch in the split between her legs and rub my lubed Johnson up and down the crack of her ass. "Whew. Baby, your ass feels so good." I'm humping in between the space between her cheeks, but I need some type of cushion, so I smack her hands. She knows what to do.

She squeezes her buttocks together, sandwiching my dick like it's a hot dog. "Ah, I love this shit," I say as I'm sliding up and down, confined inside her warm and luxurious ass cheeks. I don't go inside her asshole because I'm not a faggot. Dig me? I keep my dick restricted to a certain area of the ass.

On my upstroke, I bust my load. Fuck! I forgot all about drinking that Chinese ginseng shit. Now I'm slipping around in an ass full of cum. My dick is soft but if I keep stroking, I know it's gon' pop back up.

I have a better idea. I get up on my knees. "Sit up, Evette. I need my dick sucked."

CHAPTER 40

A ll of a sudden the door bursts open. Evette lets out a
terrified scream. She's yelling so loud, I have to cover
her mouth up before somebody calls the cops and
reports a murder in progress.

I forgot about that fucking Munch. Damn! I'm doing all right,
and I don't even need him anymore.

"Yo, man. This ain't a good time for your bullshit. Take your
ass back downstairs and finish getting high."

He's got that crazed look in his eyes and talking to him is a
waste of breath.

Evette's panicking and screaming. Her eyes are bugging out of
her head; I'm damn near sitting on her chest, trying to hold her
down. "Be quiet, Evette. If you keep screaming, somebody's gon'
call the cops. I'm on probation…you tryna get me locked up?"

She's not listening to me. She's out of her mind with fear, and
still yelling. With my hand clamped over her mouth, the sounds
are muffled, but I can feel the vibration of her screams against
my palm.

Munch is making a lot of noise, too. This nigga is going berserk
between Evette's legs.

Even worse, Munch is naked except for the dog collar. What
the fuck! I don't know what possessed him to take his clothes off.
That glue got Munch going bananas.

I glimpse his Johnson because it's hard to miss. Ol' Munch has the nerve to be holding down there. This fool is blessed with a big-ass, horse dick. The dumb bastard is hung, and don't even reap any benefits.

"I know you scared, Evette," I tell her, trying to calm her down. "Munch got problems and I'ma handle him when he gets back to his normal frame of mind. But I can't do anything with him right now. So I need you to cooperate. Stop fighting and open your legs for him. He won't hurt you. He's messed up in the head. Nigga got a pussy-eating fetish. Give him some pussy, baby. It'll be over soon. Aye?"

Evette refuses to calm down. She's still struggling with me. Shaking her head in defiance. Thrashing, trying to get Munch off of her. She's acting so wild, I think she might be in pain. I'ma fuck Munch up if he's down there biting on her shit without my permission.

Does this nigga realize he might get me in a world of trouble if I get caught up in a sex-related offense?

Munch is acting real vicious down there on Evette's coochie. I peek down to see if there's any bloodshed. To my relief, everything looks cool. I still can't take my hand off Evette's mouth because she's trippin', screaming like she's being murdered.

"Shut up, Evette," I say, seething. I'm not trying to go back to jail over this nut-ass broad.

She keeps yelling, so I slap her. I slap the shit out of her. "If you don't be still and let this man eat your pussy, I'ma give you something to yell about." I ball up my fist. "You want me to crack your head open?"

She blinks rapidly, and I can see fear in her eyes. She quiets down. "Get a grip, Evette. Now open your legs like you got some sense. I'm not going to jail for your fucking ass," I hiss.

She gets her act together and spreads her legs wide. Now that Munch doesn't have to fight for his food, I hope he'll hurry up and handle his business. I know one thing; this nut bull ain't gotta worry about me extending another invitation to my house.

While Munch is slurping, he's growling as usual and damn near howling. I don't know what's wrong with this nigga. How much glue did he sniff? I got Evette quieted down and now Munch is going bonkers.

While Munch is doing his thing, he pushes her legs up. Out of curiosity, I lean to the side to get a good look at what's going on. I grimace. It seems like this nasty nigga is lapping up the cream that's dribbling out of Evette's ass.

Aw, shit. My Johnson is starting to act up. It's throbbing—giving me the kind of aching sensation that's a cross between pleasure and pain. Damn, it's crazy how the most unexpected shit gets my dick hard.

I'm stroking my dick while I witness Munch eating my nutt out of Evette's ass. The crazy thing is, dude don't even realize what he's slurping. *Eat it, Munch. Lick my nutt up. That's some sexy shit right there. Mmph!*

Munch gets greedy and suddenly flips Evette over. Now he's spreading her cheeks and sucking cum straight out of her ass.

"Whoa! Goddamn!" My dick is pulsating. This nigga can't be so far gone that he doesn't recognize the change in flavor. Munch is a freak. This nastiness has me so worked up and furious at the same time, I'm jacking off and sporadically cussing.

"Lick it, nigga," I blurt out loud. "Ooo, shit! Get all up in that ass." I don't know why I can't keep my mouth shut. I'm verbally expressing the kind of shit that needs to stay inside my head. Fuck it! Munch ain't listening. And Evette won't pass judgment. She already knows that I get off on all types of freaking behavior.

I'm overheated. Angry and aroused by all this filth and lust. I'ma have to whip her ass when Munch gets finished. Then I'ma invite Munch to jerk off with me. Together, we gon' give this smut broad a cum shower.

From the corner of my eye, I detect a flurry of motion. "Oh, hell no! You taking this too far, Munch. Get the fuck off of her!"

This nigga done pulled Evette to her hands and knees and he's fucking her from behind. Munch is grunting and talking real nasty. "You're my bitch, bitch. And I'm your dog," he grunts. His balls are swinging like an animal's while he's thrusting into my bitch.

"Grab it," Munch groans.

"Grab what?" Evette responds breathlessly.

"Yo, nigga. You outta pocket, don't be telling her what to do."

I grab Munch by the loop of the collar, tryna choke this mufucka, but he's steadily dog-fucking Evette and she's giving it back. Her pussy acts like it's starving, swallowing up Munch's horse dick and shouting the crazy bullshit that he tells her to say.

"I'm your bitch; you're my dog." Evette is chanting those stupid words. I can't believe they're fucking like two stuck-together mutts.

This is a disaster. My plan to hurt and humiliate Evette is backfiring. What was I thinking when I brought Munch home with me tonight?

As I watch my world collapse, I'm so distressed I feel dizzy. I'm even tottering somewhat as I anxiously pace while Munch is smashing my girl.

I pull myself together. If you can't beat 'em, then join 'em. So I pick up where I left off, and continue stroking my dick. When I'm ready to bust, I aim my dick at those two dogs in heat. I spray 'em with my dick juice, a last-ditch effort to try and separate them.

My nutt is trickling down the back of Munch's thigh and pooling inside the hollow of his knee. But that nigga acts like he don't even notice.

I shoot out some more cum. It lands on the sole of Evette's foot. That freak bitch is wiggling and moaning as if her sex experience is heightened by the wet splash of jism.

Nothing is stopping these doggish fools. They're still going strong—fucking like rabbits.

I'm beside myself with fury. I feel like peeing on these two nasty mufuckas. I bet a blast of hot piss will bring 'em back to their senses.

CHAPTER 41

I invite Munch to come have a beer with me. I'm being the bigger person, tryna let him know that there ain't no hard feelings over the wild night he had with Evette. "I know you had no idea what you were doing…being high off that shit and whatnot."

He looks at me with a puzzled expression. "Whatchu saying, man?"

"I'm saying that I'm not holding no grudge over the way you came to the crib and went wild, guzzling up Evette's pussy and even fucking her right in front of me. I couldn't stop you."

"Why do you care? Ain't nothing between you and Evette. She's your boarder, right?"

"Nah, it's a little deeper than that. Evette and I got a lil' something going on. I keep it on the low…you know, because her face is all jacked up."

Munch gawked at me. "Ain't nothing wrong with her face; it looks good to me."

Now it's my turn to look bewildered. "Yo, man. I know that you two were going at it like two dogs in heat, but you had to notice she got that Bell's palsy disease."

"Nah, I ain't notice nothing. Evette's a good-looking woman." Munch gets up and goes in the kitchen. He opens the fridge.

I'm frustrated over Munch calling Evette good-looking. He ain't all there, mentally, but the nigga ain't blind. In addition, I'm offended at the gall of Munch, acting like he lives here. First, he comes over here sucking and fucking my woman right in my face; now he's taking liberties, going in the fridge and whatnot. "Whatchu doing, man?" I ask him, aggravated.

"I'm about to throw something together for dinner. Surprise my baby with hot grub when she gets home from work."

"Nah, that ain't gon' work. Evette got responsibilities to me as soon as she walks through the door."

"Man, you crazy. Evette ain't got no responsibilities toward anyone, except me and her. We're talking about getting married."

"Married! You just met!"

"Love at first sight."

"Munch, you really haven't seen her. You were so busy fucking her doggy-style, you ain't look at her droopy face."

"Man, I know what she looks like. I'm getting her a ring first of the month, when I get my social security check."

"You get a check?"

"Yeah, man. It comes in my mother's name, but I'ma switch it over to Evette's name as soon as we get married."

I knew this mufucka had mental health issues. But still, the news about him and Evette is staggering. I don't let it show. I keep my astonishment and anger to myself. While Munch is fiddling around in the kitchen, I call Fawn. Maybe she'll pick up the phone and come around here and comfort me. After the third ring, she picks up. *It's about damn time!*

"Whassup, Fawn? Where you been?"

"Hey, Kaymar. Uh…I've been meaning to call you and let you know that I'm back with my ex. So…I'll be around sometime tomorrow to pick my stuff. Is that cool with you?"

"Back with your ex? What ex? You never told me nothing about a mufuckin' ex," I bellow.

"I don't have to run down my whole life story for you. We were only messing around; why are you tryna act like we were into something serious?"

"Bitch, I was serious."

"Well, that's too fuckin' bad. Matter of fact, I don't even want that bullshit I left in your bedroom. Keep it and have a good fuckin' life!"

Fawn hangs up. Shocked, I hold my cell for a few minutes, trying to figure out why my life is suddenly falling apart. I let Fawn's pretty face and candy-flavored coochie knock me off my square.

On some real shit, I need to beat the crap out of Evette, though. That cock-eyed ho has a lot of nerve, dumping me for Munch.

I catch a sudden whiff of what Munch is cooking. Smells like something with garlic and onions. Shit smells good. But my pride won't allow me to sit down and share a meal with him and Evette.

I hear Evette's keys outside the front door.

Munch suddenly starts singing that Usher song, "There goes my baby!" Apparently, he can hear the jangle of Evette's keys, too.

I'm totally disgusted. I stand in the living room with my arms folded, ready to cuss Evette out for tryna play me.

She walks in. And you could've knocked me over with a feather. Evette's face is normal. That fuggly droopy side of her face is fixed. She's actually looking kind of pretty.

"What happened to your face?"

"I don't know," she responds. "It was like this when I woke up this morning. I think it was all that good loving Munch put on me. The doctor always told me the situation could reverse."

This is unbelievable. Her mug ain't twisted around anymore due to all that healing semen she got from all those blowjobs she gave me. Weeks of me smearing cum on her mug has healed her condition, but she wants to give Munch all the credit.

"It was really nice of you to hook me up with Munch. Real

nice, Kaymar. Thanks." Evette is all smiles and I wanna slap her.

I brought Munch over to assault her with his mangy-dog ways, and this smut bitch done fell in love. Man, this shit has backfired on me in every way possible.

"Are you cooking dinner?" Evette asks, giving me an odd look.

"Nah, that's your new man. Munch is in the kitchen making you some grub." I have my mouth turned down in disapproval.

"Really?"

"Yeah, he's in there cooking and carrying on," I say with a fierce scowl.

"Listen," she whispers. "I don't want Munch to find out about us. Can you get your stuff together and be out of here by tomorrow?"

I feel my fist balling up. I'm so mad, I'm spitting and sputtering. I can't even get out the litany of cuss words I want to hurl at her because Munch is calling from the kitchen.

"Hey, Evette! Baby! Come on in here! I got a surprise for you!" Munch shouts.

Grinning, Evette races away from the sucker punch I'm gearing up to deliver.

"Is my boo-boo here fixing me dinner?" she coos and then runs into the kitchen.

I stand there, steaming. A few minutes later, I stroll into the kitchen. Shit, I'm hungry. Angry or not, my stomach is on "E." In the kitchen, my mouth literally drops open. I can't believe my eyes. That quick, Evette is leaning against the kitchen sink with her skirt around her waist, and Munch is down on the floor licking and sucking between her legs. Now Evette is lowering herself down, getting into doggy-style position.

Disgusting! I can't watch these two mutts start their bullshit again.

So, I slam the door and leave. Planning to drown my sorrows in alcohol, I walk around the corner to the bar.

CHAPTER 42

Feeling sad and lonely, I take a seat on a barstool. I look around the bar to see if any bitches are checking for me. Nope. These hoes ain't paying me a damn bit of mind. I bet if I was flashing a knot, these cunts would be breaking they necks to sit down next to me. *Bitches!* I take a big, angry gulp of Budweiser. Then I remember I gotta drink slow…make this shit last. I'm down to my last five dollars!

I hate bitches. Haven't I been through enough in my young life…doing a long bid at a tender young age? Why bitches still making life hard for me? And when am I gon' finally gon' catch a break and become the paper maker I know I can be?

I think about calling my mother, but she's not going to allow me to stay at her house. She blames me for everything—says the crime I got caught up in ruined her life.

I'm the one that spent all those years in prison. Damn! Bitches get on my nerves. They make my life a living hell.

I look around the bar again, but this time I'm looking for a cunt to follow out of the bar. Yank her into an alley. Put a choke-hold on her. Take all the pussy I want.

As I'm brooding and nursing my Budweiser, I notice this big, tall dude standing in the back of the bar, near the pool table. He ain't flashy or nothing, but I can see a knot in his pocket. Plus, I can tell by the confident way he's carrying himself, dude got bank.

He strides over to the bar. The barmaid was just about to approach me to find out if I want another beer, but the minute she notices dude, she forgets about me and races over to him. "Whatchu drinking?" she asks with a wide smile.

"Henny," he answers and takes the empty seat next to me. Smiling and giving him a flirtatious glance, the barmaid pours him a drink. "This one is on the house, big man," she says as she pushes the shot glass toward him.

Dude points a finger at me. "Give my man whatever he's drinking," he offers.

"Thank you, man." Now a nigga is feeling good.

Every broad in the bar is looking in our direction; they're strategizing…trying to figure out the right approach to get with the baller.

I straighten up my shoulders, feeling famous by association.

"My name's Kaymar, man. What's good?" I offer him my hand.

"Brick, man. It's all good."

Brick? Sounds like the name of a rapper. But I never heard of him. Maybe he's underground.

Brick squinted toward the barmaid. She's at the far end of the bar. "Yo, cutie!" he bellows. "Hit my man over here up with some Henny! Give everybody at the bar a drink on me!" my new friend, Brick, offers.

"Good lookin' out, man." I nod enthusiastically. Dude must have major paper to throw around. I'm impressed.

Thirsty chicks sitting at the bar are all smiles as the barmaid starts pouring free drinks, courtesy of Brick.

Now this is more like it. This is exactly how I imagined rolling when I first got back to Philly. Fuck Evette, fuck Fawn, and fuck Munch. I don't need none of them broke-ass niggas. I only fucks with ballers.

"It was nice meeting you, dude. But I'm about to roll out. This part of Philly is too slow for me. These women…" He flips his hand back and forth. "They only so-so. I like to keep company with strippers. Big, fake-ass titties turn me on. You know what I'm sayin'?"

I nod. I never touched a pair of fake tits. But I'm sure it's freaky. "Where you from?" I ask; curiosity is killing me.

"Atlanta. But I'm originally from Philly."

"When you going back?"

"Tomorrow."

I almost want to plead with this bull to take me to ATL with him. Put me on with the rap scene. I'm not sticking around in dull-ass Philly. Shit, it's a free country, and I should be able to go wherever I want. I can register with the sex offenders' list in Atlanta. On the low. Keep that information under my hat. Everything ain't for everybody.

He chats briefly with the barmaid and then returns his attention to me. "Yeah, my flight leaves tomorrow, but tonight I'm tryna have some fun. It's dead in here. And I can't find any good weed." He shakes his head.

My mind is racing, tryna think of who might have some good weed. Pretty Boy keeps some green, but I'm not introducing him to my new friend. I learned my lesson with Munch. Shit, next thing I know, Pretty Boy will be part of Brick's entourage and I'll be out on my ass, living in a shelter.

Brick throws back the shot of Henny and stands up. "Good talking to you, man. I'm heading over to Delilah's Den." At that moment, his cell phone goes off.

"Whassup, my man? You got something for me?" he says into the phone.

I'm impressed by his style. I heard about Delilah's Den. That's where Yeezy's pretty, ball-headed ex used to dance. They got only gorgeous bitches up in that piece. I wanna go!

He glances at me. As if it were an afterthought, he says, "You wanna roll out? My man came through. He got that B52. I only smoke the best, baby."

I smile dumbly. I never heard of B52, but I been locked up so long, there's a lot of shit I don't know. This dude seems like he could be a sort of like a mentor. Seems like rolling with him would be a party every night. Liquor, quality weed, and big-titty bitches.

My big welcome home freak bash with strippers is getting closer to becoming a reality.

I got my swagger back. With a dip in my stride, I'm walking next to Brick, heading toward the door. The females are gazing at us sorrowfully, like they're mourning the fact they didn't get a chance to ride our dicks. I don't feel sorry for none of 'em. If they want a high-profile dude like Brick or me, they better invest in some breast implants. We only like big-titty bitches.

Brick pulls out his cell again and hits a button. "Take the limo around the block a couple of times. I gotta make a transaction. I'll hit you up when I'm finished."

"We're going to the strip club in a limo?"

"For sure. Females give up booty, head, titty fuck…anything you want when you give 'em a ride in a limo." He laughs. "Watch how I operate when we get to the club. I'ma school you, young bull."

"Aye," I say. Dude don't look much older than me, but I'm not offended that he likes calling me young bull. I'm grinning, ear-to-ear.

I'm getting outta Philly. Going to Atlanta. But I get a little uneasy when I imagine my parole officer giving me grief about relocating to Atlanta. I don't wanna stay in this boring city. Ain't nothing here for me. They got it poppin' in ATL. I wonder if

Brick hangs with T.I. or Jeezy. I'ma ask him about his crew after he finishes with the transaction.

A dark-colored hooptie pulls up. A female is driving. Brick nudges me. "Hold up, young bull; lemme go handle the transaction with this chick. Dude done sent his woman, thinking she gon' sweet-talk me out of more money than I'm willing to spend. Give me a few minutes. I'll be right back."

He takes a few steps and then looks back at me. He waves me over. "You ain't gotta wait at the curb. I gotta test this shit, so we might as well spark up together."

I'm honored. Brick is extending so many courtesies because he can see I have potential. Munch and Evette can have each other. They deserve each other. Two sick, twisted mufuckas, fucking all over the house. The only position I've seen them fuck in…is doggy-style. Umph! It's bad enough Munch wants to act like a dog, but watching Evette come down to his level of sickness is more than I can stand.

But fuck all these Philly niggas. From now on, I'ma be hanging with fly, ATL niggas. Smoking and drinking free. I bet Brick is gon' share all the pussy he gets with me.

I shoot a glance at the car. If the bitch at the wheel acts anything like those thirsty bitches in the bar, Brick and I both gon' get our dicks sucked before the limo takes us to the strip club.

Brick gets in the front. I climb in the back.

"Who's that?" the bitch asks, frowning up her face as she looks back at me. She got the motor running, but she ain't moving.

"Oh, that's my man, uh…my man, Kaymar."

"Why you bring him?" the bitch asks in a disrespectful tone.

"Yo, watch your tone, shawty. You ain't talking to a kid; that's a grown man that you're disrespecting," I tell her, narrowing my eyes. I'm fit to be tied, and I just got in the damn car. Bitches!

"It's all good, roadie. Lemme handle this business," Brick says in a calm voice.

He's talking low to her and I'm glaring at her from the back seat. Something about this snotty bitch is irking me. We need to take that weed off her and ram our dicks down her throat, and then give her a nice warm cum shower. I'm thinking all kinds of lewd thoughts while Brick is sniffing bud from a sandwich bag.

"Smells good," he says. "You wanna spark up with me and my man?"

"I ain't got time for that. Here's the weed; now pay me. I know you ain't make me drive over here for nothing."

Her voice is so irritating, I feel my temper flaring. "You gon' get your money. Now stay in your lane, bitch!" I can't help my outburst. Shawty's out of pocket, talking to Brick all greasy.

The bitch turns around and gives me a frown. "Fall back, nigga," she says. "Don't make me call my man."

Now it's my opportunity to show Brick I'm fearless. A good soldier. He could probably use me for security when we get to ATL. "Fuck your man. Call him! I'll fuck you and your man up!"

The bitch pulls a cell phone out of the cup holder. "I'm calling him!"

"Nah," Brick intervenes. "We ain't gotta get violent. I'm tryna get high and have some fun."

"Hmph. I don't appreciate the way your friend is talking to me. And I don't think my man is gon' appreciate it either." She pushes some buttons and then turns around to look at me.

I'm so sick of bitches. I feel like hurting this girl. I wanna plunge my dick in her pussy. Smack her face and piss on her. I never pissed on a bitch before, but there's always a first time. All Brick gotta do is give me a head nod, and I'ma yank that ho back here and fuck that lil' pussy until it cries.

Damn, my Johnson is poking out, making a tent in the front of my pants. I peek at the bitch to see if she's feeling me. I'm not worrying about Brick. I got control of this situation. Just like with Theodore. When I started raping that nurse bitch, my partner in crime wasn't expecting me to take it there. I didn't let him in on that part of the game. Hell, I didn't know I was gon' want some pussy until I saw how scared she was. Her fear made me feel powerful—got my Johnson hard.

Theodore thought we were only gon' jack the nurse's car. Raping, robbing, and finally bodying that broad was an afterthought. All my idea, but I let Theodore take the fall. Shit, that nigga was legally an adult. I was only minor.

He wasn't innocent, anyway. After he got over the initial shock, he took those sloppy seconds after I got off the bitch. One thing about niggas, they ain't got no morals or scruples when there's some available pussy to be had.

I bring my thoughts back to the present and I notice that one minute the bitch in the driver's seat is calling her man, telling him to come fuck me up, and the next minute she's twisting around in her seat, acting like she's tryna hand me the phone.

I recoil. "I don't wanna talk to that nigga!" I look at Brick, expecting him to take control of this situation; the bitch is taking shit too far. But Brick is still fucking with the plastic bag filled with weed.

"Bitch, you crazy," I say. She's actually jabbing me in my shoulder with the phone, trying to get me to say something to her man.

Suddenly, I feel a jolt of the most profound pain that I've ever experienced. I'm going berserk. Jerking like I'm being electrocuted. Shit hurts like a mufucka. What the fuck! I can't get my mouth to form any words.

After five or six incredibly long seconds, she finally pulls that fucking phone away from my shoulder. I'm tryna make sense of this. My mouth is about to cooperate and talk...and goddamn it, the bitch jabs me on the thigh.

This time, I piss my pants.

CHAPTER 43

I feel a pair of powerful arms pulling me out of the car. I'm dazed, but I sense foul play. "What's going on?" The words come out slurred, like I'm drunk. No one responds. I guess they can't understand me.

"Damn, this fool done peed on hisself!"

I recognize Brick's voice and realize he's dragging me across gravel.

Where is he taking me? I wonder, growing hysterical. I struggle as best I can, but I'm too fucked up to put up a fight.

A creaking door opens and I instinctively go wild—thrashing and trying to dig my heels into the ground. The dude gives me a hard yank. Now I'm inside a dark, cavernous place.

A light shines, blinding me. The bitch is holding a big flashlight, the kind that you carry with a handle. I look around, and it seems like I'm in some kind of an abandoned warehouse.

"Ew! It stinks in here, Brick," the crazy chick says. "What's that smell?"

"That's sewage."

"Did you hear that noise? Oh, my God, Brick! What was that?" she whispers in a scared voice.

"Probably mice," Brick says. "Nothing to be worried about. Ain't nobody in here but us."

"This place is creepy," she comments in a shuddering voice.

I'm a little dazed right now, but as soon as I get my head right,

I'ma fuck Brick up for tryna play me. He's a muscular dude, but I ain't no lightweight. He got a little bit of height on me, but I'm cut and chiseled my damn self, and I hold my own in a fair fight.

While the chick is complaining about the smell, I realize my pants are soggy. Overwhelmed by the smell of my pissed-up pants and the rank odor inside this joint they brought me to, I'm close to vomiting.

Brick is dragging me all crazy, banging my head against shit. He ain't got the least bit concern about my well-being. I'm furious that this big brute is handling me like I ain't nothing more than a rag doll.

What the hell did I do to these two nuts to deserve this kind of treatment? I tried to defend dude when the bitch was coming at him, talking all greasy, and this is the thanks I get? That bitch played me. She was pretending to talk on a fake cell phone. That fucking cunt kept tasering me like I'm some kind of wild animal.

I need some answers, so I speak up. "What's this shit about?" My voice is surprisingly clearer now. "This shit y'all doing ain't cool," I say in a bitter hiss.

That nutty broad gives me another hot zap on a piss-stained part of my pants. There's a terrible sizzling sound. "Agghhhh!" I yell in agony as I drop into a heap on a concrete floor. I know the cunt is crazy; I don't know why I even opened my mouth.

Everything hurts. My leg she zapped feels like it's being fried. My heart is booming so hard, I think I'm about to go into cardiac arrest.

"No more. Please! Stop using that stun gun on me," I beg when my body stops jerking and twitching. I hear chains rattling behind me. I wanna yank my head around to see what dude is doing behind me, but my body parts ain't functioning right. This bitch is fucking up my nervous system, tasering me with that fake phone every time I open my mouth to say something.

"Hold the light up," Brick says, harshly.

Moments later, he's pulls me up on my feet, roughly yanks my arms up over my head, and binds my wrists together with a chain. *This is bananas!* I think as I'm being hoisted upward. They got me hanging by a hook or something. I'm not up too high; my feet are dangling only a few inches from the ground.

"You drawlin', man. I ain't do nothing to you."

"Shut up!" Brick's face is hard. I'm thinking the chick must be his woman. Maybe he's upset by the way I came at her in the car.

"This is kind of extreme," I tell him. "Yo, man, I apologize. I ain't mean to disrespect that bitch."

"Did you hear what he called me?" the bitch says.

Brick doesn't say a word. He's smiling in a sinister way, like he's about to go ham on my ass.

"*Bitch* is only an expression. It don't mean anything." That's some real bitchassness that just came outta my mouth, but I can't hold up against another zap from that stun gun.

"Oh, it don't mean nothing? Seriously?" The bitch's tone is sarcastic. She hands the dude the flashlight and pulls a gun out of nowhere, cocks it real quick, and pulls the trigger.

"Ahhh! Goddamn," I shriek as the bullet tears through my sneaker, striking the top of my foot. "What the fuck you do that for?" I look down at my sneaker, and gawk at the small circle of blood. I'm freaking out now, jerking and thrashing, trying to break free of this fuckin' chain.

"Let me down, yo!" I holler. "I gotta get to the hospital and let a doctor look at my foot! And my chest…man, it's hurting real bad! My heart ain't beating right!"

The bitch turns her mouth down and shakes her head. "Who's the bitch now?"

My foot is throbbing so bad, I don't even wanna *think* the word "bitch," let alone speak it!

"Seriously. I need medical attention. Whatever I said that pissed you off, I apologize, Miss," I say to the chick in a sincere tone. Then I appeal to Brick. "I don't want any problems, man. I ain't got no beef with you. Just let me go—let me outta here."

"You're not going anywhere," the broad says. She walks toward me with the gun. I start jerking and flinching, expecting her to fire the weapon again. It's frustrating not being able to shield my face with my arms.

"I got beef with you!" She's smiling and smirking like she's proud of herself.

"This gotta be a mistake. I ain't never seen you a day in my life!" I turn my attention to Brick. "This is a joke. Y'all punking me, right?"

"Take a good look at me. Don't I look familiar?" She steps closer. Brick shines the light on her mug; there's nothing familiar about her face.

"Some people say I resemble my mother."

I begin to shake a little. The pain in my foot is killing me. Plus, what this broad is saying about resembling her mother is creeping me out.

"You and Theodore Belgrade thought it was funny when you were throwing stones at my mother," she says, looking me in the eye.

Now I know who she is, and the knowledge has me shaking like a leaf. She's shaking, too—from anger—not fear. One side of her mouth is twitching like she's about to go into an epileptic fit. This chick is carrying a horrible grudge.

"That wasn't me. I mean, that situation wasn't my idea. Theodore was the mastermind," I blurt.

"Shut up, liar." She looks at Brick. "You ready to do your thing, Brick?"

"Whoa, whoa! I was only a kid back then. I'm rehabilitated. I swear to God. Ask my therapist."

Brick is bending, taking something out of a dark bag. I have no idea what he plans on doing to me. My mind is racing, trying to come up with a way to get out of this predicament. There's gotta be a way for me to save my ass.

Brick backs up a little and aims something at me. It's so dark, I can't make out what it is. Assuming he's holding a gun, I squeeze my eyes shut and prepare to die.

Something small and hard hits me in my forehead. "Ow! What the fuck you doin', man?" I can feel a knot swelling up on my forehead.

"Bull's eye! You see that shit! I got him smack in the middle of his forehead," Brick brags to the lunatic chick.

"You enjoy hitting women with stones, huh? Well, I thought I'd give you a taste of how it feels." He puts a crazy-ass, high-tech-looking slingshot in front of my face.

"This is high-powered shit. I'm taking it to another level; using steel ball bearings instead of stones."

"Help!" I yell as loud as I can, twisting and kicking, jangling the chain.

"Stop whining like a little bitch!" Brick punches me in the gut.

CHAPTER 44

The assault knocks the wind out of me. I groan and gurgle as I try to catch my breath.

"Shut him up!" the chick says and hands dude a roll of duct tape. I'm struggling to get away from him, but I can't. He wraps the black tape around my mouth and the back of my head. Not once, not twice…this nigga done wrapped this shit around my head three times! Now I'm completely vulnerable.

"This is retribution, man. An eye for an eye." He steps back, aims and fires. Ping! The next piece of steel hits me in the left eye. *Son of a bitch!* Blood is trickling. That ball bearing ain't no joke.

"Wow, Brick. You got skills," the slut says. "You messed his eye up!"

I feel like my eye is hanging out of the socket, but I can't move my hands to investigate. I wanna touch my eye, and wipe the blood away. I need to find out what's what with my vision. I'm moaning and groaning, terrified I don't have my sight. I swear to God, I don't wanna end up blind in one eye.

Ow! He just hit me in the nose with one of those fuckin' little balls. My nose is bleeding. What kind of savage mufucka uses a high-powered slingshot on a mufucka? This shit is bananas. This bull is really tryna kill me! I gotta wiggle off this chain some kind of way, and get the hell out of this slaughterhouse.

He hits me in the other eye. *Ahh! God! Fuckin' hell!* Goddammit, now I can't see shit. Please, God, please...I can't be one of 'nem blind mufuckas walking around tapping on the sidewalk with a fuckin' stick. And I don't wanna be tugged around by a mangy-ass, seeing-eye dog, either.

I tell myself that my eyesight is fine; it's only blood blocking my vision. No way in the world that a cool dude like me can go through life selling pencils...holding out a cup, and begging mufuckas for spare change.

I'm tryna beg these two lunatics for mercy, but they can't understand a word I'm saying. If I get a chance to plead my case, I'm sure I can convince this wacko broad that Theodore raped and killed her mother. The jury believed me, so why is she going to the extreme to get vigilante justice?

"It's my turn," the whore's daughter says.

It's her turn to do what! I feel her presence. She's standing close to me. I don't know what to expect. Is she gon' shank me now. Cut off my dick? Gripped by fear, I tremble as if convulsing.

"My mother was a decent woman. She never did anything to you," she says in a voice that's brittle and unforgiving. "What happened to make you an evil monster at such a young age?"

I can't talk, so I shrug.

"My mother told you animals she had a family at home. A husband and a daughter. Me! I'm Anya. It was my name she screamed while you stoned her. She was screaming, thinking of the life I'd have to live without a mother!"

Pop! Pop! I wasn't prepared for the sudden gunshots. With a slug in each kneecap, I go into a state of shock that leaves me numb for a few moments. I'm not aware of sound or pain. But the calming numbness doesn't last forever. My bullet-punctured body is seized by unbearable pain that causes me to writhe and utter miserable sounds.

I want to cry, but my tear ducts are fucked up. Instead of tears, blood trickles from my eyes. I'm bleeding all over. I can feel sticky warm blood oozing from the top of my foot and seeping down into the sole of my shoe. My pant legs are sopping wet from a mixture of urine and blood. The stench wafts up to my nostrils.

Despite the circumstances, my will to survive is stronger than ever. I refuse to go out like this. I muster strength, twisting and struggling to break free from the chain that holds me.

"Should we leave him here…let him bleed out, or should I finish him off?" the crazy chick asks in a matter-of-fact tone.

"That's your call," the dude says. They're conversing in calm tones like they're discussing the weather.

I grunt and flail. Long, frantic minutes go by. Suddenly, the tape is ripped from my mouth. "I'm sorry," I say in a coarse, agonized whisper.

The girl pushes the barrel of the gun to my lips. "Suck it. Like it's a juicy dick. Wet it up; I wanna see a lot of slobber." Her voice is husky, seductive, and vicious. "Do it right and I'll let you live."

Hope ignites like blazing fire. I'm gon' live. I'm about to get out of this jam. I submit like a bitch, and suck the hot barrel. I put my heart into it, sucking like it's the sweetest dick I ever tasted.

She taunts me, slowly pulling and pushing the barrel in and out of my mouth. Desperate to please her, I lick up and down the barrel, trying to work up some saliva. Then it dawns on me; she's saying the exact words I said to her mother. I gulp, refusing to believe karma is in action. This is merely a coincidence.

"Suck it!" she yells, and then the nutty broad rams the barrel down my throat.

I choke, cough, and gag, putting a terrible strain on my injured eyeballs. She's getting entirely too rough with the pistol, yanking it around so harshly, it clanks against my teeth. As if aroused by the sound of metal against teeth, she pulls the barrel out and bangs my mouth with the handle of the gun. My lips split and multiple teeth crunch and crack. Tooth fragments float in blood and mucous that pools inside my mouth. I try to spit the teeth out but I can't. My lips are swollen and busted.

"So what's the verdict? We gotta get out of here," Brick says.

I'm somewhat in a daze, but I'm alert enough to know that I don't want to die. I moan for them to please forgive me.

"I still have some bullets left."

"All right. Use 'em. Put a bullet between his eyes, and it's a wrap for ol' boy. But I'm not disposing of his worthless body."

"Why not?"

"I'm not hurting my back, carrying dead weight. He can hang right where he's at."

"But his body is evidence," the chick says, sounding alarmed.

Body! I wish they'd stop referring to me as a body. Goddamn! I'm still alive and kicking and I plan to stay this way.

"There won't be any evidence after the rats get through with his remains."

"Rats! You told me there were only mice in here," she says in a high-pitched voice.

"Fuck if I know what's running around in here. Rats…mice…a little bit of everything. I'm ready to roll out. This place stinks. And that killer is adding to the stench."

"I know, right? He's reeking of piss and blood," the cunt says. "I'ma need a long, hot shower to get his smell off of me."

Are those two cold-blooded killers seriously gon' let me hang on this chain until rats find me? Don't leave me in here! I scream in my head.

At that precise moment, I desire a quick death more than I've ever wanted anything. Sex and money…the two things I've cherished most in life, don't mean shit to me. If my lips weren't swollen up and my teeth knocked out, I'd yell out the truth to those two crazies: "I'm still a menace to society. I might strike again if you don't give me a bullet to the dome!"

More shots ring out in quick succession. *Ah! Shit! Ow!* My thigh, my hand, and my stomach are hit. I've never hated anyone as much as I hate this trigger-happy bitch!

"Good job, Anya," Brick says, praising the slut. "Aye, we out. Ol' boy can hang in here with the sewage and the vermin."

I hear their footsteps as they hurry away. The door creaks open and then closes.

Leaking blood, I pass out.

ഇൻരു

I wake up but my eyes can't see anything. There's only darkness and silence. I don't know if I'm dead or alive. Waves of pain inform me that I'm still alive. Head to toe, every part of my body is hurting; especially my stomach. That broad shot me in the gut. I'm still hooked up by a chain. But I refuse to go out like this. Somebody had to hear all that gunfire. A rescue team is gonna be here any minute to take me to the hospital.

I feel something crawling on my sneaker. A rat? *Aw, shit. Come on; don't do this to me!* Nah, it ain't no rat. It's something small. I wiggle my foot, tryna get it off of me. That sucker runs inside my sneaker…moving all crazy, squeezing down into the sole of my sneaker. I wish it was like an insect or something, but I can tell that there's a little-ass mouse, fucking around inside my sneaker.

I shake my foot, hoping to knock my sneaker off, but my laces are tied tight and my sneaker's not budging.

Oh, my God, I feel two more mice, burrowing into each side

of my sneaker. Now there's a swarm of them nasty suckers, squirming around, fighting to get in.

Some are crawling up my pant legs now. *God, help me. I don't deserve this.* They're slithering into the holes on the knees of my pants. Hordes of mice are crawling all over me. I can't get 'em off. They're nibbling and biting on my wounds. They're feasting on my foot, my kneecaps, and my stomach.

Aye, I've had enough of this crap. For real, I'm not playing. *Do you hear me, God! Take me! I've had it. I'm ready to die!*

God isn't listening to me. I must be in hell. Something large and menacing is moving at a fast and determined pace. Sharp claws dig into my skin as this thing…this… I know what it is, but I don't wanna say it. This fat fucker is clinging to my shirt as it chews on the open wound on my shoulder—razor-sharp teeth taking bites.

Oh, fuck. It's moving to my face. *Get the fuck off me. Shit, shit, shit. A big-ass rat is fucking with my face, gnawing on my bloody eyeball.*

As death finally claims me, I feel great relief. My life flashes before me. Childhood days. My first kiss. Cruelty to animals. Stealing money from my mom's purse. Gang-banging. Car-jacking. Rape and murder. Prison life. When I finally get to my last moment in life, I'm ready to meet my Maker, but there's a click and a freeze-frame.

Nooo! I'm not going forward. I'm trapped in the warehouse. Stuck with the horrible sensations of rodents nibbling on me. I cry out in outrage and pain, my voice seeming to echo throughout eternity. I plead and wail as I wait for a benevolent God to please have mercy on me.

CHAPTER 45

I n the cover of night, Brick lurked in the shadows, watching and waiting. He knew that a mama's boy like Cash Money couldn't go very long without seeing his mother. Brick smiled when he saw the scrawny dude slip out the back door.

With his cap pulled down, Cash Money trotted down the dark alleyway.

Brick was parked at the foot of the alley. When Cash Money drew close, Brick stepped outside his nondescript, dark car.

"What's good, Cash Money? What it do, man?" Brick smiled.

Cash Money stopped in his tracks. He grimaced and jerked his shoulders in agitation. "Fuck! Not you again! Come on, man. I told you everything I know."

"Let's take a ride. I got some more questions to ask you."

Cash Money made a quick motion, preparing to make a run for it. Brick zapped him, and then threw his spastic, lanky body into the back seat of the car.

"Fuck you do that for?" Cash Money groused after he stopped quivering.

"We can do this the easy way or I can go hard. It's up to you."

"I got enough problems. Why you keep fucking with me? You took my phone. What more do you want from me?"

"There wasn't shit in that phone that was helpful, except your mother's number. Yo, I got my tools on me this time. They in the trunk. A brand new collection of interesting weapons...all designed to produce pain. And a slow death."

Cash Money groaned.

"I wonder how long your lil' frail ass will linger after I start working on you?" Brick shook his head grimly. "Probably not long. It don't seem like you're built to last, but I'll figure out a way to prolong your life and make you suffer."

"I told you everything. What else do you wanna know?"

"I been all through your cell; and I'm coming up with blanks. No leads to Smash Hitz."

"Ain't no numbers for him in my phone because I'm tryna steer clear of that psycho."

"Where'd she meet Spydah?"

"The hotel where he was staying when he did a show in Philly."

"I can't picture Misty hanging out at a hotel tryna rub shoulders with a celebrity."

"I was with her when she met Spydah. She was chasing that paper. One of the dudes that worked for her put her on with Spydah."

"What dude?"

"Man, I don't remember. Misty had a revolving door of niggas that worked for her and some of 'em lived with her at the apartment. Dudes named Sailor, Izell, Lennox, and Horatio. But they're all from outta town. I don't know how to get in touch any of 'em."

Brick scowled at that information. "Okay, back to Spydah. Is he on the down low? Was he looking for a dude to trick with?"

"Nah, he didn't even know the extent of what Misty was into. That night she met him, he wanted ten groupies to come through and entertain him and his crew."

"Misty don't fuck with females, so how did she find ten groupies?"

"She called a stripper that used to work for her. The chick's name is Felice. Felice called on some of her stripper friends and they came to the hotel, expecting to get paid a certain amount."

"Okay. Any reason why I should consider the stripper chick as a suspect?"

Cash Money scratched his head. "Now that I think about it… yeah. Felice ended up having beef with Misty."

"What happened?"

"Felice brought the other strippers. Misty told her that she would pay Felice and all the girls—"

"Hold up! Why would Misty offer to pay for Spydah's strippers?"

"Spydah didn't request strippers. He wanted free pussy from groupies. And since Misty wanted to get close to Spydah, she offered to pay the chicks."

"That don't even sound like Misty…getting chicks together in order to rub elbows with a celebrity."

"Misty wasn't interested in Spydah. She only used him to get to the big man…Smash Hitz."

Brick nodded. Now *that* sounded more like Misty. She was always scheming and looking at the big picture. "Aye, so what happened with the strippers?"

"It was all good. Everybody had a good time. Then, the next morning, Felice was blowing up Misty's phone, but Misty wouldn't take her calls."

Felice? The name wasn't familiar. Brick frowned, trying to think back to his days with Misty. She had one female working for her, but the name Felice didn't ring any bells.

"Felice dances under the name Juicy. Her pussy is fat, man. Real swelled up, like a piece of ripe fruit." Cash Money closed his eyes in fond reminiscence.

Juicy! Yeah, I remember that name. Now shit was finally starting to add up. Misty did have a hooker named Juicy selling pussy for her once upon a time. Misty posted the chick's fat pussy up on her website, and customers were feening to get between those big, juicy lips. Brick frowned as he recalled the incriminating pictures of himself that he'd allowed Misty to post online.

"Misty promised the stripper chick a lot more dough than she actually gave her. And she told her she could get her tickets to Spydah's show. She promised a whole bunch of shit that she didn't deliver. Misty thought it was funny that she burned Felice."

"Misty had a malicious streak, there ain't no doubt about that. And could be shady from time to time, but it sounds like she had a personal problem with that stripper. Any idea what that was about?"

"Payback. Felice fucked her ex-man, Dane…back in the day."

Hearing Dane's name put a sour taste in Brick's mouth. "Yeah, that nigga dead, but he deserved a fate worse than death," Brick said bitterly.

As though spooked by Brick's irreverent words, Cash Money looked around fearfully. "Yo, let that man rest in peace. Why you talking bad about the dead?"

"Fuck Dane," Brick said with his face contorted. Not only did Dane steal Misty from Brick, he stole Misty's SUV, her money, and he destroyed her business.

Brick shook his head, clearing his mind of Dane. "Getting back to the stripper, Juicy. I need to holler at that broad. Where's she dancing at now?"

"Juicy came up! She's not stripping anymore."

"Whatchu mean?"

"She works for Smash Hitz. That right there lets you know Juicy is the last bitch I'm tryna bump into."

Brick scowled excessively. "What kind of work is she doing for Smash Hitz?"

"Provides him with strippers."

"I'm confused. Why does he want strippers? Isn't he on the DL?"

"He goes both ways."

Brick nodded in understanding. "How did Juicy get in cahoots with Smash Hitz?"

"Through Spydah's crew. They told him about her unusual pussy. Misty never knew Juicy had a little side business going on with Smash. He put Misty on with all his friends and connections on a national level. But he only used Juicy's services when he was in the Philly area."

"How do you know about his business with Juicy?" Brick asked skeptically.

"She came to the crib he was renting when he was in Philly. I was there with him."

"Smash Hitz sucked your dick?"

Cash Money nodded. "He's a freak, man. He's into all kinds of perverted sex acts. He was supposed to be getting into a three-some with me and one of Juicy's chicks; that's why Juicy brought the stripper to the crib."

"Why'd he change his mind?"

"I don't know. He let them come upstairs. He met with them in this outer room that was attached to the bedroom. The bedroom door was closed but I could hear the conversation. He told Juicy that he didn't need her services. He said he'd catch her the next time that he was in town. Juicy kept tryna convince him to at least try out the new girl. Smash told her he wasn't interested. I don't think that Juicy knew Smash prefers men because she told the girl to take off her clothes and give Smash a sample."

"A sample?"

"I don't know what sampling involved, but while his attention was diverted from me, I kind of borrowed his chain." Cash Money gave a soft groan. "That's how all this shit got started—that damn Juicy!"

"Nigga, shut up. Ain't nobody tell you to steal that man's chain."

"I bet Juicy has Smash's chain. All this time, I thought Smash had one of his people get the chain out of Misty's car. But now I think it was Juicy."

"Okay, I'm starting to feel this. But I don't want to focus on Juicy only. Think hard, man…what other chicks did Misty have beef with?"

"Besides Juicy…uh…only Baad B and the tranny."

Brick's thoughts drifted. He looked at Cash Money. "How would Juicy know Misty was going to see Smash in the wee hours of the morning?"

"I'm only guessing. She persuaded Smash to try out the stripper chick. I know that for a fact because when he came back in the bedroom, he told me that he'd get back with me again some other time. After I left Smash's room, the stripper went in."

"What was her name?"

"I don't know. He didn't introduce us."

"What did she look like?"

"I can't remember."

"No? Well, I got tools in the trunk that might help to jog your memory," Brick said threateningly.

"She was a light-skinned chick," Cash Money blurted. "Oh, wait a minute. I remember her name because Smash laughed a little when Juicy introduced them."

"What's her name?"

"Redbone."

"Redbone?"

"Yeah. Smash only agreed to get with her because he liked her name so much."

"Where can I find this Redbone chick?"

"I don't know. You gotta get in touch with Juicy."

"How?"

"It all goes back to Smash Hitz."

"Before I go after Juicy, did any of Misty's male workers know Smash on a personal level?"

"Yeah."

"Who?"

"Too many to name. But one in particular was Horatio. He went to Miami with Misty, pretending to be her bodyguard. But after they got there, Smash preferred Horatio over Misty. That's when she first found out Smash was into dudes. And she milked his obsession, giving him a smorgasbord of young, muscular dudes."

"And what happened to Horatio?"

Cash Money shrugged. "I'm not sure. I remember that Misty and Horatio had a big argument over Smash Hitz. Horatio thought he deserved some extra bread for helping Misty find out the man was on the low. Misty wouldn't give it to him. I think he quit, but then again, Misty may have fired him. I don't remember, man. Like I said, Misty had beef with damn near everybody that worked for her.

"But Horatio wasn't no killer. That dude was big as a linebacker, but he was sweet. None of Misty's workers were killers. If you find Juicy…you'll get to the truth. Juicy hated Misty and I know that for a fact."

"How do you know that?"

"Dane told me. He said that Juicy wanted everything that Misty had."

CHAPTER 46

The expression "poor little rich girl" finally made sense. Anya left the lawyer's office several million dollars richer. The money was supposed to make her life easier. But this blood money, the result of a civil suit against the security company that had been contracted to keep her mother's workplace safe, didn't make her happy.

Tears sprang to Anya's eyes as she imagined Kaymar and the other merciless savage accosting her mother inside the parking garage and forcing her off the property. The terror and hopelessness her mother must have felt brought tears to Anya's eyes.

There'd been cameras around the grounds of the health care facility where her mother worked, but the security company neglected their duties. They weren't looking at the monitors nor were any of the team members outside, patrolling the parking lot during shift change, and acting as a visual deterrent. Instead the security team was inside the facility, drinking coffee, laughing, kicking it with each other while her mom was being kidnapped.

Had they bothered to glance at the monitors, they would have been able to stop the assailants. Because of their negligence, her mother was no longer alive.

Anya's aunt and other extended family in Indiana talked bad about her father; called him a drug addict, a bum, a deadbeat dad. Said he blew a million dollars on fast living and drugs.

It was true; he went through the money fast. He abandoned Anya, but no one took into consideration that he was in severe emotional pain.

Now Anya knew the truth. The lawyer told her today that her father was awarded several million, and it was his idea to put the bulk of the money in a trust fund for Anya.

She learned from the attorney that her mother's heinous and brutal murder had left her father a distraught man. He was guilt-ridden for not driving her to work as he usually did. The NBA playoffs were in overtime, and he told her to take the car. Her father's drug habit became an escape from the constant emotional pain.

This was another piece of the puzzle that Anya hadn't known about.

The sweet revenge of ending Kaymar Crawford's miserable life had given her great satisfaction for a while. Now the emptiness was back.

I want to get far, far away. Start a new life. Maybe in Trinidad; I can reconnect with my mother's relatives. Find my roots. Finally get a sense of kinship. But I can't pick up and go until I find my father. I have to make sure that he's straight.

And I don't want to leave without Brick, either. I need him in my life.

⅋⅋⅋

Anya was peering at the screen of her iPad when Brick returned to the motel. "Hey!"

He kissed her on the cheek. "I talked to your boy, Cash Money, tonight," he said. "Caught him creeping out the back door of his mother's crib."

"Oh, yeah? Did you get any new information out of him?"

"Sure did."

"What did he say?"

"He's terrified of Smash Hitz, but he's tired of hiding out and looking over his shoulder. He wants that man off his ass. I told Cash Money that I can help him out if he cooperates with me. I asked him to think real hard about all the females Misty had beef with."

Focusing all her attention on Brick, Anya closed the iPad cover.

"He kept saying he only knew about the tranny. His memory was jogged after I made a few harsh threats. He told me that he remembered seeing a female stripper at the mansion that Smash was renting on the same night that Misty got attacked."

"Do you really think that a woman attacked Misty?" Anya asked, looking incredulous.

Brick nodded. "I found it hard to believe, too. When she told me that a lone female rolled up in a sports car, got out and beat her with a tire iron, and you know…ran over her." Brick winced at the mental imagery. "I thought Misty was hallucinating, you know…delirious or something. I'd always figured the perp was a man. I never imagined a female would be out in the middle of the night with the intention to kill. After talking with Cash Money, I found out at least two women had grudges against Misty. But only one was in the Philly area that night."

Anya shook her head. "Misty's on the brink of dying, and if by some miracle she survives, her life will be hell on earth. Whoever did that to her needs to suffer."

Guiltily, Brick looked down; laced his fingers together. "There's something I need to tell you," he said. "The reason my wife wants to divorce me… The reason she's tryna get me locked up…" He looked up, his eyes locked on Anya's. "I'm the person responsible for Misty's condition."

"What do you mean?"

"Misty begged me to help her end her suffering. Even though it was over between us, we still shared a bond. I couldn't watch her suffer."

Anya scowled. "What did you do to her?"

"It wasn't my idea. It was Misty's. She pleaded with me to help put her out of her misery. She was tired of living inside a body that didn't function anymore."

Anya expression softened. She nodded in understanding.

"Misty was paralyzed but she had the partial use of one of her hands. And she had a strong will. Somehow, she managed to store a mixture of pills. Her stash was scattered under the bed."

"Wow. That took a lot of effort."

"She was serious about checking out. She asked me to gather up the pills and put 'em in her mouth." He took a deep breath. "So, I did what she wanted. But instead of slipping into the peaceful death that she wanted, Misty ended up in a coma."

Anya rubbed Brick's hand. "You tried, babe. You did what she asked you to do."

"But her mom… She's looking at it from a mother's perspective. And I get that. Believe me, I didn't want to lose Misty, either, but she claimed she'd seen the other side. She said a better life was waiting for her."

"Do you believe in life after death?"

"I don't know, man. Misty believed it, so it doesn't matter what I think about it."

"I hope my mother's in a better place," Anya mused. "And I hope Kaymar Crawford is rotting in hell," Anya said with her mouth twisted in hatred. "His partner in crime—Theodore Belgrade—better pray he stays locked up for the rest of his miserable life. If he ever gets paroled…" She shook her head. "He's gonna end up as rat bait, too."

Thinking about his situation, Brick zoned out for a moment. "Yo, it's time for me to make some moves. But I don't want to leave you in this motel. Maybe you should consider reconnecting with your people in Indiana. That way, I'll know you're safe."

"I wouldn't feel safe."

"Why not?"

"I only feel safe when I'm with you."

"You can't get involved in this. Dealing with Kaymar was easy; wasn't nothing to it. But Smash Hitz has a squad he pays to protect him. Touching that man is gonna be complicated. And dangerous."

"I thought you narrowed the suspects down to a particular female."

"True. But I don't how to get to her. The only information I have on this chick is that she works for Smash Hitz."

"My money came through. I can help you."

"Nah, I'm good," he said, although he didn't know how long his money would last.

"You helped me in so many ways. Let me return the favor, Brick."

"No! I couldn't forgive myself if something happened to you."

"I'll be all right. We're good together. Let me help you." She caressed Brick's face. "I got your back. You know I do. Besides, I've never been to Miami. It could be a working vacation." Anya gave Brick an alluring smile.

CHAPTER 47

"I was looking at some old blogs and I came across some information," Anya said.

Brick looked at her curiously.

"You can rule out D.B. Spydah and Baad B as suspects. On the night in question, Baad was big and pregnant and she and Spydah were both at her baby shower—a grand event held in Miami. The photos were splashed all over the internet the next day."

"Okay. I'm not surprised. I didn't think they were involved."

"I also checked Smash's current concert schedule, to see if we could catch him on the road, but he only has two shows left on his tour."

"Where?" Brick asked.

"He's playing in Boston tonight; the final show is tomorrow night at the XL Center in Hartford, Connecticut."

"It's too late to get to Boston, but we gotta make the show in Hartford."

"Suppose he leaves Hartford right after the show?"

"There's no other choice. It's not like I have the man's home address. I gotta get to him the best way I can."

"Going to Hartford might be a wasted trip, though. Lemme check something else." Anya perused the iPad screen. Brick waited. "Ah, here we go."

"Whatchu find?"

"This coming Saturday, Smash Hitz is gonna be making an appearance at a nightclub in Hollywood. We can get a table and bottles in the same VIP section that he's in."

Brick grinned. "Wow, you on the ball. Is he gon' perform at the club? Might as well enjoy his talent one last time."

"I doubt it. He's paid to just show up, mingle a little, take a few pictures...have some drinks. The good thing is, a couple of stacks will buy us a table real close to the man."

"What else do you get for two G's?"

"Not that much. You have to pay for bottle service and the liquor is pricey," she said and chuckled.

"How pricey?"

"Like...three hundred a bottle."

"Wheeeeew," Brick uttered, grimacing.

"I know, right? And you have to commit to buying at least two bottles. We'll get a better table location if we order an impressive amount of bottles in advance."

"Umph! They robbing mufuckas!"

Anya laughed. "At least we won't have to worry about making trips to the bar. We'll have our own personal server throughout the night, mixing our drinks and keeping our table clean. While we're enjoying the scene, we can keep our eyes on Smash Hitz."

"Aye, aye. So how much we gon' need. What we talking altogether?"

"We gotta spend like ballers to get close to Smash Hitz. So you already know we have to come with the money."

Brick briefly pondered Anya's words. "Yeah, well, that nigga can expect to get a couple bones crushed for making me blow a bunch of unnecessary dough."

"Don't worry, babe, I got this. Money's not an issue anymore. Remember?"

"This isn't your problem, Anya."

"Yes, it is. You helped me and I'm glad I can return the favor. To fit in with Smash Hitz' crowd, we're gon' have to go all out. Flashy jewelry, clothes, and a limo. I gotchu, Brick. Let's do this!"

Brick took a deep breath and exhaled. He didn't argue with Anya.

৪০৩

Hoping to get shots of A-list celebrities before they were whisked inside, paparazzi stalked the front and back entrances of the upscale nightspot.

Anya and Brick were both blinged out in luxurious jewelry, and were dressed to impress. Wearing an attention-grabbing cocktail dress that showed off her sexy curves and shapely legs, Anya could easily be mistaken for someone famous. Brick looked extra handsome in an untucked dress shirt and a pair of four-hundred-dollar jeans. Anya noticed the paparazzi trying to figure out who she and Brick were as they exited their limo.

Bouncers closely guarded the velvet rope entrance, where a long line had formed. Having reserved a table, Anya and Brick were on the guest list, and were greeted by a host who escorted them inside the club.

It was still early, but the club was already packed; the music was blasting. The host ushered them past throngs of people, guiding them to the posh section they'd be sharing with rap icon, Smash Hitz.

Settled into soft leather seats, the VIP section was a relaxing and intimate haven away from the chaos. Their table was set up with candles, a bottle of Patrón and a bottle of Belvedere vodka. Also, a colorful assortment of garnishments, juices and soda were arranged on the table.

Glamorous people milled about and Anya noticed numerous famous faces, but there was no sign of Smash Hitz.

"Is that the bull from that new show on Cinemax?" Brick's eyes darted to the left.

Anya's eyes went in the direction of Brick's gaze. She smiled as she recognized one of the hot male stars from *Zane's The Jump Off.* "Yup, it sure is," she said. "That's one of the frat brothers from Zane's new show." Her eyes appreciatively scanned the actor from head to toe.

"You like what you see?" Brick asked.

"He's a hot piece of chocolate, but he doesn't excite me the way you do."

Brick took a sip from his drink, stifling a smile. "Did I tell you how gorgeous you look tonight?"

"Yes, but I don't mind hearing it again."

"You look beautiful. This is your element—the kind of lifestyle you could be leading all the time." He looked down, and then pointed to himself. "A guy like me...I'm just a regular dude. Hand me the remote after work, give me dinner, a few beers every now and then, and I'm good."

"I wanna fight over the remote and share those dinners and beers with you."

"But you got money now."

"So! Money isn't everything."

Brick looked around. "Seeing you in this environment is giving me a change of heart about everything. I don't want you to get involved in this, baby. After I make contact with Smash...if the nigga ever gets here..." He looked around in disgust. "I want you to go back to the hotel, pack up and start all over. Find your family in Trinidad."

"We're doing this together, Brick."

"I screwed up my life; I'm fucked. But you…" He caressed her hand. "It's not too late to back out of this, Anya."

Anya shook her head. "I told you…I'm all in."

Over the loudspeaker, someone announced that Smash Hitz was in the house. There was a big commotion as Smash Hitz and his entourage entered the VIP area.

Anya felt a rush of excitement, smiling like an adoring fan. She grew up listening to Smash's music and, on one hand, she was excited to see him up close and personal, but on the other hand, she was itching to beat the shit out of him—if that's what it took to get the information that Brick needed.

Smash's entourage consisted of six tall, well-built, gorgeous men and three beautiful women. Knowing of the rapper's predilection for men, she wasn't sure if his entourage were there to protect him or merely eye candy. Though muscular, the men in the entourage seemed too handsome to be throwing punches. They looked more like male models than bodyguards.

CHAPTER 48

Not wanting to openly stare, Anya and Brick furtively watched Smash Hitz as he shook hands and mingled with the VIP guests. Every step he made, he was flanked by two men on each side.

Anya searched the faces of the two women, trying to decide if either female was actually a transvestite.

"Let's make a move," Brick said. Anya and Brick stood and then walked over to Smash Hitz' table. Using fake names, they introduced themselves to the famous rap artist.

"I can't believe I'm actually meeting you in person," Anya gushed.

"It's an honor, man," Brick said, graciously. Smash Hitz took in the love, smiled, and then headed for the stage.

Back at their own table, Brick and Anya watched Smash Hitz take the stage performing his latest song. The crowd was going off, reciting Smash Hitz' lyrics for him. For a moment, Anya and Brick were caught in the music. They swayed and rocked with the crowd until Smash yelled, "Peace," and then exited the stage.

Instantly, they went into a panic. "I know that nigga ain't split already," Brick said as they noticed he didn't return to his table. "That's it?" Brick asked in surprise.

"I hope not."

"He was only here for an hour." Brick looked down at his new, diamond-encrusted watch. Anya looked over at what was left of his entourage. The women and a few of the men were still sitting there laughing, talking, and drinking.

"He left half of his entourage behind. I'm sure he's coming back. If not, we'll get to him through his people." Anya stood. "I'll be right back."

Feeling bolder without the larger than life presence of Smash Hitz, Anya strutted over to his table. "Did Smash leave?" she asked one of the men.

"That's confidential information," he said and smiled. The dude's teeth were even and white; he'd obviously spent a fortune on his smile. He perused Anya and then shot a glance over at Brick. "Is that your man?"

"Yeah, we're together."

"Do you party together?"

Anya detected some sort of hidden message, but went along with the conversation. "Oh, we definitely like to party."

"If you can leave your inhibitions here at the club, both of you are invited to Smash's private party at a secret location."

"Really?" Her eyes lit up.

"Give me your number and I'll text you with the address after I clear it with Smash."

"Okay." Anya rattled off the cell number from the disposable phone that she was using while in L.A.

"I'm Bradford, by the way."

"Hi, my name is Kenya," she said, using her alias.

"Okay, sweetheart. You'll hear from me later on tonight."

Anya sashayed back to her table. "We're invited to a private party at Smash's crib. It's on the hush-hush. That dude I was just talking to is going to text me with the secret location. "

Brick broke into a grin. "That's what I'm talking about, baby. Now we're getting somewhere."

"He instructed us to leave our inhibitions here at the club. I don't what to expect, but it sounds to me that we should prepare ourselves for something super freaky, " Anya said, looking a little nervous.

"Don't worry about those freak niggas, baby. I'll fuck a mufucka up if somebody tries some shit with you. I got something real special in store for that freak, Smash Hitz, but he ain't gon' like it."

Brick rubbed his hands together as he imagined inflicting bodily harm on Smash Hitz and everyone else that was involved in hurting Misty.

&)(&

When the text came through with the address to the secret location, Brick tipped the limo driver and sent him on his way. He and Anya switched to an inconspicuous rental car, and drove to Malibu.

They parked in front of a mansion, and were met at the gate by a brawny, security dude. "Name?" he asked, stone-faced.

"Kenya and Stone," Anya replied. Brick noticed the slight tremor in Anya's voice. He put his arm around her waist, reassuringly.

The guard looked at the screen of his phone. "Okay, you're on the list. Go ahead," he said, stepping aside.

Nothing could have prepared Brick or Anya for the bizarre world they walked into.

"What the fuck!" Anya whispered.

"Damn!" Brick muttered.

They both gawked at the two nude men that held trays. Both men were dark complexioned, with close-cut, platinum-colored hair. One wore green contact lenses and the other wore blue. Most startling, however, were their full, jiggling feminine breasts—a stark contrast to their humongous dicks that swung pendulously as they moved about.

"Champagne, Patrón, or Grey Goose?" the green-eyed blonde asked Anya. "My name is Malaysia and I'm your server tonight."

Uh…uh." Staring at the man's enviable breasts, Anya was stuck as her eyes roved from the tray to the curious, male/female fusion named Malaysia.

Dick and hips swaying, the "fusion" with the blue eyes sidled up to Brick. In his hand was a tray filled with dildos, condoms, dick rings, nipple pincers, and an assortment of sex-themed party favors. "Help yourself," he said, giving Brick a flirtatious wink. "Call me Trixie." He switched the tray to his other hand, prompting his long and thick dick to gently sway.

Brick's expression didn't change. He grabbed a handful of condoms. "Thanks," he said.

Still stammering, Anya had not yet selected a drink. "We're both drinking vodka," Brick told Malaysia.

Trixie batted his lashes at Brick. "The showcase is in the ballroom. You two can follow me," he said, and strutted ahead. Prancing like a long-legged stallion in seven-inch platforms, his perfect, hard mound of an ass made figure eights as he moved.

Anya looked at Brick and raised a brow quizzically. "Showcase?" she mouthed. Brick shrugged as they trailed behind the naked pre-op, transsexual man.

"Excuse me, Ms. Thang," Anya blurted. "Is Smash Hitz gon' perform at the showcase?"

Trixie whirled around while delicately placing a large hand on a narrow hip. "Honey, this is not the kind of venue where Mr. Hitz performs. But I'll let you in on a lil' secret," he said, leaning forward conspiratorially. "After the guests loosen up and interact with the performers….a special couple will be selected and then sent by limo to Mr. Hitz' home in Beverly Hills. Honey, if you think this place is something, you should see his sprawling mansion in Beverly Hills. This ain't nothing but a playhouse compared to the big crib. Now, follow me."

"Hold up. Who picks the couple?" Brick asked.

"We do. All of the staff observes closely and then we select the most adventurous pair, and the lucky couple gets to spend the night with Mr. Hitz."

Brick gave Anya a significant look. She nodded in understanding. They both were thinking the same thing: *After all this trouble, Smash Hitz ain't even here!*

Anya returned her attention to Trixie. "Could you put in a good word for us? We're big fans; it would mean a lot," she said in a tiny voice.

Trixie adjusted his stance, deftly balancing the tray as he shifted to the other foot. "It don't work like that, sugah. You gotta earn ya spot with Mr. Hitz."

En route to the main room, where the party was already in progress, Brick and Anya exchanged looks as they passed corridors and other areas that were blocked off with signs that firmly stated, "Forbidden."

Trixie waved his arm in an extravagant gesture. "Here we are. Feel free to shed those clothes after you get nice and comfortable." Eyes latched on Brick, Trixie pinched his nipples. They hardened almost instantly. "We're completely uninhibited here at The Playhouse. And sometimes the staff joins in the fun." He blew Brick a kiss and sashayed off.

"Someone has the hots for you," Anya murmured. "I'm the jealous type, so I hope I don't have to whip Miss Thang's ass and use that anaconda dick he's rocking as a punching bag."

"Nah, babe. He ain't no competition. This is all you," Brick said and ran a hand over his thickening groin.

CHAPTER 49

Anya and Brick stood dumbfounded at the entrance to the ballroom. They looked in the room and then back at each other, sharing embarrassed smiles.

In the center of the room, a light-skinned woman with long, butterscotch-colored, spiral-curled hair, was oddly positioned in a sex swing. In front of her, a man slid his dick in and out of her pussy, while another man fucked her from the rear.

Perpendicular to the sex-swing act was a man lying on his back on top of a pallet. He was apparently a contortionist with both legs pulled behind his head, his ankles bound to his wrists. Fully exposed, his anus was wide open and ready for penetration. His erect penis pointed outward, visibly pulsating.

"Oh, my God!" Anya whispered.

In another area, a woman stood against a wall with her legs spread while she stroked her oversized, erect clit. With her eyes locked on a couple sitting on a nearby sofa, the big-clit chick smiled, silently inviting the couple to come join her.

"What the hell is all this? A sex circus?" Brick mumbled.

"I don't know, but I'm mesmerized. Don't hold it against me, but I'm kind of turned on…in a real weird way. This is disturbing," Anya said with a soft giggle. "It's a damn shame we're here for business instead of pleasure."

"Stay focused, babe. Let's go on in…sit down and watch this freak show. Smash isn't here, but we still might stumble on to a lead to put me in touch with Juicy." Brick reached for Anya's hand as they crossed the room together.

Couples were snuggled together on settees, chairs, and sofas, watching the various sex acts in a kind of wide-eyed rapture.

"I recognize some of these couples in here. Most of them were at the club earlier tonight," Brick mused.

Anya looked around at the spectators. "Yeah, I see a few familiar faces, too. I wonder why Smash only invites couples."

"I heard he's into watching live porn. This so-called 'Playhouse' is proof that the man is the biggest freak on the planet."

"I know, right? I'm glad we didn't try to track him down in Miami. This dude has mansions all over the globe."

The gender-bending serving boys pranced gaily around the ballroom, plying the guests with more liquor and offering condoms.

Pleasant-sounding murmurs from the guests signaled that everyone was having a naughty good time.

"Ooo, look at that shit over there!" Anya pointed to the woman that was openly playing with her pussy. "The more she rubs on it, the bigger her clit is getting. It's swelled up to the size of a baby dick," Anya whispered, enthralled by the unusual sight.

Apparently aroused, an attractive couple seated near Anya and Brick began to murmur excitedly. Deciding to get involved in the action, the female, a voluptuous dark-haired beauty, set her drink down and rose from her chair. "You coming?" she said to her man, her eyes sparkling with sexual mischief.

"No, not yet. I just wanna watch. Go on over there, Tiffany. Do you!" he encouraged.

"I will. I'm not shy about my sexuality," the woman stated. Dressed in a body-hugging short dress, she took off across the floor, swinging her long weave and her hips.

Moments later, Brick, Anya, and the encouraging bashful husband were all leaning forward, watching Tiffany, on her knees, sucking the baby-dick clit.

"Damn, Brick. This *is* a freak show, and it's getting to me. We gotta hurry up and get outta here. With all this going on…" She looked around at the debauchery and gazed at Brick. "Babe, this freak shit has me craving one of your special punishments," Anya said, squeezing her thighs together.

"I gotchu," Brick assured her. "After I handle this business."

"I want Smash to hurry up! After you finish interrogating him, and you know, whatever else you have to do…are you gonna take care of my pussy?"

"I promise," he whispered. "You gotta chill, though."

"Okay. Just know that I want you to pound my pussy until I start speaking in tongues."

Brick chuckled. "Stop making me laugh. This is serious business."

As they both laughed softly, a big, beefed-up bald dude came in the room. Wearing a stern expression, he rushed past the guests, heading toward the servers. He was dressed in jeans and a wife beater that showed off arms with muscles like boulders. Oddly, he had a silk scarf flung around his neck, and was wearing heels. Expensive heels with red soles.

With great authority, he marched over to Malaysia. "Redbone's getting sloppy! Tell her I said to get off that swing and take a break."

"What the fuck!" Brick's head swiveled back and forth from the girl on the swing to the beefy drag queen.

"I know, right?" Anya said. "That's a big-ass drag queen. This place is a zoo. But who's he supposed to be? The supervisor?"

Brick went silent as he watched the girl disengage from her sex partners and climb out of the swing. "That's Redbone!" Brick murmured.

"Redbone? Who's she?" Anya asked. She was momentarily distracted as the girl in the swing was replaced by another naked female with oversized implants.

"It's about to get ugly in here," Brick said, looking serious.

"What happened? Did Smash Hitz come through?"

"Nah, I'm about to have a word with Redbone."

Anya looked surprised. "Why?"

With a determined look in his eyes, Brick pushed out of his seat and followed Redbone, the chick that Cash Money had told him about.

ℰℬ

Barefoot and naked, Redbone lifted a tarp and trotted down one of the "forbidden" corridors.

Looking from side to side and over his shoulder, Brick stealthily followed her. He didn't see the supervisor dude or either of the servers. No one was around. *Good!* He peeked in an opening of the tarp and watched until Redbone and her buttery-colored curls had disappeared from view.

He scanned the area again; there was Trixie, carrying a tray. The server did a double take when he noticed Brick.

Smiling sheepishly, Brick said, "I wanna get into something private with Redbone. How much to keep you quiet?"

"For you, handsome?" Trixie looked up in thought. "Three hundred dollars and a taste of your personal goodies when the showcase is over." Trixie gazed at Brick's crotch.

Those days are over, mufucka, Brick thought, but said, "You got it, boo." Brick peeled off three bills.

Trixie took the money and walked away.

Brick lifted the tarp and stepped behind it.

The hallway led to a room with an arched entryway. Sliding along the walls of the corridor, Brick crept toward the dimly lit room.

Eyes squinted, he scanned the room, making note of a ladder, piles of sheetrock, and cans of paint on top of the thick protective plastic that covered the hardwood floor. He quietly edged his way into the room, noticing that furniture was pushed into corners and covered with drop cloth. The room was obviously in the process of being renovated. Another fetish room, Brick surmised. Smash Hitz would probably transform the entire residence into a sex-themed showpiece.

In a dark corner in the rear, he spotted the red spark of Redbone's cigarette as she took a leisurely drag, and then sipped her drink. Reclining on a tarp-covered chaise lounge, she was giving her aching pussy and sore ass a well-deserved break from all that nonstop fucking.

Moving quickly, Brick's boots crunched noisily on the plastic floor covering.

Startled, Redbone leaned forward. Eyes wide with alarm, she snuffed out her cigarette, dropping it into her drink.

CHAPTER 50

Redbone observed Brick, and her bewildered gaze quickly changed to irritation. "Can't you read? This area is off limits, asshole! The bathroom for guests is inside the ballroom." She shooed him away, gesturing with her hand.

"When's the last time you saw Felice…or maybe you know her as Juicy," Brick said in a low tone.

Redbone's delicate features contorted. Her thin lips twisted in disgust. "Who's asking?" She flattened her hands against the tarp-covered cushion, lifting herself up.

"A friend of a friend," Brick said coolly as he approached her.

"You're an asshole," she snapped. Moving swiftly, the naked stripper attempted to get past Brick.

He grabbed her by the arm. She opened her mouth to scream. "I'ma fuck up that pretty face permanently if you scream," Brick threatened, prompting Redbone to shut her mouth. "You understand me?" Brick gave her arm a harsh jerk.

She nodded quickly.

"Where's Juicy?"

"I have no idea. What's this about?" she said in a whispery voice.

"I'm asking the questions. Are you still working for Juicy?"

"No."

"Who do you work for?"

"What's it to you?" she snarled. "You got a lot of balls, coming in here. Do you know whose house you're in?"

"I don't give a fuck. If you come out your mouth all greasy one more time, I'ma knock your teeth out the back of your head. You hear me, ho?"

She twisted her face angrily, and reluctantly nodded.

"Let's start with a different question." Brick paused a beat. "What do you know about Misty?"

At the mention of Misty's name, Redbone's eyes grew large. She wrestled free of Brick's grasp. Barefoot and naked, she fled to the entryway.

Anya stepped out of the shadows. "Where you going, bitch?" Anya shoved her so hard, Redbone stumbled backwards.

Brick caught Redbone and slapped a palm over her mouth. "I'ma ask you again…what do you know about Misty?" he persisted. He had only wanted to question the woman about Juicy, but her reaction led him to believe that she was much more involved than he'd suspected.

Before he removed his hand to allow Redbone to talk, Anya had moved to a clutter of worker's tools and grabbed a nail gun. In a blink of an eye, she shot a spiked nail into the top of Redbone's foot. The stripper's mouth widened as she tried to release a piercing scream. But Brick tightened his hand around her mouth, smothering the sound.

"Try to run somewhere now, hooker!" Anya spat.

Anya was ride or die! Brick looked down at the spike that held Redbone frozen in place. Blood oozed around the head of the nail. "Remind me never to piss you off," Brick told Anya.

Anya gave a wry smile. "Now you know," she remarked.

"How'd you know I was back here?" Brick questioned.

"Miss Thang. I had to pay him a stack to let me join you in a ménage for an hour. Guess what Miss Thang said?"

Brick lifted a questioning brow.

"Miss Thang said, 'I expect you to turn a blind eye when your man and me get together after this soiree is over.'"

Brick laughed. "Yeah, I gassed him up. So how much time do we have with Redbone?"

"The crowd's gon' be here for at least another two hours."

Redbone trembled. Her tears trickled onto Brick's hand. Brick spoke softly in her ear. "I'm taking my hand off your mouth, but if you yell, she's gonna nail your other foot to the f—"

"Fuck that other foot," Anya cut in. "Hmph. I'ma aim for her fake-ass titties. I wonder if we'll hear a '*sssss*' when I burst them bitches like balloons."

"You hardcore, babe!" Brick said. Anya was a little spitfire. Her fearlessness reminded Brick of Misty.

Forcing the end of the nail gun into Redbone's right breast, Anya repeated Brick's question. "Whatchu know about Misty? Don't make me have to ask that question again."

Lips trembling, teeth chattering, Redbone moaned from pain, unable to produce coherent sound.

Alerted by the clatter of stilettos coming in their direction, Redbone yelled, "Help!"

Brick and Anya dove for cover, hiding behind covered furniture.

"You're supposed to be back on the swing," boomed the familiar voice of the stilettos-wearing supervisor. He suddenly gawked at Redbone's impaled foot. "Ooo, chile, what the hell did you do to yourself? And why you back here fiddling around with the tools and shit?"

Redbone sniveled. Eyes darting to the area where Anya and Brick were hiding, she frantically wiggled her foot, trying to work the nail out of the floor. "I…didn't… Redbone stuttered. The pain was so severe, she was unable to get her words out.

"Stop twisting your foot around. You're making it worse." The supervisor rubbed his bald head in aggravation. "I don't know how to get that nail out of your foot. I can't bring unwanted attention to the Playhouse, so you can forget about an ambulance."

"Please," Redbone moaned the word.

"No! I'm not losing my job over this. Smash is not gon' appreciate the way you done fucked up his showcase. I'ma go get Malaysia...see if she can help me get this thing out."

"No, don't leave me, Horatio! They're behind the couch," Redbone shouted, miraculously regaining her ability to speak clearly.

Horatio! The supervisor bull is Horatio, the bodyguard dude that Misty took to Miami! Brick snatched Anya's purse, without explaining, whipped out her fake cell phone, and then leapt out of his hiding spot.

No questions asked, Anya was right behind Brick when he zapped the supervisor twice. Horatio fell into a twitching and heaving mound.

Crying and moaning, Redbone attempted to yank her foot from the binding floorboard. Instantly, the large head of the nail disappeared and became embedded inside the top of her foot. Blood spurted, yet Redbone remained fastened to the floor.

"Hand me that tape." Brick pointed to a spool of electrical tape that laid amidst the construction crew's tools.

Anya grabbed it. "I got this." She began unraveling tape. Mimicking Brick's actions in the warehouse, she wrapped the tape three times around the mouth and head of the shuddering and sobbing stripper. After silencing her, Anya dragged a chair over to the naked girl. "Take a load off. Have a seat."

Brick zapped Horatio again. "I need the tape, babe," Brick said as his victim lay twitching.

Anya tossed it to him. "We should get Redbone to call Juicy. Lure her to us."

Brick smiled as he taped Horatio's mouth. "We don't need Juicy. This high-heel-wearing punk-ass is the mufucka I've been looking for all along."

Anya frowned in confusion. Brick picked up the nail gun. He stretched out one of Horatio's arms, and shot a nail into the middle of his palm. Horatio screamed in anguish, but the sound went unheard as it reverberated behind his taped mouth.

Brick repeated the process with the other hand. As the spike entered his hand, Horatio banged his own head against the floor, groaning in agony.

"I'll put a spike between your eyes if you bang your head again." Horatio nodded, and mumbled incoherently. His legs curled up involuntarily as he tried to endure the excruciating pain.

Anya's eyes drifted down to Horatio's ankles. As if reading her mind, Brick said, "Nah, the nail won't go through his ankles. They too thick."

"Lemme try it," she said, reaching for the nail gun.

Brick gave it to her.

Panicked, Horatio kicked his legs and squirmed wildly, causing the Christian Louboutin stilettos to fly off his feet.

Anya scooted down to his feet. "If you kick me, I swear to God, I'ma nail your dick and your balls inside your ass."

Horatio became completely still. He squeezed his eyes closed as Anya widened the space between his legs, bent his knees and then placed the soles of his feet flat against the plastic covering on the floor.

Two nails were fired into each foot, ensuring that Horatio stayed put. The big man howled, but the contractor duct tape was doing an excellent job muffling the sounds.

Anya waved the thick roll at Brick. "Yo, babe, this is some good shit right here. We should cop a couple on the way out."

"Uh-huh," Brick responded absently as he got down on one knee and looked Horatio in the eyes. "You're the one who fucked up Misty. Did you really think you were gon' get away with it?"

Horatio's eyes widened.

"You fucked with the wrong one when you came at Misty." Brick looked the man over sneeringly. "Look at you...wearing high-heels and dressed like a bitch. It's Judgment Day, nigga!"

Horatio murmured in denial and shook his head violently.

"Take the tape off his mouth," Anya suggested. "Let him plead his case." She looked at Horatio. "We spent a lot of bread to get this private session, so don't be wasting time. Ain't no rescue team coming back here looking for your ass."

After hearing that no rescue mission was in progress, Horatio and Redbone both groaned in distress. Horatio writhed in pain. His eyes began to roll into the back of his head.

Brick smacked his face. "Ain't no time for passing out. Wake up, nigga. You got some explaining to do." He ripped the tape from around Horatio's mouth, tearing off pieces of a mustache and other facial hair, along with some skin in the process.

Anya grinned as she mused, "That tape is some real good shit!"

CHAPTER 51

Anya held up the cell phone as a warning to Horatio. "Holler, bitch. Please!"

Wide eyes and trembling lips, Horatio quietly whimpered.

"Misty was a paper maker," Brick said. "You didn't like that, did you?"

Unable to disguise his disdain for Misty, Horatio's mouth curled viciously. "She was shady; always tryna beat somebody out of what they earned."

"And so you tried to kill her over a coupla dollars?" Brick said with contempt.

"I wasn't trying to kill her; I wanted to make sure she couldn't keep using her looks to scheme and connive. She always had an unfair advantage. I just wanted to give her some permanent imperfections. You know, even out the playing field."

"And you wanted her out of the picture, so you could have Smash Hitz to yourself," Brick added.

"I wanted my fair share; that's all."

"So how does Redbone fit into the picture?" Anya asked.

"Juicy got burnt by Misty, too."

"I asked about Redbone." Anya nodded her head toward the shivering stripper.

"Redbone and Juicy had a thing."

"What kind of thing?" Brick barked.

"You know…they were messing around together. So they cooked up a scheme where Redbone and I would put on a sex show for Smash Hitz. But Misty messed it up by sending this skinny bull named Ashy Cashy to the crib."

"Cash Money?" Brick asked.

"Misty called him Ashy Cashy."

Brick had only heard Misty refer to Cash Money as Troy, but being that the bull always looked dusty, he could understand how Misty had come up with that nickname.

"I'm in a lot of pain, man. You gotta take these spikes out my hands and feet." Beads of sweat dribbled from Horatio's forehead. He closed his eyes and bit down on his lip, trying to fight the pain.

"Nah, I'll pull those nails out with a pair of pliers after you finish talking."

"Please."

Brick ignored his plea. "So you were supposed to get down with Redbone over here, but Smash didn't need you because he had Misty's worker. And you were jealous and full of hatred."

"Yeah, man. If it wasn't for me, Misty wouldn't have been all in with Smash Hitz. She used me to get to him, and then she dumped me—like I was trash."

"I have another question. How'd you know Misty was taking Smash Hitz' chain to his crib? And by the way, what happened to the chain?"

Horatio looked stunned that Brick knew about the medallion. "Redbone. She was there with him. She overheard Smash on the phone arguing with Misty. She heard him tell her that she had a half-hour to bring his chain back."

"Where's the chain?" Brick asked again, more forcibly.

"After I took it out of Misty's car, I called Juicy and told her I had it. She told me to take it to the crib with me and slip the chain to Redbone. That's what I did. I swear to God, I thought they gave the chain back to Smash Hitz."

Anya didn't waste any time yanking the tape from around Redbone's mouth. "Start talking, bitch."

"I...me and Juicy..." she stammered. "We were supposed to split the money after she sold it. But I never got paid."

"Where's that bitch, Juicy?"

"I heard that she's sick. In a hospice program, dying of AIDS."

"Ew. All y'all nasty, diseased mufuckas is fucking and sucking each other. This Playhouse should be quarantined and condemned."

Brick's eyes went vacant for a brief moment.

"Brick?" Anya said with concern in her voice. She patted his hand until Brick blinked a few times. "You zoned out for a minute, babe."

"Oh, yeah? I've heard enough of this lying nigga's mouth. Now it's killing time. Shut him the fuck up," Brick instructed Anya.

Brick had been reliving what Misty must have experienced on that fateful night at the hands of this big, angry faggot. He had brutalized Misty and left her for dead on that lonely road. Left her beyond unrecognizable and only suitable for a closed casket. But Misty was too strong to go out like that. No, this man didn't kill her. But he had done much worse. He had killed Misty's spirit and her will to live.

&ⱷ

Anya tugged the long, flowing scarf from around Horatio's thick neck and stuffed it inside his mouth. Wild-eyed and bucking his body, Horatio made a futile attempt to escape his fate.

Brick reached inside his boot and pulled out a dagger. Brick walked briskly toward Redbone.

Surprised, Redbone recoiled. "Any last words, bitch?"

"I didn't hurt that girl. Horatio did it. He's the one that's supposed to die—not me!"

"Whatever, trick," Brick said, coldly. He grabbed a handful of butterscotch ringlets and yanked her head back.

"No...wait! Please!" Redbone scratched and fought to no avail. A slash across her throat sent blood spurting from the gash, closing her eyes forever.

Horatio had been momentarily captivated by the sight of blood pulsing from Redbone's gaping neck. So much blood. Gushing like a geyser. Horatio gave a sigh of relief that Redbone had been sacrificed instead of him.

"Now it's your turn, nigga," Brick promised as he made strides toward the man that he'd skewered. From his other boot, Brick withdrew his Asian-style knife.

Terror once again filled Horatio's eyes. He erroneously thought that he'd been given a reprieve. Groaning like a madman, he shook his head wildly from side to side.

Brick shot a dark look at Horatio. "I've been waiting a long time to get some justice for Misty. Not only did you ruin her life, you destroyed the only family that I ever had. Now it's time for retribution." Brick released a sigh. "This is gon' be long and painful. I'ma take my time." Brick closed his eyes blissfully. "Gon' savor every moment."

Brick gave Horatio a close look at his two sharp weapons. "You like competing with females, so I'ma help you out. Give you some surgery on your genitals. Turn you into the bitch that you are." Brick paused and began cutting open the crotch of Horatio's tight jeans. Horatio bucked upward, ripping flesh from his impaled hands.

"Calm down, Horatio," Anya joined in, rubbing the perspiration from Horatio's forehead in a feigned act of tenderness. "We can't have you bleeding to death while you're on the operating table. You gotta be still while the doctor works on you."

"Now listen up while I explain the procedure. My nurse over here is gonna get rid of your dick and your nutt sac." Brick paused while Horatio went wild again, frantically trying to rip his hands away from the hardwood floor.

"Don't worry, I'ma free your hands up after I slice off every one of your fingers," Brick assured him. "After that, I'ma amputate your toes. But it's your lucky day, mufucka. You're getting a face peel—no charge. You gonna look refreshed and so damn pretty after I slowly peel all the skin off your fuckin' face."

Brick handed Anya a knife. "Do your thing, mama."

As Anya went to work, Brick whispered in the suffering man's ear. "I'm getting ready to fillet you like a fish, mufucka. And then gut you like a pig."

ഊൠ

Horatio was dead long before Brick got a chance to cut his belly open. Splattered with the dead man's blood, Brick and Anya escaped through a window. In the cover of darkness, they jogged to the rental car, satisfied.

CHAPTER 52

"This is where we part, baby."

"No!" Anya was horrified by the suggestion.

"Have to," Brick said, firmly. "I gotta turn myself in. Serve whatever time they wanna give me."

"Why would you do that?"

"For my son. I can't keep running. I can't let my flesh and blood grow up thinking that I deserted him. I have to own up to what I did to Misty. I figure, the sooner I get it over with and do the time, the quicker I'll get to be with my son.

"Even if he hates me...I at least want the opportunity to tell him that I love him. That I'm here for him."

"I can't argue with that," Anya said. "But why do we have part ways? I can help you. Get you a good lawyer—"

"Nah, you don't understand," Brick interrupted.

"I understand that I love you. Even if you end up having to do a bid, it won't be that long. I'll wait for you, babe. Visit you and keep money on your books. I would never abandon you while you're down. I got your back. You know I do."

Brick solemnly nodded. "C'mere, baby," he said, his arms stretched out.

Crying, Anya stepped into his arms.

"Remember when you told me, 'no strings attached?'"

Sniffling, Anya nodded.

"Well, I'm holding you to your word. We both got the revenge we were yearning for. Now it's time to move on."

"But...I thought—"

Brick interrupted her. "Concentrate on finding your pop. A while back, you mentioned hiring a detective. You have a lot of money now. You can get a top-notch private investigator. Someone experienced with tracking down missing people."

"You're right," she reluctantly agreed.

"As for me..." He paused. "I gotta do everything in my power to reestablish the bond between me and my son. He's only a toddler. I gotta do this jail time so I can hurry up and get back with my son."

"Are you sure you're not trying to impress your wife...you know, a last-ditch effort to save your marriage?"

"No. It's over between Thomasina and me. I know that for a fact. She'll never forgive me. And I accept that."

"Can we be friends—you know, stay in touch?" Anya asked, her voice cracking a little.

"I don't think that's a good idea. What's done is done. Why drag it out?"

Anya couldn't argue with Brick's reasoning. As badly as it hurt, she had no choice but to let him go.

ഇൻ

Realizing that law enforcement had most likely been provided with their descriptions, the pair decided to travel separately.

Brick took a flight out of Las Vegas to Philadelphia.

Disguised in a long wig, Anya drove to Las Vegas. From Vegas, she planned to book a trip to Trinidad. Maybe she'd luck up and connect with family members on her mother's side. And hopefully, a private investigator could reunite her with her missing father.

Separating from Brick hurt like losing a limb. Tears welled. *No more tears!* She wiped her eyes. From the very beginning, Anya had realized that she and Brick would eventually part ways.

CHAPTER 53

Before turning himself in, Brick wanted to say goodbye to Misty. Brick walked into the hospital with a heavy heart. He was barred from visiting her, but with nothing to lose, it was worth the chance to attempt to slip in. He was surprised when none of the hospital staff tried to prevent him from entering Misty's room.

Misty! There she was, lying in the hospital bed, surrounded with all sorts of equipment that facilitated her tenuous hold on life. Looking around the room, he noticed a vase filled with flowers, and knew that they were placed there by her mother. Knowing Thomasina, she probably brought fresh flowers every day, hoping to somehow brighten her daughter's day.

Brick gazed at Misty and winced. She was so frail and helpless. He'd really screwed up. Misty had wanted the peace of death, but here she was after all this time, still alive but comatose.

As broken and tortured as she'd been, her previous condition seemed a lot better than this.

A deep, damning shame came over Brick as he drew closer to Misty. Gloomily, he sank in the chair next to her bed. He looked at Misty's shrunken face. Her complexion was a sickly shade of gray. She seemed barely alive.

Brick shook his head hopelessly. "Misty. This is not... I'm so sorry," he uttered, giving a halted, mumbling apology.

He couldn't blame Thomasina for hating his guts. There was

no getting around the truth; he'd screwed up what was left of Misty's life and had destroyed his marriage.

He'd assumed that getting revenge on Misty's assailant would bring some relief from his inner turmoil, but he was still a tortured soul. Brick pictured himself being handcuffed and, instead of resisting the idea, he welcomed it. He needed to pay for what he had done and deserved to be arrested. He should be put underneath the jail!

Distraught, Brick covered his face with both hands and silently wept.

A painful moan that was followed by the sound of difficult breathing entered his awareness. Brick hadn't made a sound; his sobs had been muffled by his hands. Confused, he pulled his hands away and looked around. He glanced at Misty, and noticed her facial muscles forming into a frown.

"Misty?" he whispered with urgency.

Her eyes blinked and then opened. Brick shot up from the chair and hovered over her. "Misty," he repeated her name again, this time in a hushed, awestruck tone.

Her eyes moved back and forth, taking in the surroundings. Her lips moved.

Brick grabbed the call button and pushed it repeatedly.

"Brick," Misty mouthed, gazing at his face.

"Misty, baby. You're back!" Brick lifted her contracted hand to his lips, kissing it prayerfully with tightly closed eyes.

His prayer of gratitude was interrupted by Misty's raspy and barely audible voice. "Water, please."

The water that Brick quickly provided quenched Misty's great thirst and soothed her parched vocal chords.

Finally able to speak, though haltingly, she said, "Didn't want to come back. Shane said...not my time."

Overwhelmed with joy and astonishment, Brick hovered over

Misty. "Shane was right, baby. It's not your time. You belong here with your family that loves you."

"He said…my life partner…waiting…when I return." She frowned slightly, cleared her throat and swallowed. "He's supposed to… to guide me through. Through challenging times…ahead."

Brick smoothed back the hair that had fallen in her face. "Don't worry, Misty. Everything's gon' be all right."

Perplexed, she crinkled her eyebrows. "Was he talking about you, Brick?"

He shrugged. "I don't know, but I'm here for you. You're my first love, Misty. You know you always had my heart. Nothing's changed," Brick said while tears ran freely from his eyes.

A young nursing assistant entered, responding to the call. "Can I help you with something?" she said to Brick. The nurse stopped cold when she noticed that Misty's eyes were open. "She's awake! I have to get the charge nurse, and call her doctor." She rushed out of the room.

"What about you and my mother?" Misty asked after the nurse left.

"She hates me. Can't forgive me for giving you the pills. Our marriage is over," he said solemnly.

"I'm sorry."

"It's for the best. I cared deeply for your mom, but the whole time we were married, I never stopped loving you. Trying to be a good husband, I tried to bury my feelings for you. But I couldn't."

"But I'm paralyzed, Brick. Can't do anything for you. My face…it's all messed up. How can you be happy with a disfigured invalid?"

Brick cupped her face, caressed the side that was injured. "Having you back makes me happy. And your face? You'll always be beautiful to me, don't you know that, Misty?" Brick said with conviction, assuaging Misty's insecurity and fear.

He clasped her hand tighter. "Misty, listen…most people don't get a second chance in life, but for some reason, we get to try it again."

"I'm gon' show you that I've changed. I learned a lot about love."

Brick eyed her tenderly. "I can feel the change, Misty, baby… and I love you, girl. I always have; always will."

Misty smiled faintly. "I've always loved you, too, Brick. Just had a dysfunctional way of showing it."

"Forget about the past, I promise you…we're gon' get it right this time," he said, looking at her with love and adoration.

In those brief moments before a team of doctors and nurses made a stampede to Misty's room, a stunned Thomasina stood in the doorway, holding a fresh bouquet of flowers. With her mouth agape, Thomasina listened as her husband and her reawakened daughter declared their undying love for each other.

Thomasina's hand dropped limply to her side. The flowers that she'd lovingly clutched to her chest began to fall to the floor, one by one.

Brick looked up and saw his wife in the doorway; he saw the hurt and pain in her eyes. With Misty's hand in his, he looked at Thomasina with sympathy and apologized with his eyes. *I never meant to hurt you. I'm so sorry. I love Misty; I can't help myself.*

Thomasina's hand covered her mouth as she held back sobs. She whirled around. Whisking past doctors and nurses that hustled into Misty's room, she made her way to the elevator.

Why? Thomasina asked herself. *I've done everything for that child of mine. Everything! But all she does is bring me pain.*

What kind of monster comes out of a coma, scheming and conniving? Baron is too blind to see what I've known all of her diabolical life. He's destined to find out the hard way, that Misty is incapable of loving anyone but herself.

ABOUT THE AUTHOR

Allison Hobbs is a national bestselling author of seventeen novels and has been featured in such periodicals as *Romantic Times* and *The Philadelphia Tribune*. She lives in Philadelphia, Pennsylvania. Visit the author at www.allisonhobbs.com and Facebook.com/Allison Hobbs.